Last Stop: Paris honored as finalist for Best Indie Book of the Year

Shelf Unbound, a leading magazine covering independent publishing, has chosen Last Stop: Paris as one of six finalists for its "Best Independently Published" award for 2015. More than a thousand books were considered in the judging.

The award was announced in its December-January issue, which can be found online.

Early praise for *Last Stop: Paris*

A full-throttle adventure through modern Europe and the Mediterranean in a book that's part thriller, part mystery and all rollicking ride... Pearce again accomplishes every thriller writer's aim: creating characters that the reader can root for and a believable, fast-paced story line... An exhilarating journey that will satisfy the most avid thriller reader.

- *Kirkus Reviews*

John Pearce's first novel, *Treasure of Saint-Lazare,* set a high bar for international mystery, but his second, *Last Stop: Paris,* easily meets and surpasses it. This novel captures the very soul of contemporary Europe, crossing borders with apparently effortless aplomb. And his enterprising character, Eddie Grant, continues to fascinate with his combination of European sophistication and American ingenuity. But Paris too is a main character; Pearce must know that city even better than he knows the back of his hand.

- *Ronald Rosbottom, author of "When Paris Went Dark," finalist for the American Library in Paris 2015 Book Award*

In *Last Stop: Paris*, Franco-American Eddie Grant, aided by his beautiful partner, Sorbonne professor Aurélie, crosses Paris - and Europe - in hot pursuit of the killers of his wife and son ten years earlier. Eddie's Paris, which ranges from the sophisticated salons of the Île Saint-Louis to the rue Picpus in a working class neighborhood takes us beyond the usual tourist stops; as one who has lived in the City of Light for decades, I applaud the author's knowledge of its varied quartiers. An intriguing romp - and now I get the double treat of going back to his first book, the prize-winning historical mystery *Treasure of Saint-Lazare*, of which this is a sequel. How did I manage to miss it?!

- *Harriet Welty Rochefort, author of "French Fried, "French Toast", and "Joie de Vivre" (St. Martin's Press*

A gripping novel of mystery and intrigue taking us across Europe and into all its sordid dens of iniquity. A complex and riveting achievement. It brings Europe alive.

- *James Goldsborough, author of "The Paris Herald: A Novel"*

John Pearce knows Paris: its glittering splendor, but also its shadowy underbelly, its sorrow, double dealing, and mayhem. *Last Stop: Paris* follows a twisting and turning course across the globe. It's a gripping and complicated tale of international intrigue, terror and revenge.

- *Peter Steiner, author of "The Resistance" and the forthcoming "The Capitalist." New Yorker cartoonist known for "On the Internet nobody knows you're a dog."*

John Pearce has done it again: taken us back to Paris and Florida for his latest cosmopolitan thriller. And Eddie Grant, the lovely Aurélie, and the temptress Jen return with a cast of pals and thugs to whisk us from page to page. Will the Nazi-filched Raphael be found at last, or will this crafty wordsmith save it for another spell-binding sequel?

- *Bill Carrigan, author of "The Doctor of Summitville"*

The second time Pearce surrounds us with all the flavor of Paris wrapped around an intriguing plot filled with captivating characters. The vivid scenery and international espionage keep the reader engaged while delivering a veiled history lesson at the same time. An enjoyable read, Édouard's adventures are always endearing!

- *Barbara Krier, Sarasota, FL*

If gold, the Russian Mafia, CIA, Vladimir Putin, sex, and exciting world travel are not enough for you, John Pearce proves in his latest action novel, *Last Stop: Paris*, that he once again has the ability to create plot lines that both thrill and captivate.

- *Stewart Stearns, author of "Lorenzo's Rules: Lord of the Ninth Underworld"*

LAST STOP: PARIS

THE SEQUEL TO *TREASURE OF SAINT-LAZARE*

John Pearce

Alesia Press LLC, Sarasota

By the Same Author:

Treasure of Saint-Lazare

Last Stop: Paris is a work of fiction. The names, characters, places and incidents portrayed are the product of the author's imagination. Any resemblance to actual persons, living or dead (with the exception of certain historical figures) is entirely coincidental.

ISBN: 978-0-9859626-2
Ebook ISBN: 978-0-9859626-3-0

Published by

Alesia Press
PO Box 51004
Sarasota, FL 34232
Publisher@alesiapress.com

Cover design by JD Smith, www.jdsmith-design.co.uk
Editing by Jen Blood, www.adianediting.com

For Jan

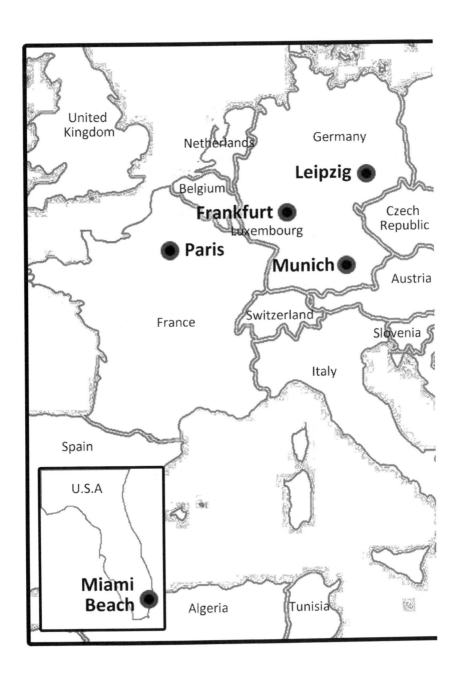

CHAPTER ONE

Paris, Île Saint-Louis

The truth of it was, if Icky hadn't twisted his arm Eddie Grant would be home making love to Aurélie instead of following a rented butler into Henri Gascon's gilded living room.

Aurélie knew precisely what he'd rather be doing, and felt much the same way. She squeezed his arm harder and pulled him into the buzzing crowd of middle-aged men in business suits and women in cocktail dresses, who paused every few minutes to extend their glasses to a passing waiter. They drifted apart, only to regroup and resume their bright gossip about the next weekend in the country or Christmas in Antibes — the holidays were only three months away and the late-afternoon air gusting gently through the open windows already carried the snap of winter.

"Ah, the well-mannered Paris cocktail party," Eddie murmured to no one in particular as the butler handed them off to an elderly waiter, who extended a silver tray.

"Monsieur Grant, Madame Cabillaud. May I offer you the last two glasses?"

Eddie looked up in surprise. "Georges! I thought our Christmas party was your last. Did you decide not to retire?" He took the champagne and handed one glass to Aurélie.

"I did retire, but I still do the occasional party just to round out my month."

Eddie looked around the crowd in search of friendly faces. It would be a few minutes at most until Aurélie was lured away to debate her new book dissecting the effects of the French Revolution on the ordinary citizens of Paris. She loved the give and take, and defended herself with *vivacité d'esprit,* a quick-witted energy that could charm the most curmudgeonly academic. The attention and the public acclaim were her oxygen.

"There's Jeremy," she whispered after they found a place near an open window, "over at the piano. You can talk to him until the dog-and-pony show begins."

As the pianist shifted to Mozart, their friend Jeremy Bentham worked his way toward them.

"Jeremy," Aurélie said. "Édouard is very glad you're here. He doesn't really like talking to bankers."

"I don't usually run into you at affairs like this, I suspect for the same reason," Eddie added. "Have you seen our host?"

"Henri is bending somebody's ear over near the piano. He called to invite me and I have a little money to invest, so I thought it would be a nice way to see how the really rich live, and maybe have a little ice cream at Berthillon," Jeremy replied. He dissembled easily for the benefit of the guests around them; in fact, both he and Eddie were at the party as a favor to their friend Icky Crane, a CIA department head. Icky was a college friend and Army buddy of Eddie's and both had served under Major General Bentham in the first Gulf War.

Their host Henri Gascon ("the Fourth," he reminded everyone he met, sometimes more than once) was president of Banque Privée de Normandie, whose defense of its clients' privacy stood out even in the close-mouthed fraternity of European private banks. To the general public, he was known mainly for his dual-purpose cocktail parties. They attracted the wealthy of Paris, who came to see and be seen in his rambling and over-decorated apartment on the ultra-expensive Île Saint-Louis, with its view over the Seine to the buttresses of Notre Dame Cathedral, the Eiffel Tower shimmering in the distance beyond. They delighted in complaining about Henri's choice of champagne, but they kept coming. Having to listen to his latest investment pitch was a small price to pay.

∫

Jeremy moved closer and said, in a whisper only Eddie could hear, "Henri's exchanging final words with the speaker — there, under the chandelier. Tonight we're going to hear from the American goldbug, Lee Filer. The hedge fund manager couldn't make it, I'm told."

"How did he ever get on TV with a figure like that? No woman would."

"I understand he has an unexpected charisma. That, and his mix of very right-wing politics and goldbuggery, especially since the price of gold seems to be going straight up, or at least it did until recently. He thinks there's no end in sight." The tips of Jeremy's mustache turned up slightly at the mild joke.

"Sounds like he'll fit right in with Henri," Eddie said.

"He's nowhere near as reactionary as Henri. If the German Army marched down Pennsylvania Avenue, Filer would change his tune in a heartbeat, while Henri would stand on the curb waving their flag. Henri still thinks the wrong side won the war.

"The other surprise is that Henri has a special guest — his half brother, the congressman from Texas who wants to run for president, Dick Tennant. They don't see a lot of each other and Tennant isn't officially involved in the bank, but he does like gold. I'm told that in his social circle he doesn't talk much about his French mother."

Henri was the latest in a line of Gascons that went back to great-grandfather Henri the First, who founded the bank before World War I. The family had come very close to losing control in the aftermath of World War II when Grandfather Henri, the Second, was locked up in Santé Prison for five years, which many Parisians thought was inadequate punishment for his ostentatious collaboration. At first there was talk of simply taking him to the execution ground at Montrouge, but cooler heads reasoned that the bank was too important to leave in the hands of a six-year-old — Henri's father.

Grandfather had stayed out of sight after his release, but schooled his son and grandson rigorously in the secret arts of protecting the money of the rich. He died young, still inveighing against victors' justice and the "indignity laws" that had denied him the right to vote or be involved in civic affairs. Henri the Fourth paid him homage by adopting his toothbrush mustache.

"And here they come," Jeremy whispered as Henri led the speaker through the crowd toward them.

Henri extended his hand and said, "Eddie, I was delighted when you called to say you could come. I'd like you to meet Mr. Lee Filer, the well-known American TV personality and expert on the gold markets.

"Lee, this is Eddie Grant, who I've told you about, and his fiancée, Aurélie Cabillaud. And you've met General Bentham."

Jeremy said, "The fund manager couldn't make it, I understand. I was looking forward to hearing him."

"Claude Khan is like a dog after a bone where gold is concerned. He's not just a numbers man — he has a real emotional connection with bullion. Sometimes it's a little scary," Henri replied. "He heard there was a new seller somewhere in the Mediterranean and went to find him. He should be back in a few days. You can meet him then."

Filer threw his best TV-star smile at Aurélie and asked, "Aren't you the people who found the treasure of Saint-Lazare? The papers were full of it for a while."

"That was us plus a lot of other people," she responded. "In fact, that was the reason Henri was able to persuade Édouard to come listen to you tonight." She smiled sweetly at Henri.

Eddie worked to keep a straight face as he recalled the one time he'd seen Filer pontificate on gold and a grab bag of his favorite conspiracy theories. It had been an hour's amusement one night in Florida, when he couldn't sleep and had resorted to channel surfing in his hotel room.

Later, he and Aurélie had found millions of dollars in Reichsbank gold bars hidden in the sub-basement of an apartment building not far from Gare Saint-Lazare, but a priceless Raphael self-portrait they'd expected to be with it was not there, and so far hadn't been found. The newspapers had gushed for days about the find, and the American tabloids and cable networks went crazy.

∫

Aurélie touched Eddie's arm and whispered, "I'm getting the high sign from one of the editors of *Le Monde* so I'd better go see him. I owe him for the good review."

Filer watched impassively as she wound her way through the crowd toward a gray-haired man, the only one in the room wearing a tuxedo.

"And I need a whisky," Jeremy said as he headed toward the tiny bar tucked into the corner of the next room. "Please excuse me."

"I understand you hadn't invested in gold before," Filer continued. "That surprises me, because Henri tells me you're an active investor."

The man had done his homework. Eddie's investing skill had made him and his mother Margaux even richer than they had been at his father's death ten years before.

"Gold has always seemed the ultimate refuge of the pessimist, which I'm not. There's no shortage of opportunity elsewhere. And it doesn't really do anything, which in my lexicon makes it a speculation."

Henri said, "I hope we can change your mind." He turned to Filer and said, "Meet me at the piano in a couple of minutes. We need to start so all these people can go to dinner. I'll be sure everyone is ready."

As Henri walked away, Lee forced a smile and murmured, "Icky Crane gave me your name. I don't know how much you know about his job now, but I need to get a message back to him. Unfortunately, I haven't been able to get away from my colleagues for the last couple of weeks. Can you help me?"

"I have his cell number and talk to him occasionally." Eddie reached into his jacket pocket for a card, which Filer quickly palmed and slipped into his pocket. The smile never left his face, but his gaze fixed on a chunky man across the room, leaning casually against an antique table richly decorated in gold leaf, under a framed antique Persian scimitar.

No wonder Filer is nervous, Eddie said to himself. That's a serious goon if I ever saw one. What sort of mess has Icky put me in this time?

"Khan cancelled the minute he heard you were coming," Filer said quietly as he started to walk toward the piano, "and his men are keeping me away from email and my phone, but I'll figure out some way to call you tonight."

Henri walked briskly toward the grand piano and stepped up on a small stage covered by an oriental carpet just as the last chords of Mozart died and the pianist moved away toward the bar.

"I'd like to introduce my brother, the American congressman from Texas, Richard Tennant. Many of you know him already. Dick, would you like a word?"

The congressman raised his hand in the crowd and smiled at the scattered applause. He was well known as a hard-line goldbug who had once run for president and had shown an interest in running again next year.

Jeremy returned, drink in hand, and leaned over to whisper to Eddie. "Icky told me the congressman is really sprucing up his image. He got a neck tuck and has become a big believer in Botox. You can see that he found a new hairdresser. I think the bookworm glasses are an effort to look professorial but, believe me, he's not. At least he left his cowboy boots at home."

"Howdy, everybody," the congressman bellowed. "Henri, thanks for inviting me. And the rest of you good folks should know that both Henri and I have invested in this fund. We're confident it will make us a lot of money, and quick."

Eddie heard a woman to his left whisper to her husband, "*Qu'est-ce que c'est* howdy?"

Filer took the stage to explain that he was recommending the investment fund because he believed gold — bullion, not paper or futures contracts — was the final redoubt of value in a threatened world. His long-time associate, the well-known international businessman Claude Khan, was seeking investors in a special fund whose only investment would be gold bullion, the price of which he expected to rise dramatically in coming months as Europe slipped from recession to depression and became more and more unstable.

"Remember that the assassination of an archduke plunged Europe into the worst war the world had seen up to 1914. While we don't have archdukes any more, we do have all sorts of opportunities for political instability. But even without that, doubts about the financial system will continue to drive people to gold as the ultimate reserve of value. It's the Armageddon investment.

"And there's not an unlimited supply of gold. If everyone in the world converted all their wealth into gold, it would make a cube a lot smaller than any of the Egyptian pyramids. But in fact, there's only enough gold available to cover ten percent of all the world's wealth."

Filer's pitch was familiar to his American viewers but bizarre to the mainly French audience. He talked about bankrupt societies, too much government spending on the poor, and the obligation of the rich to be certain their countries ran smoothly, then went on to thank his friend Congressman Tennant, who had been a staunch supporter of the gold movement for years.

"While he made most of his money in oil and cell phones, I'm pretty sure he's added a lot in the gold markets over the past three or four years," Filer added, as the congressman nodded in agreement. Henri beamed approval.

∫

"Could there be any doubt now that speculation is back in full flower?" Eddie asked Jeremy in a whisper. "This whole thing gives me the creeps — I'm going to find Aurélie and get out of here. Can you and Juliette join us for dinner?"

"She'll be off work in an hour. Can we meet you then?" Juliette Bertrand was a prominent news presenter on French TV, and Jeremy's live-in companion.

"We'll go to Les Ministères and keep a place for you. Filer whispered that he needed to talk to me, for Icky. I had no idea he was involved, but I gave him my number."

"Filer? This is starting to get odd. We'll definitely meet you as soon as we can."

Eddie knew Henri would call him to make a more detailed pitch for Khan's investment fund, so he went in search of Aurélie and found her in a niche close to the bar. She and a young philosophy professor good-naturedly argued one of the points she'd made in her book.

The philosopher, a flamboyantly handsome man frequently in demand for the heavy panel discussions popular on French television, pulled at his unbuttoned cuffs and brushed his blond pompadour back with one hand.

"I don't see how you can conclude that the proletariat didn't support the Revolution," he told her heatedly. "They loved the public executions."

"I never once used the word proletariat because it picked up so much freight in the twentieth century. I said the ordinary citizens had very little hope that the revolutionaries who brought down the king and executed the nobles would treat them any better. Look at the Vendée, which had a bitter armed counter-revolution. In fact, that's my next book — the Revolution as seen from the provinces."

"We can agree to disagree, and I've never yet won a fight with a beautiful woman. I do wish you'd studied philosophy, though. You would brighten up our dowdy department in so many ways." He turned and walked away without acknowledging Eddie.

Eddie was surprised anew every time they attended one of the intellectuals' parties that were part of Aurélie's circuit. She reveled in the limelight and vigorous academic debate, while he preferred to stand back and let her shine. He'd done his best to give her the bulk of the credit for finding the Nazi treasure, since she'd been the one to puzzle out where it was hidden. His mother thought he inherited his reticence from his father, who had learned to blend into the background when he was an American military spy behind German lines during World War II.

"Can you go now?" he asked. "We have reservations at Les Ministères."

"We just got here, for God's sake. There are a few more hands to shake. Ten minutes?"

A half hour later, Filer's audience had dwindled to a handful, so the tiny elevator was full. As Eddie and Aurélie turned toward the stairs, a small blue shape hurtled out of a door nearby.

A toddler's high voice reverberated in the marble hallway, taunting someone behind the door. "You can't catch me," she piped, then ran squarely into Eddie's leg, fell, and started to cry noisily.

Without thinking, he reached to pick up the little girl. She looked at him in wonder and immediately stopped crying.

"I wish I had that effect," said the young woman who followed the toddler, carrying a diaper.

Aurélie had moved to Eddie's side to admire the baby.

"What a lovely child," she said. "Yours?"

"Mine and the congressman's. I'm Gloria Tennant. Thank you for catching my adventurous Emily." She looked frankly at Aurélie, as many women did.

"You should thank Édouard. He's wonderful with small children," Aurélie said with a smile, extending her hand. "I am Aurélie Cabillaud, and this is my fiancé Édouard Grant. He's Eddie to our American friends, at least those I can't convince otherwise."

"So you're French?"

"I am, Édouard is half and half, but he has lived in Paris most of his life."

"Lucky man. Well, thank you for rescuing Emily. I know Dick would thank you, too."

The elevator carried them down in silence. Then, arm in arm, Eddie and Aurélie walked slowly along the stone wall that separates Quai d'Orléans from the metallic sheen of the Seine, fanned into small whitecaps by the stiff fall breeze. The flying buttresses of Notre Dame gleamed gold against the darkening indigo sky. In the distance, the white beacon atop the Eiffel Tower swept over the city.

Aurélie sighed and pulled her scarf closer around her neck. "She is a beautiful child, but why do you suppose that pleasant young woman married such a crude man?"

"They say power is the greatest aphrodisiac."

"Édouard..." She stopped in mid-sentence.

"What is it, chérie?"

"It's important, I think. Are we going to do that?"

"I've been asking myself the same question. Little Emily made the idea seem very attractive, didn't she? It's probably time. You're young, but if we wait too much longer I'll have a child in school until I'm seventy. But what about your career? You want to travel, write, teach here and in the States."

"Being pregnant isn't like being sick. Women have been doing it since the dawn of humanity. You of all people should know by now that I can do two things at once."

They turned to cross the Pont de la Tournelle and walk down Boulevard Saint-Germain to the restaurant, a half-hour promenade that would get them there soon after its 8:30 opening.

At the Left Bank end of the bridge, they stopped briefly to look down at the line of barges tied under the angular statue of St. Genevieve. "I wonder what it would be like to head out to sea in a boat like that, just the two of us?" she murmured with a sigh as she squeezed his arm tightly to her breast. "There. I've wanted to do that since we got to that awful party. Are you really going to do business with that dreadful banker and his cowboy brother?"

"Kiss me and find out," he replied with a smile she could barely see in the deepening twilight. She wrapped both arms around his neck as he pulled her close for a long kiss. Then they stood silent for a long moment, watching a tour boat pass slowly below.

"Not if I can help it. I was there because of Jeremy, and he was there because Icky is interested in something about that gold fund. That fund manager and his emotional bond with gold sounds really spooky — he may be the one Icky's interested in, not Henri. He seems like one of those guys convinced the world is going to hell, with raging inflation and riots in the streets. His gang has been wrong about that for the last three or four years, but show no sign of changing their minds. If I ran my business that way I wouldn't have anything left."

They walked in silence until, shortly before they reached Rue de Poissy, his phone rang. They stopped so he could answer.

"Hello, sport." Icky had long since given up trying to rid himself of his Down East accent or his endless repertoire of preppie expressions.

"I tried Jeremy, but he's probably off with his new girl. God knows I wouldn't want to talk to me, either. I have to ask — is that gorgeous creature with you?"

Eddie quickly shifted mental gears into English.

"Of course. She was the star of the show. The rich intellectuals were circling around her like moths. They either love her new book or they're jealous of it. And they're asking about her next one — she's heading out to the country in a couple of days to start her research."

"Well, remember you have to recommend me when she kicks you out." It was their standing joke.

"Jeremy's going to bring Juliette and meet us for dinner in an hour or so. But tell me why Lee Filer would want to talk to me about you. Why the hell are you dealing with a washed-up TV pundit?"

"In my world, you take information where you can find it," Icky said. He paused, and Eddie heard him cover the phone and cough before he continued. "Coming down with something. Anyway, the congressman is a good friend at appropriations time, but otherwise he's a devious jerk. He asked if I knew anything about Claude Khan or his hedge fund because he was thinking about buying in. I didn't, but he knows I'm very interested in Nazi gold. When a strong buyer comes into that market, it sometimes brings out stuff that's been hidden in attics for the last sixty-five years. He recommended Filer, who of course was up for a free trip to Paris. He does have a lot of cred among the goldbugs."

Icky went on to explain that the cocktail party was on a schedule Filer sent when he arrived in Paris a month before. The arrangement was that he would go on tour with Khan, lending his reputation to the sales effort and being paid well for it, while secretly reporting back to the congressman. Even more secretly, he was to report directly to Icky, who mainly wanted to know what other investors had signed up or shown interest, plus the source of the gold.

"He sent me emails regularly until two weeks ago, but then they stopped and I don't know why. That's why I asked you and Jeremy to go see him. It was the only place I could think of where you could talk to him in a public place."

Eddie said, "It was strange. Henri obviously was surprised when Khan didn't show up, and Filer was just as obviously frightened by the nasty-looking bodyguard type who was keeping an eye on him from across the room. And then the last thing he said was that Khan cancelled when he heard I would be there.

"He whispered something about not being able to get away from his colleagues for the last couple of weeks, but we had to break off and he's supposed to call me later tonight. What did you tell him about me?"

"Just that you were my old buddy and could show him around Paris. I might have told him you were richer than the Queen, but it was definitely all public domain stuff. But I'm glad to hear he made contact. Call me as soon as you hear from him. Anytime." The connection ended abruptly. Icky thought goodbyes were a waste of time.

∫

Aurélie took his arm again as they stepped off the curb. The crowd had thinned, leaving them momentarily alone in the street except for a young man in a red hoodie, dancing ahead to the beat of his own private music, a figure of grace and lightness who seemed to float a few inches above the pavement.

Halfway across, Eddie paused and turned to Aurélie for a kiss. He pulled her even closer and she turned eagerly to meet him — and glimpsed a dark sedan, headlights out, as it pulled quickly from behind a parked taxi and careened around the corner toward them. At the same moment, the taxi started to pull away and its front bumper caught the left rear door of the sedan, whose driver ignored the scream of tearing metal and tried to speed up, his front tires bucking and bouncing on the pavement. Aurélie instinctively tightened her grip on Eddie's arm to pull him out of the street.

"Go!" she cried urgently as the car bore down. Together they took one long step before it was on them. At the last instant, Eddie pushed her forward and she landed in a heap on the curb. He almost escaped untouched, but the car's left mirror scraped heavily across his hip. He staggered and fell next to Aurélie as she shook her head, beginning to sit up.

The sedan roared away from them at high speed and ran a red light as it turned onto Quai de la Tournelle along the Seine.

The cab driver jumped out and ran to them. "Are you OK?" he asked. "Should I call an ambulance?"

Eddie rolled slowly onto his back and moaned. Aurélie moved closer and asked, "Édouard?"

"I think I'm OK, but my butt's going to hurt," he said. He looked down and added, "These trousers have had it, but I don't think anything is broken. Did anybody get that bastard's license number?"

"It looked like he'd put something over the plate," the cab driver said. "I couldn't make it out."

The driver crouched at Eddie's side. "Those two guys made me suspicious as soon as I parked. They were loud, and loud in Russian. The driver was going on about their boss and how he really wanted to take care of somebody named Grant.

"I guess that's you, because they got really excited when you started to cross the street."

Aurélie asked, "Are you Russian?"

"Me? Russian? Not on your life. My mother is Romanian and my father is French. I grew up with her, then lived in Moscow a year, which is why I'm OK with the language. Believe me, anybody from the old Soviet satellites can spot a Russian from a mile away."

An hour later, they sat in the emergency room of the Hôtel Dieu, the old stone hospital next door to Notre Dame Cathedral, which has accepted the sick of Paris since the seventh century.

Aurélie's father, Philippe Cabillaud, a semi-retired police commissioner who kept getting called back for special projects, met them at the hospital. He pressed Eddie and Aurélie for the details again and again — Philippe was well known for his intense and detailed interrogations.

The taxi driver was a young man named Thierry Delabie, who had moved from Bordeaux with the hope of joining the National Police.

"I've been thinking back over what they were saying when I passed," he told Philippe. "They were clearly aiming at Mr. Grant, because they called his name. But as I replay their voices, I'm more and more certain their accents were Chechen, from far south Russia. Does Mr. Grant have any enemies from there? They were blowing up Moscow apartment buildings when I was there, so I know firsthand that they can be brutal."

"Eddie and Aurélie were in the headlines a lot three years ago," Philippe told him. "They found a trove of gold bars hidden in an old cellar since World War II, but the people they had problems with were mostly Americans. They thought the Russian mafia in Miami might be involved, but everybody lost interest and no one followed up."

Thierry remembered that the Peugeot had been waiting for at least ten minutes, because he had passed it on the way to drop off a fare a block farther down Boulevard Saint-Germain. After that, he circled around the block to look for a parking place close to his favorite crêpe kiosk, where he wanted to buy his dinner and wait for the next fare.

"I got there just as another cab pulled out," he said. "I think the guy in the Peugeot wanted to move up closer to the corner because I saw his brake lights come on, but I got there first, so he had to go around me. I got a call at the same time he saw Mr. Grant. He had no lights, so I couldn't see him and I hit him as I was pulling out.

"I think this might have worked out different if he hadn't had to swing out into traffic. He almost got hit by a city bus — too bad."

Eddie lay uncomfortably face down on an examining table listening to the questions and answers, covered only by an ice pack, when Jeremy arrived with Juliette on his arm.

Thierry recognized Juliette instantly. He shook her hand enthusiastically and told her he almost never missed her newscast, for which she thanked him graciously.

Jeremy, meanwhile, was patting Eddie on the shoulder. "You picked a hell of a hard way to get out of a dinner, pal," he said. "You could have just called."

"*Comment?*" Juliette asked him. "What?" Her English was not strong and she had missed the joke.

"Sorry," Jeremy said, switching back to French. "Just a joke."

A half hour later, Eddie was released with a bottle of strong pain relievers and instructions to sleep on his stomach for two days. Aurélie escaped with a sore knee and a ruined skirt. Philippe delivered them to their home at the Hôtel Luxor at 11 p.m., but not before Eddie gave Thierry his business card and made clear that he would pay for repairs to the taxi.

"Damn," Aurélie said as they prepared for bed. "I had high hopes for tonight."

"Me too, but I don't see any reason to disappoint either of us. The pills are working..." He gave her a wolfish grin.

"I'll be right back," she said with a happy smile.

CHAPTER TWO

Paris, Rue Oudinot

When Josep Darnés moved into the small apartment building as a boy, he tormented the neighbors by running up and down the spiral staircase like a young mountain goat. Now, worn by his years, he crept down as silently as he could, clinging with his right hand to the thin wooden railing while his left curled protectively around the small white dog nestled under his arm. Halfway down, he gripped the dog's muzzle gently to prevent the yips and cries he knew would come when the medicinal smells from the dentist's office enveloped them on the second-floor landing.

"Just another minute, Odette," he murmured gently to her. "We're almost there. You can already smell the fresh air."

Josep's young parents had packed their meager possessions on a worn-out bicycle and pushed it from Catalonia to Paris looking for a better life and an escape from the desperate hunger that followed World War II. They trudged slowly through the ruined landscape, dependent on the kindness of farmers as poor as they were for food and shelter. Josep was the result of a careless night in a barn a few miles south of Limoges, where the farmer had given them a bottle of rough local wine.

When he became a man, Josep began a solid career in the French National Railway near the end of the *Trente Glorieuses*, the thirty years of economic boom that followed the war, but in retirement his life became lonely and hard. His wife, who'd been a sleeping-car attendant when he met her on the Paris-Marseilles run, had died ten years before, far too soon after they'd retired together. Their son followed him into the civil service, but left to work for an international bank and now lived in Brussels. He did not often visit his dour father.

Odette was Josep's final link to his past. She was the last in a long string of small white dogs his wife had pampered beyond all reason, and when she died Josep had rechristened the puppy in her honor. Odette the Second was no genius, but eventually learned to answer to her new name.

As she'd aged her bladder had weakened, so she had to be taken out frequently. Those outings were the only times she didn't have to wear the small red diaper Josep's Belgian daughter-in-law had sewn after she'd come for a visit and found the apartment reeking of dog urine.

Josep closed the door quietly behind him, then placed Odette gently on the narrow sidewalk. "Where shall we go tonight, old girl?" he whispered as he bent over her to stroke her head and pick up the leash, a greasy length of braided leather his son had made as a teenager. "Let's go see our friend M. Duclair." He pulled the old gray jacket closer against the September chill, straightened his cap, and followed his dog down the sidewalk.

Odette wandered unsteadily back and forth, stopping at every post and doorway to sniff for other dogs. She found many. Josep followed her the hundred yards to the corner, where the lights of a neighborhood restaurant still glowed at two o'clock on a Wednesday morning. Behind the broad glass windows, the owner wiped down the last of the dozen tables in preparation for his final task, mopping the small black-and-white hexagonal tiles of the floor. Sometimes M. Duclair would invite Josep to share a glass of wine, but tonight he simply gave a friendly wave and went back to his tables.

Disappointed, Josep stopped at the corner to ponder his next step. To the left were broader sidewalks and brighter lights leading to Boulevard des Invalides and Napoleon's Tomb, where a few taxis still passed. To the right, the street was more residential — a comfortable, quiet neighborhood. He decided for no particular reason to go to the right and tugged gently on the leash. In seconds, he passed from the brilliance of M. Duclair's restaurant windows to the gloom that could have been almost any residential street, if not for the darkened Republican Guard barracks and, a few doors down, a commercial building whose windows had been bricked up for so long Josep had lost all memory of who occupied it.

Odette pulled him toward a familiar place on the curb just beyond the front door of a building much like his, with a carved stone doorframe and wrought-iron balconies.

She squatted next to a Peugeot and Josep imagined just for an instant that he heard a contented sigh. As he moved a half step closer to relieve the tension on the leash, a drawn-out cry of pure fear came from above. He looked up in panic to see a man falling past the second floor, his arms and legs flailing madly. Josep jumped back an instant before the man's head struck the car's fender and split, spraying blood and brains in every direction, but mainly on Josep's face and treasured old jacket. His body fell squarely on Odette.

CHAPTER THREE

Paris

The rising sun began to paint the towers of Notre Dame Cathedral a rosy gold as Eddie and Aurélie started on their second cups of rich café au lait, a breakfast tradition they shared every morning. They sat close together on a small teak love seat Aurélie had found in the basement a month after she moved into the penthouse atop the Hôtel Luxor, Eddie on a soft cushion he'd taken from a dining room chair. A marble table held the broken remains of a baguette and a pot of tart cherry jam. Behind it spread a postcard view of the zinc rooftops and terra-cotta chimney pots of the Right Bank.

"I always enjoy this part of the day," she told him with a smile, pulling the heavy white robe closer about her otherwise naked body. "But I feel guilty about it. We should be out running along the Seine."

As she leaned forward for the last slice of ham, he reached inside the robe to caress her breast and roll her stiff nipple between his fingers.

"Careful there," she warned with an impish smile. "Are you sure you're ready for seconds?"

She pressed her small hand over his large one and leaned forward for a kiss just as one of the two iPhones on the table behind them trilled.

"Damn. That's Philippe's ring. Better talk to him." Her father's semi-retirement had become considerably less semi since their mutual success in finding the millions of euros in Nazi gold bars. Even so, at eight o'clock most mornings he would still be in bed, usually with one of several women — Eddie's mother Margaux occasionally among them.

It was not a social call. Aurélie hardly had time to say "bonjour" before she stopped and listened intently, nodding occasionally.

She put the phone back on the table and turned to Eddie with a puzzled frown. "Bizarre. It seems my tenant threw himself off the balcony last night."

Aurélie had owned an apartment on the Left Bank since her student days and kept it as a safe haven through her bad but mercifully short marriage. Now, she rented it to foreign tourists from time to time to pay its costs and add a little to her salary as professor of French literature and history.

"I don't understand why Philippe called me, though. The gardienne has a key, unless maybe she's on vacation. In any case, I have to meet him there in an hour, less if possible. Want to go? We can finish this tonight."

"I have a lunch, but there should be plenty of time. Let's jump in the shower."

"You in yours and me in mine. Otherwise we'll never get out of here."

∫

From the Saint-François-Xavier métro station it was only a short walk to her apartment on Rue Oudinot. They waved at Philippe as he paced impatiently, talking rapidly into his telephone and gesturing with his free hand at the Peugeot parked in front of the building. As they drew closer, they saw its fender and the curb near the front tire were covered with dried blood.

Philippe shook Eddie's hand then gripped Aurélie by both shoulders. "I'm sorry to have to get you out on such short notice, but the gardienne doesn't answer and I don't want the forensics people damaging your door, so I thought it would be easier if you came over. Do you have classes today?"

"At eleven, but Édouard can stay a little longer. Madame Toulouse is probably visiting her sister in the south."

"Let me tell you the background, and make a little confession," Philippe said.

"Around two o'clock, a man fell from one of the balconies." He pointed up to the fourth floor. "We're sure it's yours because the people in the others know nothing about him. His head hit this car first, which is what killed him. Unfortunately he also killed an old man's pet, a little white mixed breed named Odette, who thought she was safely taking a crap on the curb. He barely missed the owner."

"That's terrible. Was it suicide?"

"That's what the gendarmes think, but it looks more like murder. Odette's owner saw two men walk away from the building just before the police arrived. Before we go up, you need to walk around this Peugeot and look at the other side."

"It's the same car," Aurélie said quietly when she saw the damage the taxi's bumper had caused.

"And take a look at the wing mirror. I'm lucky to be walking at all," Eddie added.

Philippe nodded and said, "Now you know what I know, and for now it's between us. Let's go upstairs?"

At the top of the stairs, a uniformed policeman touched his cap at Philippe's approach.

"This is my daughter, the owner, and her fiancé, M. Grant. She will give us access to the apartment," Philippe told him. Aurélie unlocked one of the burglar-proof locks, then put her key into the second and turned it.

"This one isn't locked. That's unusual, because the rental agent always tells tenants they should lock both of them. The insurance company would not be pleased."

A short hallway led to a double living room on the right. The tall window overlooking the street stood open, its sheer curtains flapping in the gentle breeze. Philippe looked over the wrought-iron balcony railing and said, "This must be the place. I don't see how it could have been anywhere else."

He asked her to look at several pictures on his iPhone. The first showed the man's body sprawled next to the car, the head bloody. A small white paw stuck out from under his hip.

The second was a close-up of the man's face. "Is this your tenant?" Philippe asked. "This was taken early this morning and it's pretty gory, but we need to be sure. I need to be sure."

Aurélie took the phone and said quietly, "Édouard, look at this." She held the screen up so he could see it clearly.

"It's Filer!" he said.

Then, to Philippe, "This is the goldbug we met at Henri Gascon's party last night, just before our adventure on Boulevard Saint-Germain.

He told me at the party he needed to talk to me, he had information for Icky. I see now why I didn't hear from him. I'd better tell Icky about him right now."

An hour later, they sat on the sunny terrace of a café facing busy Rue de Sèvres, waiting for their expressos to arrive. To their right, the grand old Hotel Lutetia loomed over the broad intersection like an art deco ocean liner slowly approaching its dock; across the street, homeless men and African nannies in long bright-colored dresses shared a small park. On two of the green benches, students sat hunched over their laptops, taking advantage of the free WiFi service Paris installs in its parks.

"A computer. That's what's missing," Eddie said. "Icky told me Lee Filer communicated with him by email until two weeks ago, then stopped. Today he's killed and there's no computer. It's possible, barely, that he lost it, but I think he'd have bought a new one. There's a store on every corner in Paris. If we find that computer, I believe we'll find the killers.

"Also, I gave him a card at the party and saw him drop it into his jacket pocket. The jacket was thrown on a chair in the bedroom but the card isn't there. Maybe it's nothing, but it wouldn't take much imagination to connect me with Icky. We have to assume that whoever killed Filer knows there's some connection with me."

Philippe said, "I'd hoped that part of your life was in the past, but maybe it's not quite yet. Both of you need to be careful."

"The bastards!" Eddie exploded. "It's not enough that they wiped out my family, or tried to take a shot at me. But I can't stand them threatening Aurélie. She's an innocent in this and it makes me feel like I can't protect her."

Aurélie covered his hand with hers and said gently, "No, mon chéri, I'm not an innocent. I'm part of your past, present, and future, just like you're part of mine. We have each other's backs." She rested her head on his broad shoulder for a long, silent moment.

"Now I have to confess something." Philippe looked directly at his daughter after the waiter left. "The only reason I'm involved in this at all is Icky. He asked me to find a safe house, and the only one I could think of on short notice was Rue Oudinot, so I sent him to your rental agent. I flagged the address, so when the emergency call came in I heard about it. It took a while, so Filer's body had already been moved when I got to the scene."

"So now it's doubly obvious Icky has something going here," Eddie said. "What is it?"

"I'm not sure what it's about," Philippe responded, "but he thought it was important so I helped him out. Any of us would have."

"It would've been nice to know my apartment was being used as a CIA safe house," Aurélie said with some heat. "I mean, I know Icky was Eddie's college buddy, and he's my friend too, but it's my apartment. Thanks for that."

Philippe tried to mollify her. "I am sorry, Aurélie, but I thought it would be completely uneventful. The man was something in the American gold markets, a goldbug or pundit of some sort, and Icky used him just for this one trip.

"But that means it was probably — almost certainly — murder, especially since the car that ran you down is parked in front of the building. I talked to Icky four hours ago, and now I'll wait to see what he thinks we should do. I'll have to report my involvement, which won't be fun. We get along well with the Americans, but this will look like freelancing."

"Poor Dad. Worst case, you'll have to actually become a retired policeman. Maybe you can take up fishing." She smiled, her flash of anger forgotten.

Philippe's impatience was legendary. "That's a terrible thought. Waiting for a fish is my idea of purgatory."

Aurélie stood and picked up her bag. "I must go, or I'll be late. Édouard, don't forget it's my weight-training day at the gym, so look for me around seven. It's your turn to cook."

∫

Eddie was the third generation of Grant men to serve in the U.S. Army, excluding their distant relative, the Civil War general and president. He left Paris after high school to attend college in the United States, and graduated at the right time to be a Special Forces company commander in Operation Desert Storm. His lapel displayed both his Bronze Star ribbon and the narrow red thread of the Legion d'Honneur.

When he returned from the Army, he searched for a way to follow his father into business and settled on a language school with a proud history but troubled present, whose owners were desperate to sell it. As soon as it was profitable again, he began to buy others like it. He owned at least one in every major French city and had named the entire enterprise Gran'Langue, a play on his own name and their function.

Thousands of French business managers had passed through their doors and come out speaking English; other thousands of tourists and expats had come to learn French.

His friend Thomas Jefferson Crane, who had picked up the nickname Icky early in life because his tall, gaunt frame reminded his brother of Ichabod Crane in the Washington Irving story, had been his executive officer in Desert Storm, but had chosen to join the CIA rather than return to the family textile business.

Soon after he left Philippe, Eddie sat suffering through lunch with a long-winded Londoner, cursing himself for leaving his pain pills at home. The man worked through a bottomless stack of spreadsheets and charts, explaining each in more detail than Eddie would ever remember — certainly more than he would need until he could sit down quietly and examine them on his own.

He congratulated himself for choosing the Bistro Auvergnat, an atmospheric wood-paneled place with a genuine zinc bar on the Rue Vivienne behind the Palais Royale. It had good enough food, but its main appeal was quick service, and for that reason he frequently ate there when he was alone. He chose it for this lunch because the tables were small and close together and didn't leave much room for paper, so he was spared the full effect of the over-detailed pitch. After an hour he held up his hand, promised to look carefully at the proposal, and scooped up the entire stack. He was more than halfway convinced to buy the school, mainly because it was in Bordeaux, one of the few cities where Gran'Langue had no presence. But he would do it only on the condition that the boring Mr. Barnes take his money and go away.

He'd been back in his office only a few minutes when his iPhone chirped. The screen told him Icky was calling from his personal cell phone — unusual because he usually depended on the CIA's secure communications system.

"We were just talking about you today..." Eddie began, but Icky cut him off.

"Just listen. This isn't a secure line, but I'm home with a really bad bug of some sort and I need you to do something right away." He sounded sick but deadly serious, and Eddie recognized the urgency in his voice.

"You remember when Carole Westin told you some of the odd parts of her job were overlapping? All of a sudden, the pieces seem to be coming together, and Filer's murder is a very important one.

"Go see Ahmed. I would do it myself but it will be a couple of days before I can travel, and I have some political problems with it on this end. Ahmed needs help, and for a lot of reasons you're the best one for the job. Indispensable, in fact."

"How soon?"

"He booked you on a five o'clock Air France flight that will arrive Munich around six-thirty. He'll meet you. You can stay in his guest room so you won't need a hotel."

"What's the connection between Ahmed and our dead goldbug?"

"I'm not a hundred percent sure yet, but there is one, and I hope your trip will pin it down. Call me when you arrive."

"Icky, you know I promised Aurélie I wouldn't chase the gang behind the treasure. Will this trip run me afoul of that promise?"

Silence. Eddie felt his heart beat three times before the response came.

"Eddie, I can just about guarantee Aurélie wouldn't object. I have pretty good information someone wants to put out a contract on you with the Russian mafia in Nice, and I can't do much about it officially because that asshole congressman you saw last night has my boss convinced it would get in the way of good Franco-American relations, by which he means his magic hedge fund. It's something we should let the French police handle, he says. I'll eventually work around him, but for now you're my best bet, because you know some of the players."

"That helps make clear why a couple of Russians tried to run me down last night. It doesn't seem I have much choice. Ahmed can brief me tonight."

"I got my information from a Russian restaurateur in Miami. I suspect he wasn't entirely truthful with me, but I doubt he was making it up when he said someone wants to hurt you. Be careful.

CHAPTER FOUR

Munich

As the Airbus climbed away from Charles de Gaulle Airport, Eddie sat back to think seriously about what might be going on. Why would Icky send an untrained agent to Paris, especially on a dangerous job?

He reasoned through the small amount of information he had, coming at it from every direction, and by the time the plane pulled up to the gate in Munich he was certain the search for the Raphael painting had come back to haunt him. There was nothing he would rather avoid.

Eddie did not much care about the treasure they had unearthed near Gare Saint-Lazare. The gold had gone to the French government and the paintings stored with it turned out to be pedestrian eighteenth-century Teutonic landscapes of the sort Hitler favored, not the glorious sixteenth-century self-portrait by Raphael they'd hoped to find.

Eddie could count on one hand the positive things that had emerged from that adventure. At the top of the list was Aurélie, of course, followed by learning that a single man was probably behind the death of his father as well as his wife and son, all of who died in 2001. With Aurélie's help, Eddie had found the German mobster who'd helped kill his father and set the man up for execution by his own people, but he hadn't been able to identify the shadowy force behind the entire evil enterprise — that remained a deep mystery. For six months, Eddie had crisscrossed Europe looking for clues, to no avail.

Aurélie had pleaded with him to drop the search for the sake of his own internal peace and their increasingly passionate love, and he'd acquiesced — but he'd made up a reason to visit Icky in Washington, and resumed taking volunteer assignments of the sort he had quit accepting after his family was killed.

Eddie and Icky had been classmates at a small West Texas college. When they graduated together in 1987, both went to the Army as second lieutenants, then through exhaustive Special Forces training.

Desert Storm brought the action the two young soldiers craved. Eddie had been executive officer of a front-line company when the captain commanding had been struck by appendicitis on the flight to Saudi Arabia. He got the promotion he'd wanted and Icky, as the next senior and most promising platoon leader, replaced him as number two. They worked together through the short war and left the Army soon thereafter — Eddie to return to Paris with his pregnant wife, Icky to his family's textile business in Massachusetts. The CIA tried to recruit both but only Icky signed on, mainly because he could see clearly that the future of the textile business was in Asia, not the United States. And Icky had personally recruited their classmate Ahmed Matossian to be his unofficial window into the roiling political chaos that followed the collapse of the Soviet Union.

Ahmed inherited his father's export firm in Austria, but later moved it to Germany. He said he moved so he could be closer to his suppliers, but Eddie knew he had financial problems in Vienna and had found a new investor in Munich.

Eddie found Ahmed waiting at the escalator. He hadn't changed much. His once-black hair was now shot through with gray, but still swept back from his high forehead into a pompadour. A carefully trimmed mustache curved downward beneath his thin, aquiline nose, giving him a look that, combined with his quick wit, had been catnip to a long line of college girls. His sharply cut blue pinstripe suit, finished with a beige shirt and light-blue tie, made Eddie feel underdressed. "Very distinguished," Eddie had told him at their last meeting two years before. "But I can't decide if you look more like a distinguished symphony conductor or a distinguished Hungarian pimp."

"The pimp, for sure," Ahmed shot back. "I flog washing machines in the Balkans, and in that world an orchestra conductor would starve."

Ahmed, the diminutive and charming descendant of refugees from the Armenian genocide, had used the seduction skills he'd once practiced successfully on Baptist college girls to build a thriving export business specializing in German washing machines and refrigerators, which he sold mostly in the Balkans. Icky had once told Eddie he suspected Ahmed's original success came from brokering Russian weapons to both sides of the brutal Bosnian war of the '90s. In any case he had proven to be an especially good source of information about the questionable money that sloshed among the reputable banks of Europe, which was the main interest of Icky's department, and of his deputy Carole Westin. Icky wasn't inclined to be picky about his sources.

Ahmed greeted Eddie soberly. "This is a strange one. Let's head to the office and I'll brief you as we go."

He led the way to a silver Mercedes sedan parked in a crosswalk, then made small talk until they were well away from the airport and he'd checked his mirrors carefully. He turned to Eddie with a serious look on his face.

"Two days ago, I was at the airport waiting for one of my Russian contacts, but he didn't get off his flight from Moscow. I waited for the next one but he wasn't on that, either. I called Icky, and it only took him a couple of hours to find out my man had been murdered that morning — killed by a bomb in his car as he and his wife drove to the airport." He shook his head sadly. "They were my friends, and they were on the way to the first vacation they'd had in two years. Gregor was going to spend a day helping me figure out if there's something going on in my business that shouldn't be. He said he'd learned some things I should know about.

"He was an FSB agent, very senior, who'd been posted in a lot of Western capitals. Somebody put enough plastique in his Lada to destroy a tank then set it off remotely — probably from a car ahead of them. Icky doesn't think it was an internal fight or another intelligence service. He's still checking, but that sort of thing hardly ever happens anymore. Putin just puts his political enemies in jail. There was the polonium poisoning in London, but he thinks this one was something private."

"How would that involve you and Icky?"

"Because Gregor Ashkenazi was someone I've trusted for a long time. He sent a message just last week, said he had material Icky and I needed to see and would bring it out himself, since he was already planning to come for a vacation with his wife's sister. He doesn't know Icky's real name, of course. He only knows him as Andrew. But he said

Andrew had to know about some things going on in Greece and Bulgaria. That's my territory, where I sell things, which is why I knew Gregor in the first place. He and I worked a little together, with Icky's blessing. I know he wouldn't have called for a meeting unless it was important."

"Icky thought your dead Russian had something to do with the man who fell from Aurélie's apartment in Paris last night," Eddie said. "I'm still trying to figure out what I'm doing here. What is it I need to know?"

"Icky is suspicious that one of my customers is moving bullion and maybe weapons secretly around Eastern Europe. I think the guy is about half too sharp for his own good, and I wouldn't be surprised if he's moving dirty money, because he's a well-known goldbug, but Icky's very concerned about it and now I am too after what happened to Gregor. He's also an important customer..."

∫

Eddie's iPhone interrupted. He looked at the screen and said, "Sorry, but I need to take this. It's a detective in Florida and he never makes social calls."

Thom Anderson was the Sarasota detective who'd investigated the murder of Roy Castor, the event that started the complicated international search for the missing Raphael painting. He and Eddie had become friends because of their common background in the Army and Thom's fascination with Paris.

"Eddie, heads up. Sonny Perry broke out of prison a couple of days ago. He was being transported back to Sarasota for a court hearing when somebody forced the prison van off the road. When we found it, the driver and guard had been shot. They took Sonny away in a van, which we found a couple of hours later abandoned at an Interstate rest stop up near Tampa. There were bolt cutters in the back, along with his handcuffs and leg irons. It was well planned, and it means we have a really bad actor on the loose somewhere, and he has smart friends. You're probably high up on his shit list."

"I'd hoped that sleazy bastard would die in jail, and soon," Eddie said. "I'll keep my eyes open. What was he doing away from the prison?"

"Another sanity hearing for his old boss. Sonny was on the way down to testify yet again about Al Sommers's erratic behavior. It'll never come to anything and one of these days Sommers will just keel over and be done with it, but for now the judge is still listening. They both used to be bankers."

Sonny and Al Sommers had played central roles in Eddie's search for the elusive Raphael painting. Sonny and his lover, a Russian mafia enforcer named Dmitri, had locked Eddie in an old fallout shelter behind Sommers's home outside Sarasota. When Dmitri tried to use Eddie as a human shield against the approaching police, Eddie set a trap and killed him.

Sommers had convinced himself that Roy, and before him Artie Grant, knew how to find the painting.

Eddie knew Sonny and Dmitri, plus the German mobster Erich Kraft, had killed Artie in 2001, but weren't the brains behind the crime. This time, Eddie had a growing feeling that he was about to cross paths with the mastermind, and the thought filled him with an exhilarating mixture of dread and anticipation. He had almost no fear for his own safety, but he was concerned that the maelstrom might suck in the people he loved, and he was determined to avoid that at all costs.

∫

Ahmed left the freeway to drive into a small industrial park just as the streetlights came on. A one-story beige warehouse with a simple black-and-white "Import-Export" sign faced a parking lot separated from the freeway by a high fence. He parked in a space marked prominently with his initials, next to a black BMW convertible.

"Everyone's gone for the day except for the sales rep I want you to meet. She picked up some information about the customer Icky suspects, and wants to tell you about it."

"Me? Do I know her?"

"She knows you. Her name is Jennifer Wetzmuller."

"What? Jen?" Eddie was dumbfounded. He and Jen had a history — a passionate three-day affair in 1988 and another brief and even hotter one twenty years later, which started soon after she arrived in Paris bearing a cryptic letter from her father, shortly after his murder — the murder for which Sonny Perry had been sent to prison. The letter contained the key clues that launched the frantic search for the Raphael and the gold.

He'd heard Jen had moved back to her native Germany after closing her art gallery. Thom told him most of her inheritance had been used to keep her out of prison for diverting money she'd owed to clients.

"I've met Jen twice, and both times we wound up in bed."

Ahmed arched an eyebrow as if to ask, "You too?"

"I left her behind in Sarasota on bad terms and have no interest in seeing her again. But I still want the man behind the gang that killed her father and mine, and I suspect she wants the same thing."

"She never mentioned that. She just said she had picked up some information that you'd understand better than anyone else. Icky suggested bringing you in and she thought it was a great idea. I think she's starting to be afraid of this guy, and so am I, but he's a good customer and I don't want to piss him off if I can help it."

"And I don't want to replay the whole treasure thing, or the Jen thing," Eddie replied.

The reception area was dark except for a shaft of light cast from a small office on the left. He could feel his pulse start to race as he saw Jen's familiar figure, fashionable in a white blouse and a blue skirt reaching precisely to the top of her knees — the same outfit she'd worn the day she arrived in Paris with Roy's letter. The effect was just as dramatic this time.

He took a step toward her and extended his hand, which she ignored as she threw both arms tightly around his neck.

"Eddie!" she said with the excitement of a woman considerably younger than her forty years. "I was afraid I'd never see you again." After an embarrassed moment he put both arms around her waist and drew her close, conscious of the pert breasts straining through the thin blouse. Her scent was delicious.

He held her for longer than he intended then backed away, trying to avoid her lips without seeming to do so.

"Jesus, Jen, you look as good as you did in Paris. How do you do it?"

"Paris? How about Sarasota?"

"There, too, but you look a little different here."

"Sure. Here I have my clothes on."

Ahmed cleared his throat to interrupt. "I'm glad you're glad to see each other, but we have serious business to see to tonight. Can we do that first?"

He sat at the head of a small conference table with Jen on his right and turned to Eddie.

"Jen has some concerns about one of our customers, and we've been talking about it for a couple of days. I've also talked to Icky about it — Jen hasn't met him but knows who he is — and he would like us to pool our information and see what we can figure out, since he's sick and can't come here yet."

He nodded to Jen as a signal to begin.

"Eddie, you know I came back to Germany when I left Sarasota. I didn't have much money left and my aunt was kind enough to take me in. She lives in a village near Frankfurt, but I didn't know her well. She was ten years older than my mother and they were separated before the war, so they weren't close."

"Lucky for you she still lives there."

"It sure was. I had a hard time finding a job and was afraid I would run out of money when she introduced me to Ahmed, who was looking for a sales representative. One thing led to another, and I now cover the firm's largest account, a man named Claude Khan, who buys appliances from us and resells them in the Balkans, mainly Bulgaria. I was pretty good at sales at my gallery in Sarasota, and I found I could learn how to sell washing machines fairly easily."

She looked across the table at Eddie and seemed to be seeking his approval.

Eddie paused and thought carefully before he spoke. "I know something about Khan. He's trying to put together a hedge fund to buy gold bullion. Just yesterday I was at a cocktail party for prospective investors, but he didn't show up."

She pulled a gold pen from the pocket of her skirt and began to twist it absentmindedly.

"Mr. Khan has become important to both of us. Ahmed leased him warehouse space in this building, so when he orders appliances from me they're basically delivered to him when we receive them. Then when the truck comes for our shipments, his are loaded at the same time, or sometimes he uses his own truck."

Ahmed interrupted. "Every week or two he sends two men over to pick up his boxes and roll them into his side of the warehouse, which he always keeps locked, then he pays me for them the next day. It's a nice deal for both of us — I get the cash right away and I can bundle his purchases with larger orders and get a discount. But it's just business."

Jen continued. "I've become friends with Claude ... Mr. Khan. I spend the occasional weekend at his country home not far from here" — Eddie thought her face reddened just slightly — "but otherwise our relationship is completely professional. He's quite a bit older than I am, or maybe I should say I'm quite a bit younger than he is, which may help explain the attraction."

"What can you tell me about his background?" Eddie asked.

Ahmed spoke up. "He's a mongrel, like most of us. He's half French and half Arab — he was born in Paris during the war and lived there until he was eighteen, then moved back to his father in Saudi Arabia. Since then he's knocked around, done a lot of things. He lived for a time in East Germany. He speaks French like a native and his German is fluent..."

"But he has that Eastern accent," Jen said. "Like the men you disarmed so neatly that night in Paris. There's no mistaking it — it's like hearing an American speak French." The gold pen twisted faster and faster.

Ahmed added, "He's also into finance. When he started the gold fund, I invested a little money in it. He says the price is bound to keep climbing, and might even jump a lot before too long."

Eddie turned back to Jen. "The first thing I need to know is, does Khan know about Icky and Ahmed's connection to him?"

"No," she replied. "Ahmed told me that would be dangerous, so I've been very careful never to mention Mr. Crane."

"Good. Icky was looking for someone who's buying up gold. That could be part of what's going on.

"Ahmed, your Russian friend Gregor said he had information about one of your customers. Do you think it was Khan? There are a lot of signs that he could be of interest to Icky and the CIA. If that is the case, the Russians will want to know, too."

Jen said, "I mentioned this to Ahmed because Claude has started acting strangely. Several weekends ago, I waited for him at his house and he never appeared, just sent a Russian who needed a shave and a bath to apologize and tell me he'd be there the next week, which he was. But then he acted like a man under a lot of pressure. He spoke pretty roughly to me. He apologized and said he was tired from negotiating some new products for the Balkans. It was the first time he wasn't a perfect gentleman. I was afraid of him."

"The Arabs aren't big on women's rights," Ahmed replied. "I suspect he really thinks you're just a tight warm place..."

"Please, Ahmed!" she said. Then, "Excuse me a minute. Too much coffee."

When he heard the bathroom door close, Eddie said quickly, "She's frightened of him, and not because of one bad experience. And she hasn't told us everything. Did she leave out anything she'd already told you?"

"What she didn't say, and she may not even know, is that her aunt wasn't the only reference that got her the job. Claude asked me personally to hire her, and said he also knew the aunt. But for some reason neither of them wanted her to know that."

They heard the toilet flush. As Jen's footsteps approached the door Eddie said, "Let me try something."

As she sat down again he asked gently, "Jen, did you know Claude Khan before you met him at your aunt's?"

A puzzled look crossed her face. "That's a question I've asked myself. When I was a child in Frankfurt, just a year or two before my mother died, she introduced me to a man who spoke German like he did, with an Eastern accent and a sort of bureaucratic flavor. I came downstairs as she and my stepfather were talking to this man. I don't remember his name, but it certainly wasn't Khan. It was something longer, something more Eastern. And that man didn't look quite like Claude. Of course, that was a long time ago, thirty years, but there's something about him that seems familiar."

"Has he ever shown signs that he knew you in the past? That would be pretty hard to conceal."

"Nothing obvious, but he's acted very familiar from the first. But it's not just me. He knows about you, too. A week ago he let slip that he knew about all the deaths in your family. He didn't say anything more about it and I didn't push him, but it made me nervous. Claude is smooth enough himself, but he surrounds himself with some rough characters, mostly Russians. I know we didn't part on the best terms, but I don't want you hurt. That's why I asked Ahmed to contact you after his source was killed. I was suspicious and a little frightened."

"I appreciate that. Tell me about the meeting with your stepfather. What was their behavior? Were they old friends just getting together for a visit, or was it something else?"

"Well, they were friendly, but it wasn't just a beer-and-schnapps meeting. My stepfather was pretty deferential, like you'd be to a boss."

∫

Eddie and Ahmed questioned Jen closely for two hours. At the end, Ahmed pulled three Amstel beers from a small refrigerator in the corner and they sat back to decide on the next step.

"Jen, Eddie and I need to hash this over, then talk to Icky. Can you come back late tomorrow morning so we can fill in any blanks that occur to any of us overnight?"

"I have a customer appointment at eleven. Early afternoon would be better."

"Then let's all be here at two," Ahmed responded.

As they walked to the parking lot, Eddie asked her, "Is that the same BMW?"

"Couple of years newer, but it performs just as well and it gets more practice here. The speed limits on the autobahns are really high, where they exist at all."

"Keep it warm. Sonny broke out of jail. You may have to outrun him again." The two of them had escaped from Sonny and Dmitri in a highway chase in Florida only because of her high-speed driving skills.

As Eddie opened the door of Ahmed's car, Jen leaned toward him. "I have some spare space if you'd rather..."

Eddie paused for several seconds. "Thanks, but we need to talk. I'll go with Ahmed tonight and see you tomorrow." He touched her hand gently. "It's nice to see you again." She beamed.

Then, as Ahmed closed his door and could no longer hear her, she turned serious. "Eddie, there's more for your ears only. Give me your number and I'll call you late tonight."

As they drove toward Ahmed's home, Eddie texted Icky to expect a phone call within the hour, then asked Ahmed, "What do you make of all that?"

"I'm undecided. I can't figure out if she's really found something important or is just puffing it up to make another pass at you."

"There's something there. I can feel it," Eddie said. "I learned in Sarasota that she doesn't frighten easily, but she's scared of something now. If I had to guess, Claude Khan is someone Icky needs to know more about — which Icky already suspects — and all this talk of new products in the Balkans is smoke, maybe covering something more sinister."

Ahmed said, "But why did she tell us, unless it's just fear of Claude?"

Eddie was silent for a moment. "If he's the nightmare he might be, she's right to be scared of him. Or she's working with him. We can't exclude that."

Ahmed guided the Mercedes smoothly into a double garage next to a gleaming black Porsche. "My wife's," Ahmed said when he saw Eddie's quizzical glance.

The house looked American, a twenty-first-century version of their professors' suburban homes during their college days. They walked through the kitchen door into a family room, where Ahmed's wife sat watching *The Tonight Show*. She rose quickly and pulled a scarf over her head, then turned off the television.

"Eddie, meet Halime," Ahmed said. She was a dark-haired beauty who Eddie calculated was fifteen years younger than Ahmed, several years younger than Aurélie. Ahmed obviously still had the touch.

He extended his hand but she did not take it.

"I should explain," Ahmed said. "Halime is more Muslim than Mohammed in some things, like not shaking hands with men, not so much in others..."

"I can tell my own story, thank you," she interrupted in fluent English, her dark eyes flashing. "You must be Mr. Grant. I am Halime, and at home I am a faithful follower of the Prophet. Outside of the house I live among the Germans in the way they expect. Sixty years ago, my father moved to Germany along with millions of other jobless Turks. I was born here, but I still consider myself a Turk. I went to college in the United States, at Columbia."

"That explains the English," Eddie replied. "In any case, I'm pleased to meet you. I went to college there, too, but Ahmed and I had to settle for that little place in Texas. Aurélie will be a visiting professor at Columbia for the spring term next year. We're looking forward to living in New York."

"It makes for an odd life," Ahmed said. "I'm a Jew, she's a Muslim, we live in a country that doesn't much like either, and I do business with some of the most vicious Arab and Balkan Muslims in the world. Not to mention the Russians, who are in a class by themselves."

"Ah, but we live in Munich because the food is so good," Halime said. Her half smile said she wasn't entirely serious. "And, of course, Ahmed has made a good living here as well. And I enjoy my work as a nurse.

"So that's all out of the way. Everyone's been introduced. Would you like a sandwich, a glass of wine, a beer? I have roast beef."

Halime was charming, there was no doubt about it, but Eddie had a feeling that seducer Ahmed might have reached too far for this one. Something told him she was the seducer, not the seduced, and from the look she gave him from under the scarf he suddenly suspected his name had just been written on her list.

Icky had texted back asking them to call in a half hour, so Eddie took his sandwich into the guest bedroom and dialed Aurélie, hoping she wasn't already in bed.

She wasn't. "How did it go, chéri? Is this the breakthrough?"

"Could be. The biggest surprise is that Ahmed's informant is Jen Wetzmuller, and she works for him now."

Silence. Eddie waited because he knew Aurélie suspected, correctly, that if Jen hadn't been too closely connected to Al Sommers and his group, Eddie might well have brought her back to Paris with him — as he wished he'd done after their first affair in 1988, instead of marrying Lauren Adams. Aurélie had treated the entire episode as something from his past to be forgotten and they hadn't discussed it, any more than they discussed her own disastrous marriage.

"What is she doing there, Édouard? That seems very strange."

"She had nowhere to go when she lost the art gallery in Sarasota and she was nearly broke, so she moved back to Germany and settled with an aunt who lives near Frankfurt. The aunt knew Ahmed a little, so helped Jen get a sales job with him. She's done well, no surprise, but Ahmed also says the aunt wasn't the only push he got. The other was from a customer who is none other than our man Claude Khan, who Ahmed thinks may be involved in something suspicious, like maybe smuggling. He's a large customer now — her most important, and Ahmed's. They even share warehouse space. So he's into both washing machines and gold. Either or both could be very attractive to a smuggler."

"What does Icky think?"

"Don't know yet. We're to call him in about fifteen minutes."

Aurélie told him her train would leave the following morning from Gare Montparnasse. She planned to stay in and around Poitiers "for about a week — or until I get too horny," doing interviews and digging in the town's historical library for information about the Vendée War, the region's spirited royalist backlash to the French Revolution. "I'll be at the Hôtel Normandie. Please call me often."

"I promise. And don't worry about Jen. She's the past and you're the future."

∫

Ahmed knocked. They sat together on the large bed while Eddie dialed. Icky answered on the first ring.

"I've called in several chits for what I'm about to tell you," he said, hoarse but less so than earlier in the day. "It's a combination of suspicion and new fact, and some of it comes from a really dirty source, some of it from the Paris police.

"First, Sonny Perry escaped from prison in Florida. Whoever sprung him killed two guards, so the state is hot on his trail."

"The detective called from Sarasota to tell me," Eddie said.

"Second, and this is mainly for you, Eddie. Somebody is moving suspicious amounts of money and gold bullion around Germany and the Balkans. As I told you earlier, someone — I think it's the same guy — is also agitating with the Russian mafia in Nice to do something unpleasant to you, like maybe a kidnapping. I can't think of any reason for that combination except the painting, can you? Too many pieces of the puzzle fit together — a frustrated goldbug could be dangerous.

"And third, two known members of a Chechen nationalist group, who were the crème de la crème of terrorists until the Middle East got hot, boarded a plane from Moscow to Paris just a few hours after Ahmed's FSB agent was killed. French immigration gave them a hard time but couldn't find enough reason to exclude them. Philippe Cabillaud confirms they haven't caught a plane out, so God knows where they are now. If the assassination of Gregor Ashkenazi and his wife was related somehow to the guy moving the gold around, it's also likely those two had something to do with throwing poor Filer off a balcony in Paris."

"What was he doing there?" Ahmed asked.

"He used to be one of the most prominent goldbugs on late-night cable TV, until his star faded," Icky replied. "We got a lead on a group in Paris that's been shipping a lot of bullion and we can't figure out why. It's not illegal by itself, but the price is pretty high now so it's suspicious. Also, we think we might run into some old Nazi assets if we cultivate people like that, or we might stumble into a terrorist financing network. Cases and cases of gold bars like the ones in that old count's basement haven't been seen since 1945, and now every one of them is worth a million and a quarter dollars. Gold was trading for less than 900 dollars an ounce then but it's almost twice that now, so it's that much more interesting to the true goldbugs of the world.

"My goldbug couldn't pass up a chance to help out his country's intelligence service, especially if it meant a free trip to Paris. He was referred to me by our favorite Texas congressman, so I hope Philippe can figure out what happened to him. The congressman makes a lot of speeches about how we ought to return to the gold standard and get rid of the Federal Reserve, and thought this guy's status would give him an in with the European goldbugs. Said his own brother was a gold buyer, too, and he's a banker in Paris."

Eddie said, "I met both of them last night at the banker's cocktail party. The congressman comes across as a windbag."

"Of course he does. He's in Congress. They have a saying for his type down there — all hat and no cattle."

"I can believe that. Anyway, Philippe is pretty sure Filer was murdered, but I don't think he knew the poor guy was a volunteer."

"I've given Philippe the name of the Russian Mafioso who's the threat. He runs a restaurant in Nice and wants you to think he's just a poor businessman, but he's in charge of a lot of the dirty stuff. I've talked once to his brother, who does much the same thing in Miami. Philippe is going to have a chat with the man in Nice and I'll send somebody to talk to his brother, in Miami."

Eddie said, "The guy who locked me up in a fallout shelter in Sarasota worked for the mafia in Miami. I'd bet it's all one big octopus with tentacles spread everywhere."

"As I recall it didn't end well for him — his friends may still be mad at you, even after three years. That's one of the reasons I don't trust these guys even a little bit."

Eddie tried to wrap up the call. "We're going to talk to Jen again tomorrow afternoon and then I'll go home, unless there's something else you want me to stay for."

"Just let me know if she has anything new. I think the next step in France has to come from Philippe. And, Eddie, you need to watch your back until we find out what's going on."

Watch his back, indeed. This was the day Eddie had seen coming, and he relished the fight. True, he had promised Aurélie he wouldn't seek it out, but now it was coming to him, and he would face it on his own terms. To do that, he needed to know more about the enemy, and he was convinced Jen was a key. It was clear she hadn't told him everything while Ahmed had been in the room. He looked forward to her call.

∫

He didn't have long to wait. A half hour after Ahmed left him alone in the guest room, his iPhone rang.

"Jen?" he asked, and that was all the invitation she needed.

"I've missed you, Eddie. I wish you were here with me now, so I could whisper all this very serious information to you across the pillow just the way we did in Sarasota." Her voice was low and sexy. He could feel himself responding just the way he had three years before.

"There's a story I need to tell you. Please don't breathe a word of it, especially to Ahmed. Parts of it will have to be our secret. Will you promise me that?"

"I can't give you a one hundred percent promise, but I won't tell Ahmed. I might have to tell Icky about it."

"Mr. Crane would be OK." Later, when he replayed the mental recording of what had happened that day, and what would happen in the days after it, he wondered how he missed such an important clue.

∫

"I wasn't down to my last dime, but I needed to find a job," was the way Jen described her life during the six months after they separated in Sarasota.

"I was still hurting over Roy's death, but everybody I knew had been involved in it one way or another. I had to do something. I'd been in Virginia, but the job ended so I went back to Sarasota, where at least I had a place to live. I had decided to come back to Germany. I still had my citizenship and spoke the language, but I knew no one except my aunt in Frankfurt.

"While I was in Sarasota, I went to see Al Sommers. He was in the hospital, in a section where they treat prisoners, and to my surprise he was happy to see me."

"You probably looked a lot better to him than the jailers," Eddie said.

"That may have had something to do with it. In any case, I asked him to help me find the man who'd bought the World War II loot Sonny inherited from his father, and reminded him he could still be caught up in that investigation, too, because he'd sold some gold church furnishings the same way. I figured anybody with those contacts would be able to help me find a job, even one a little dicey.

"He said he'd never heard a name and had no way to contact him other than through a man who owns a restaurant in Miami."

"Was this man's name Boris?" Eddie asked.

"Oh, do you know about him? He owns the Golden Samovar on South Beach. Boris wouldn't give me a name, but said he would send him a message and ask him to contact me."

This can't be entirely coincidence, Eddie mused as Jen talked on. This was the second time today he'd heard about Boris, the man Icky was confident lay at the center of the Russian mafia's activities in South Florida.

"Icky mentioned him to me earlier today. I'm beginning to see where this all is going."

"I moved to Frankfurt the next week and started looking for work, without much luck. Even in Germany, there was still a lot of unemployment. This was near the end of the recession, remember?"

"I sure do," Eddie replied. "And for a lot of people, it's not over yet."

"Then, after three or four weeks, Claude Khan knocked on my aunt's door. He apologized for taking so long and said he'd been in Eastern Europe on business, but that he thought he could help me. He took my aunt and me out to a fancy Russian dinner downtown, then asked me to visit him in Munich that weekend.

"It was funny. You know I like big men and here I was with this little guy hitting on me. And he was old enough to be my father. But there was something about him I can't quite identify. He had charm and gave me the feeling he could get important things done, a lot like you. I liked him."

"Ummm," Eddie responded, surprised at a sudden feeling of envy. "So how did the meeting go?"

"There's more. I found out later that he hadn't been in Eastern Europe all that time, because a neighbor told my aunt he'd been sniffing around for the last two weeks. I think he was checking on my movements, seeing if I was legit or some sort of plant. I really was looking for a job, so I guess I passed his test.

"The meeting was fine. He told me he'd received my name from a friend in Paris, who had heard about me from Miami but didn't have a job for me then. Claude told me he had a friend in the import-export business who was looking for a new sales rep, and if I could sell paintings I could certainly sell washing machines. So he suggested that I apply to Ahmed for the job. I did, Ahmed hired me, and I've been here since.

"I like the job and found I was pretty good at it. I don't mean Claude's part of it, that's easy, but finding new clients and making them happy. Claude is Ahmed's most important customer, but one thing you should know is that he's more than that. Ahmed got in financial trouble a few years back and had to look for an investor. Claude bought into the business. I don't know how much of it he owns, but enough that Ahmed listens to him.

"He has another business like it in Buenos Aires, but there I think he owns the whole thing. Most of my dealings with him have been long distance, except for the weekends I told you about."

"How long has he been doing that?" Eddie asked.

"Three years. He told me when I first met him that he was flying back after our dinner in Munich. He comes to Germany three or four times a year and stays about a month each time. He doesn't want people knowing he's in town."

"So if he's the man I've been looking for, it's no wonder I never found him."

"That could be it. One other thing: be careful of Halime. On the surface it looks like they have a good marriage, but Ahmed is thinking of leaving her."

"Why?" Eddie asked.

"Because she's too close to Claude. It makes me feel funny, since in a way that makes her a threat to me. But Ahmed found out they'd been getting it on. I suspect it's mainly so Claude can get information about what Ahmed's doing, but that's not the whole story. She's a very sexy lady. I'm not at all sure Ahmed's enough man for her. It may take two of them."

∫

Aurélie called Eddie the next morning shortly before she left for Montparnasse station, but he was already on the phone with Icky, planning their next meeting with Jen. When he returned the call an hour later, there was no answer. He figured the train was in an area with poor cell service, unusual in France but not impossible in the rural countryside.

They questioned Jen closely about Khan's movements, trying to connect them to Icky's timeline of known gold shipments into

Germany. Jen had only accompanied him on one trip, about four months before. It was, she said, a boring business visit to the Black Sea port of Burgas, a long and dreary flight with a change in Sofia.

"I hardly saw anything but the inside of the hotel. Claude met his customers after dinner the first night we were there, which I thought was strange. The next day he had a lunch meeting. I did some shopping, but frankly Bulgaria isn't my first choice for a vacation."

"Did he say anything about where he was meeting these customers, or who they were?" Eddie asked.

"Russians for sure," she said. "And he was meeting someone unusual at the docks. I remember he changed to jeans and a knit shirt. I'd never seen him so casual before — he's usually a suit-and-tie type. He said he had to go on an old tramp steamer to be sure none of his appliances had been stolen. It was odd that he'd meet anyone on a boat. He's scared to death of the water — I think he'd rather be burned alive than swim.

"This was supposed to be the handshake meeting for a new and important account. Of course I was very interested in it because it would be more business for me and Ahmed, but that hasn't happened yet. I asked him about it a couple of weeks ago and he said it would happen soon, but he was vague."

Ahmed said, "I remember when you went with him. He told me he enjoyed it."

"I can imagine that," she said with a fleeting half smile.

"Does he go other times?" Eddie asked.

"Sure. He's trying to build the import side of his business. It's expensive to drive a truck to the Balkans for eighteen hours and bring it back empty. His crew are Chechens and he doesn't trust them much, so he wants to be there when the truck is loaded. Now and then he will fly over and come back with the truck, but that's a long drive and he has a bad back. I think he brings back mixed cargo, but nothing we handle."

Eddie looked at Ahmed. "What's your guess?"

"Cigarettes. Somebody approached me once about selling black-market counterfeit. There's a big demand for them among the immigrants in Germany and France, where taxes are high. I've heard the newest ones are such good copies you can't tell them from the real thing, right down to the tax stamps.

"He'd better be careful, though. With the recession, the customs people are looking much harder. The French are murder on it — just about any kind of tax evasion means jail time there if you're caught."

Jen and Ahmed worked together to assemble a description of the two men they'd seen move boxes to Khan's side of the warehouse.

"Do you have any surveillance video?"

"Normally we do," Ahmed said. "But my agreement with Claude is that we turn off the cameras when he's moving his own merchandise around.

"His deal is mainly for my benefit, so I couldn't really refuse. His boxes show that they're shipped from my address, to look like they're part of my shipment. They aren't really because he has control of them before they're shipped, and he uses his own truck. I know it's a risk and he could slip something illegal into one of them, but he was just too good a customer to ignore. So I do it."

Eddie, surprised, asked him, "If you think he would smuggle cigarettes into Germany, how could you doubt he would smuggle something the other way? It puts your entire business at risk."

Jen asked, "Are you through with me? I'm taking a client to dinner and I need to get ready."

Eddie looked at Ahmed and nodded. "I think so. Go ahead. I'll come back if anything comes up."

"This won't be a long dinner. If you'd like a nightcap after ..."

"Thanks," Eddie said, "but I'm going to try to go home tonight. I'm sure I'll be back, though, and we'll have that drink. There's one more question that just occurred to me. Does Khan try to keep track of where you and Ahmed go, what you do?"

Jen said, "Not really. We hardly ever see him in the office. He did call one day last week and said he wanted to meet Ahmed a few days later. Ahmed and I share a calendar so I was able to tell him that wasn't a good day because Ahmed would be out of the office."

"Did he ask where?"

"Yes, he did, and it seemed harmless enough. It was the day Ahmed went to the airport to meet the plane from Moscow."

∫

After she drove away, Eddie sat back in his chair and said, "I think we've done everything we can do at this point. Rather than hang around until tomorrow, I think I'll go home tonight."

"OK. Halime is ready to make dinner if you'd like to stay, but I understand. If you need to go, I'll run you to the airport."

"Let me talk to Aurélie first and see how she's doing."

"Call her from the conference room and I'll check the web to see what's available," Ahmed responded.

Aurélie didn't pick up immediately and Eddie's finger was poised over the disconnect button when he heard the ringtone stop. There was silence on the line and he said, tentatively, "Aurélie?"

A chill raced up his spine as a man's guttural voice said in fractured English, "She is our guest." His first fear was that this was the threat Icky had warned about. But he wasn't the target — Aurélie was, and that filled him with a cold, determined rage, an iron resolution that the perpetrators would pay dearly.

He pushed his own emotions far into the background so he could focus on the man's voice, its texture, not just his words. It could be crucial to Aurélie's future — their future together.

"She will not be hurt if you do what we want. Return to Paris immediately and have nothing more to do with the Jew Ahmed." The line went dead.

Eddie stood for a moment, in shock, but the soldier in him worked carefully through the entire conversation. There had been street noise in the background, but nothing more than the sounds of any Paris street. The accent was generic and could be a Russian or an actor, but he would bet on a citizen of the old Soviet empire who'd learned English as an adult, and not all that well.

He walked quickly back into Ahmed's office. "Aurélie's been kidnapped," he said hoarsely. He felt like his knees were about to give way. "I need to go back now."

"There's a flight in two hours. Let's use the phone in the conference room." Ahmed grabbed a notebook and pen and led Eddie back. "You sit down and take a deep breath."

The first call went to Philippe, who Eddie knew would pass the case off to specialists. It would be a bad idea for him to lead the investigation into the kidnapping of his own daughter.

"Philippe, when I just called a man with a Russian accent answered her phone and said I should leave town and stay away from Ahmed."

Philippe paused for a moment, then said coolly, "I'll get a notepad. When I come back tell me everything you know."

Eddie could hear water run in the background and thought Philippe was wise to impose a brief delay.

"Now tell me."

Eddie related Aurélie's plan to visit Poitiers for her book research, and his efforts to call her during the day.

"First we'll find out if she got on the train or checked into the hotel," Philippe said. "Then we'll canvass to see if anyone saw her. You'd better call Icky. This is probably fallout from the treasure of Saint-Lazare and we'll need his help.

"We want to do this as quickly as we can, but we have to do it deliberately. Don't do anything without talking to me. I'll go into the office and have a car meet you at CDG."

Icky's reaction was much the same as Philippe's, except that it wasn't his daughter who'd been kidnapped.

"Eddie, I'm sorry this happened," he said. "The Paris police will do all they can, and I know what I have to do. It's only noon here, so I'm going to pay a call on a couple of dirty Russians, including the restaurateur in Miami I mentioned last night. A very pointed call. With Sonny Perry on the loose, I'd be very surprised if they're not involved. We'll find her.

CHAPTER FIVE

Paris

Kidnapping a commissioner's daughter was completely unacceptable to the Paris police. Within a few minutes detectives knew Aurélie had not checked into the hotel in Poitiers. Shortly after that, they found the conductor of the TGV and learned that her seat had been vacant from the time his train left Paris. The taxi driver had dropped her at the Boulevard Pasteur entrance of Gare Montparnasse, the one used by most TGV passengers, and had seen her roll her black suitcase into the station.

After an hour of interviewing shopkeepers, cleaners, and other staff, they had found a newspaper kiosk operator who remembered seeing a tall blonde who looked much like the one in the picture each detective carried. Her kiosk had the prime position for TGV customers coming into the station. She remembered clearly that Aurélie had picked up three newspapers, Le Figaro, Le Monde, and the International Herald Tribune, and opened her purse to pay when she was approached by a tall, skinny man with a pronounced Adam's apple. After a few heated words in English, which the witness hadn't understood, the blonde replaced the newspapers and walked back toward the door. The man pulled her suitcase, and the witness saw him push the blonde into the back seat of a blue Ford and climb in after her.

"I thought it was a lovers' quarrel or I would have called the police." She squirmed to resettle her bulky frame on the stool and readjusted her headscarf, obviously nervous to be the center of police attention. "He didn't do anything but talk to her, but just as she got into the car she kicked him in the leg, hard. It must have been very painful, and I don't think she was aiming for his leg. And then I went off for my lunch and just came back."

"So she's probably still in Paris," Philippe told Captain Alberti, who had been placed in charge of the investigation. "At least we know that much. Now we have to find out where."

"Indeed. Where among a million apartments? They aren't completely stupid, but they may be overconfident," the captain replied. "Her telephone was right next to the préfecture when M. Grant reached it. This has the fingerprints of organized crime, so we'll find her but it may take a while."

"We don't know how much time we have," Philippe said.

∫

Icky meant business. He was already coordinating action with an old friend who'd retired from the CIA five years before and lived in Nice, less than a mile from the restaurant he was sure was the direct conduit for information between the Miami and Nice branches of one of the most active Russian organized-crime families.

He also placed a call to Raul Gutierrez, a CIA coordinator who lived in Miami. Officially, Raul's job was to provide liaison with the South Florida police departments, but he'd made his reputation as a successful young agent in Cuba, his grandparents' homeland. That, combined with good spoken Russian, had earned him the promotion. He called it "a wussy desk job," but Icky knew he loved Miami.

Raul had dealt with the Miami Russians before and didn't like them at all, which Icky figured was an advantage because his plan depended on intimidating the man who'd told him only part of the truth the day before. He would pay for that.

Icky began calls the way he ended them — brusquely. "We need to have a chat with Boris Budzivoi, who owns the Golden Samovar Restaurant on South Beach. Have you dealt with him?"

"That sleaze? He acts like he's St. Augustine, but he's up to his ass in everything dirty that goes on down here, plus some international stuff."

"We lost an agent in Paris a couple of days ago," Icky said. "He was unofficial but he was still ours, and we think a couple of Chechens threw him off a balcony two days after they blew up an FSB officer in

Moscow. That poor guy was on his way to the airport with some information for our man in Munich. They killed his wife, too.

"Now somebody with a Russian accent has kidnapped the fiancée of one of our volunteers in Paris, who was also my company commander in Desert Storm. He's an all-round good guy named Eddie Grant, and his fiancée is one of the most gorgeous creatures you'll ever meet."

"Sounds like you'd like to know her better," Raul said.

"I may have wanted to once, but that won't happen now. Anyway, I called Boris yesterday after we picked up word that he was involved in getting Sonny Perry out of the state prison. The story was that somebody in Europe was trying to put out a contract to hurt Eddie because of a case we had a while back, and Sonny was to be the instrument.

"Boris told me he wasn't involved, but his brother in Nice might be. What he didn't tell me is that either he or his brother in Nice or one of their friends were involved in kidnapping Aurélie Cabillaud. I want you to find out what he knows."

"I'd like that," Raul responded. "He and his people are behind too much of the crime in South Florida. I'm guessing we'll find connections to your day job, because the word is that Boris is right at the center of money laundering. The Secret Service looked at him a couple of years ago.

"Should I go over to his place? He'll be there now."

"Wait just a few minutes. I have some information coming in about his telephone calls and emails. They might give you some leverage."

CHAPTER SIX

South Beach, Miami

A n hour later, Raul steered his black Impala slowly up Ocean Drive. The queen palms towering over the beachfront park cast shadows in the afternoon sun, giving him the feeling he was climbing an endless ladder. Tourists milled about on the sidewalks, where in a few hours crowds of young clubgoers would gather.

He found a space two doors north of his target, an over-decorated restaurant with its namesake golden samovar carved on a garish sign above the door. A few empty tables sat on the sidewalk.

He pulled open the door and stepped into the gloom of the old restaurant. The dark carpet had seen better days. It felt sticky under his feet.

"Sorry, but we don't open until six." The bartender approached him, wiping a glass.

"I'm looking for Mr. Budzivoi."

"Who's asking?"

"Raul Gutierrez. Tell Mr. Budzivoi I'm a friend of Mr. Crane in Washington. The one he talked to yesterday."

The bartender disappeared down a hallway to the right and Raul moved into deeper shadow as a precaution. As he waited he surveyed the tables, each covered with a starched white tablecloth and set with heavy silverware. A small vase with religious icons painted on two sides sat in the center of each table, filled with flowers that looked fake, but good fake. Expensive place but turning shabby, he mused to himself.

The minute hand moved past four minutes, then five, and then the bartender returned. "Mr. Budzivoi says he doesn't have time to talk to you right now. Can you come back tomorrow?"

"No. It has to be now. Tell him it's about his brother in France. He's in some trouble and I'm just trying to be sure the trouble doesn't spread to Mr. Budzivoi."

After less than a minute, the bartender reappeared in the hallway and pointed to a door at the far end. "Just go right in there."

Raul pushed open the heavy door to find Boris at a large mahogany desk, in a room dominated by a brag wall of the type normally seen behind Washington politicians. The place of honor went to a black-and-white photo of Vladimir Putin with a much younger version of Boris, taken at some sort of military parade in Red Square. Raul thought it probably dated to Putin's days in the KGB.

The modern Boris hadn't aged well. He weighed at least a hundred pounds more than the trim man in the photo, and with the weight had come an unkempt, hangdog look. An unlit cigar protruded from the side of his mouth; to Raul, it gave the room a smell reminiscent of wet dog. His salt-and-pepper hair was stiff and unruly, and he wore a ruffled shirt open at the collar. Raul could not see his trousers, but figured they were half of a tuxedo, his attire for greeting dinner guests.

"I told your Mr. Crane all I knew," Boris said without introduction. "What else do you need?"

"Mr. Crane appreciated the time you took to talk to him. He just asked me to pose a couple of follow-up questions."

"Look, Mr. — whatever your name is," Boris began. "I'm an American citizen. I've lived here for ten years. You guys assume that every Russian in Miami is part of some organized crime, but not me. I'm just trying to earn a living and take care of my family. Now get out of here!"

"I'm not leaving yet," Raul told him. The polite veneer started to slip away.

"You need to understand that this visit is important to people who could make very bad things happen to you. I know you're a big man in the Russian immigrant community here, and everybody knows you give a lot of money to charity. But I and a few other people also know you're up to your ears in money laundering, racketeering, and God knows what else, including drugs and now kidnapping. And I know you have some interesting connections in Europe, a brother who basically does what you do in Nice, and some friends who your man Putin" — he waved his hand at the photo of Boris and Putin on the wall — "would happily send off for a lifetime in Siberia, and you with them.

"You know as well as I that if you were convicted of even a little bit of the stuff you've done, your fraudulent citizenship would be gone and you'd be on a plane to Moscow. You need to know the time has come for you to decide which side you're on."

Raul knew he'd struck home when Boris sat back and slowly rubbed his right eye with his thumb. He looked at Raul, then into the distance. He started to speak, thought better of it, then made up his mind and asked, "What do you want to know?"

"How did you bust Sonny Perry out?"

"Sonny who?"

"You know goddamned well who I mean. He was your man Dmitri's lover until Dmitri got himself electrocuted in Sarasota. Now how did you get him out?"

"Dmitri got himself killed by that Frenchman, Grant, may he rot in hell. But I don't know nothing about Sonny. Last I heard he was trying to get his old boss out of jail on insanity."

"We picked up word that you're trying to get even with Eddie Grant. You'll want to be really careful with that."

"Not me, much as I'd like him dead. Maybe that stupid brother of mine, or some of his even stupider helpers. You might want to talk to them. That's what I told your boss."

"They would have come to you to get Sonny out of the country even if you weren't involved in the break."

"They didn't. You think I'm the only Russian around here with relatives in France?"

Raul decided to try another tack. "Mr. Crane is very concerned that somebody is moving a lot of gold around Europe. Finding and stopping that is his main job. It appears to be coming in from the Black Sea and then disappearing in Germany, but some of it has showed up in the Cayman Islands. I know you work there quite a bit. What do you know about it?"

It worked. Boris sat back in his chair. Raul watched him try to suppress a faint smile of relief that the conversation had turned away from Sonny Perry. He had no desire to lock horns with the Florida police. Much better to deal with the Feds, even if it might result in his being deported, and their prisons were known to be far more pleasant. He decided to offer a few crumbs, as Raul had hoped he would.

"That's not me. I don't do bullion directly, never have. But not all Russians are alike. You might take a look at the Chechens. Some of them still think they can spin off as an independent country. I know that isn't going to happen, but there's nothing like a lost cause to stir hope. Look at all the old Confederates in this country."

Chechens? Raul remembered the brutal and bloody War of Independence, when Chechnya had tried its best to declare independence from Russia and had used some serious terrorism in the effort, including bombings in Moscow and one notorious mass kidnapping and murder at a theater, but Moscow seemed to have won and installed its own pro-Russian government. Could something still be going on there?

"Do you have any idea who could be orchestrating all this?" Raul asked.

Boris stroked his cheek with his thumb, giving the impression that he was thinking.

"I don't know for sure. But I think you might want to talk to a man named Alain Alawite. He's half French, half Arab and I'm told he really doesn't like Eddie Grant. I also hear he really does like gold bullion and old artworks. I think he maybe buys church art and other stuff the Nazis looted. American soldiers brought a lot of that home, and some of it still hasn't been found."

"Where does this mysterious Mr. Alawite live?"

"Last I heard he was mainly in South America, but also spends some time in Germany, near Munich. He gets around a lot. He's lived in Berlin, had connections to the old East German government, and he's in and out of Dubai, probably because that's where so much gold is traded. And of course he's a Saudi citizen. His father was a Saudi diplomat in France during the war. He was born in Paris."

"Is that the only name he uses?"

"I doubt it, but it's the only one I know."

Raul's Blackberry beeped as a text arrived from Icky. "Ask address Boris apt Paris. Impt."

He was nearly finished in any case, so Raul went directly to the point. "What's the address of your apartment in Paris, Boris?"

"How did you know about that? I just bought the damned thing."

"Mr. Crane wants to know where it is."

"It's in the 14th arrondissement, Rue Boulard — it's right by that pedestrian street named after the photographer, Rue Daguerre. It's a duplex on the fifth and sixth floors — that would be sixth and seventh to Americans. But I just bought it and haven't even been there."

"Who'd you buy it from?"

"A guy who works for my brother, in Nice. He has a lawyer in Paris who handled all the paperwork and says he'll find me a manager to rent it out from time to time."

"His name?"

Boris pulled a notepad from his top drawer and quickly scrawled a name and address. "He's in Paris a couple of districts over from the apartment. In the twelfth."

"Give me a minute," Raul said, as he set about sending a reply to Icky's question. When he'd finished, he took out a card and handed it across the desk.

"You know what we're interested in. Here's how you can reach me if you think of anything else. I don't need to tell you how much trouble you're going to be in if you don't help us. We really need to know more about that European gold."

"I'll see what I can find, but I don't expect much. I'll call you in a couple of days."

CHAPTER SEVEN

Paris, Rue de Picpus

Three burly detectives in blue knit shirts left the small car and walked briskly into a low office building on Rue de Picpus, scarcely two blocks from its intersection with bustling Avenue Daumesnil. A fourth took up his position in front of a row of brass plaques announcing that a half-dozen lawyers had their offices upstairs.

Detective Sergeant Richard Gautier paused beside the elevator to run his finger down the list of tenants. He pointed to the name of Shamil Akhmadov, Avocat, in Suite 3F.

He pressed the elevator call button to bring the car to the ground floor, and as it descended led his small squad silently up the stairs. At 3F he knocked politely, then without waiting pushed open the door to find a jowly man seated behind a modern glass desk, talking on the telephone. Piles of legal files labeled in Russian and French flowed off the desk to tables on both sides. Even the red velour sofa on one wall was covered with paper.

Silently, the sergeant showed his police ID and signaled he should hang up. The lawyer grunted and said, "I will call you later. The police want to talk about something." To the sergeant, he said, "What can I do for you?"

"Monsieur Akhmadov, we are from the Police Nationale. I am Detective Sergeant Gautier and I must ask you a few questions."

The lawyer reached for his telephone, but Gautier put his hand firmly on the receiver. "Later, but now I require that you answer the questions."

"Of course, sergeant. You may ask any question you like. I do not guarantee I will be able to answer it."

"The first one is very simple. To whom did you lend the apartment on Rue Boulard? The one purchased recently by M. Budzivoi of Miami."

"That is easy. With permission, I lent it to a man I had not met before, an American. My client knew him and gave me permission."

"Boris Budzivoi?"

"No, the previous owner, who works for M Budzivoi's brother. He lives in Nice. His name is Vladi something. I forget. Anyway, he sent his friend to pick up the key. The friend was a very odd man. He spoke no French but a little Russian."

"And what was his name?"

"It was unusual. His name was Sonny. Sonny Perry."

CHAPTER EIGHT

Paris, Place Denfert-Rochereau

Like many Parisian apartment buildings, Boris Budzivoi's was built for maximum privacy and protection from street noise. Typical city blocks are surrounded by buildings with stores on their ground floors and apartments above, with green space in the center. Often, two or three buildings are built one behind the other, so that the apartments in the courtyard are sheltered from the noise of the traffic and over-enthusiastic Friday night revelers. Boris's was the third in one such line.

At 10 p.m., Philippe's driver turned off Boulevard Raspail onto a narrow street whose name Eddie missed, a few blocks from the statue of the recumbent Lion of Belfort that dominates Place Denfert-Rochereau. He stopped in front of a plain stone building from early in the twentieth century and Philippe led the way into the small lobby. The neighborhood had swung from unfashionable to trendy, with restaurants run by two or three generations of immigrants from the Auvergne region sharing the streets comfortably with Breton crêperies and stylish ethnic bistros. He and Aurélie had visited a few of them and liked the Japanese flavor common to the new wave of adventurous restaurateurs. The Asian influence was becoming more pronounced in Paris each year.

"From here we'll be able to see across to one of the courtyard buildings," Philippe said. "Icky got the address from the Russian in Miami, who bought it just a few weeks ago from one of the members of his brother's gang in Nice. I suspect it's been in the family for several years. Claude Khan borrowed it and Sonny Perry picked up the key.

"The place we're going is directly opposite that apartment, and we have a similar command post on the other side of the building. This has all been set up since we got the address this afternoon."

A uniformed gendarme opened the door for them when they left the elevator on the top floor. Inside, Eddie saw that cameras on tripods were set up to peer through gaps in the shutters covering the two windows.

"These are thermal cameras," Philippe explained. "Capt. Alberti will explain it. He's in charge of the operation."

The captain shook Eddie's hand then told him, "These cameras are pointed at the building where we think" — there was a faint emphasis on the word — "Mme Cabillaud is being held. They pick up heat rather than visual light. The building is made of stone too thick to allow a reading, but we can see tiny changes in the heat signature at the windows as people pass them, even through drawn curtains.

"We think there are two men in there, because we've seen their heat signatures on both floors at the same time, but there could be three. No one has come out of the building since we set up here six hours ago. We've cleared the occupants out of the two floors below the ones we're watching. One of them saw a woman they didn't recognize come in with a man who fit the description of Sonny Perry.

"We have looked at the plans for the building. The apartment covers two floors with a spiral stair between them, and on the top floor there's a little room, a sort of office, that's completely on the interior of the building, with a bathroom but no windows. The gardienne says a singer used to use it as a practice studio and it's so isolated she never bothered the neighbors. Our thermal cameras won't reach that far, but it's reasonable that they would put her there. They certainly wouldn't want her to be near a window where she could call for help, and all the rooms on the lower floor have windows. So we think we know where in the apartment she is, if this is the right building."

"What is your plan?"

"If you could see through these shutters you'd see our SWAT team on the roof of the building," the captain said. "There is a small attic above the top floor so they were able to walk very carefully without being heard and there are now two gendarmes above each window of the second floor of the apartment. In a minute or two one of them will rappel quickly down to each window and swing through it, very noisily. Suddenly there will be five very hostile flics in the room. It should be enough to overwhelm them, and we have the advantage of being able to see, using our night-vision goggles. They will surely have the lights out."

Eddie asked, "And what if she's not on that floor?"

"Then they will search the other." He could have been explaining his job to a sixth-grader. Then he turned away and raised a radio to his lips. "Report!" he said quickly into the microphone. Eddie and Philippe heard five responses, then his curt command, "Go!"

The sound of breaking glass echoed through the courtyard. The officers at the windows backed the thermal cameras away and opened the shutters, and the captain waved to Eddie and Philippe that they could go to the window on the left. Nervous as he was, Eddie appreciated that he'd been given the best possible view of the action.

The broken window glass had hardly reached the ground when Eddie heard the sound of a fight, then a heavy blow and the sound of a body hitting the floor. He was surprised at how loud it all was until he realized he'd heard it from the captain's radio, which had an open circuit from the microphone mounted on the team leader's helmet. The sound filled him with terror.

He closed his eyes briefly, wishing he could be more actively involved, but he'd learned in the Special Forces that the person with the most to gain or lose personally from an assault was the least qualified to take part in it. He was grateful that he and Philippe had even been allowed to be present.

He heard the shout "La Police," first from the team leader, then repeated by other members of the group. In the background one of the gendarmes shouted, "Madame Cabillaud! You are safe now," then told two of the policemen to check the floor below. Half a minute later, the leader came to the window and announced, "She's not here."

The sound of a blow came from the radio. Eddie saw the leader look back into the room, then turn to repeat what he'd heard. "They took her out ten minutes ago through the cave."

"Merde!" Philippe turned to the captain. "I know this block. Several of the basements are connected, and some of them lead into the catacombs. They could be taking her anywhere. But she knows the area well, much better than the kidnappers. Let's go to the basement. Now."

∫

Twenty minutes earlier, as the police moved into position on the roof above them, Sonny Perry and the two Chechens, Max and Jacob, sat quietly in the living room of the small apartment. A sullen Jacob sat next to Aurélie, who lay handcuffed and gagged on a dirty and water-stained mattress. From time to time he rubbed a sore spot on his leg where she had kicked him.

He scraped the chair ever so slightly over the once-elegant parquet floor but Sonny silenced him with a hiss, then resumed listening to the dark, nearly silent world around him. The building was deep in the center of the block, with two others standing between it and the street, so the sounds of everyday traffic were almost entirely absent. From seven stories below, he could hear two men talking to each other in English.

His phone vibrated. After a few seconds he simply grunted and returned it to his pocket. Max and Jacob moved quietly to his side.

"They're on to this place, so we have to go to Plan B," he whispered to them in Russian. Poor as it was, his Russian was better than their English.

"Max, you and I will take the woman to the backup site. Jacob, you stay here for ten minutes and then follow us. We'll take off her handcuffs or she'll never be able to go up and down the old staircases. Leave the gag. Max, you'll go first. I'm a little slow." He still limped from Aurélie's forceful kick at Gare Montparnasse.

Sonny waved Jacob away from the door and went in. He unlocked the handcuffs and put them in his back pocket, then pulled Aurélie to her feet. "We're going somewhere else, bitch. Just follow Max and you won't be hurt. I'll be right behind you."

Aurélie's wrists were raw from the handcuffs, her legs stiff from being still so long. She fought the now-familiar panic that rose in her chest at the sight of Sonny Perry and did as she was told. She was terrified that she'd never see Eddie again.

They crept down the stairs in single file. When they reached the lobby, Max unlocked the door of the basement used by the building owners for storage and wine cellars and led the way down a rough and narrow stone staircase. At the bottom they turned right to follow a moss-covered stone wall to a corner, then turned left and stopped in front of an unmarked door, which Max opened with a second key. It led to a steep stone staircase that appeared to be centuries old.

When Aurélie saw the stairs she balked, grunting her disapproval through the gag, but Max reached back to pull her roughly through the door.

From the glow of his flashlight, Aurélie could see that the basement was ancient, with nothing in it other than the columns supporting the building. She knew they must be at the level of some of the shallower catacombs, the manmade caves that began as quarries when Paris was a Roman city. She wondered how much of Paris's criminal element did business in caves like this. It gave new meaning to the term "underworld."

At the far end of the basement, an old wooden door reinforced with iron straps barred their way. Max opened it with another key and they ducked through the low doorway to a similar basement, whose walls were lined with storage lockers. Aurélie quickly calculated that they must be under a hill, where the second basement of the first building was level with the first basement of the second. In the distance, she heard the rumble of the Line 4 métro train as it braked to a stop in the Denfert-Rochereau station. An escape plan began to take shape.

The street at the top of the next stairs should be Rue Daguerre, or very close to it. Even this late at night there would be pedestrians leaving the restaurants that lined the street.

She followed as Max mounted the stairs and carefully pushed open the door. Aurélie could see the glass entrance door of a tiny lobby, then behind it a long line of mailboxes. The building was one of a row built inside the center of a city block, and they had surfaced at its front door.

Max stepped sideways around a baby's blue pram and gestured for her to follow. Sonny hung back three or four steps — out of range of her powerful kick.

As she emerged from the basement, Max turned to climb the narrow wooden spiral stairs. Aurélie hung back until he was halfway to the first landing. It was the only chance she would have, she knew — she had no idea what was in store from here, but she refused to wait and find out. She took a single focusing breath, then rolled the pram in front of the stairs and bolted toward the exit door. She pressed the button that unlocked the door and sprinted through it into a driveway barely wide enough for a small car. Behind her, she heard Sonny tell the Chechen, "I can't run. Catch her. And when you do, kill her."

Max's heavy footsteps pounded a dozen yards behind. Halfway to the building entrance, a large gray cat lay on a green garbage can, its tail waving languidly from side to side. The waving stopped as she drew closer, then the cat jumped away just as she grasped the can to pull it across the driveway in her wake. She heard Max swear as he slowed to kick at the cat, then to push the bulky poubelle out of the way.

Aurélie's fingers searched for the exit button she knew would open the heavy blue door. The first one she pressed turned on the lights, but she quickly found the second and watched the door begin to swing slowly toward her.

"Stop!" Max shouted.

She ignored him. As soon as the door had opened enough to admit her slim frame, she slipped sideways through it. As she turned, she saw Max pull a large knife from his belt.

She stepped out into familiar territory — Rue Daguerre, the bustling pedestrian street a hundred yards from the catacombs entrance. At 11 p.m., small groups of pedestrians were walking slowly away from the restaurants, either toward their homes in the neighborhood or the métro station at the corner.

Aurélie ran for the métro, certain she could lose Max in the maze of tunnels that connected three subway lines.

"Help me!" she called out, as loudly as she could. "He's trying to kill me!" Heads turned, first toward her and then toward Max, who hesitated for only an instant. He paused again when a homeless man, carrying what must have been the last in a long series of beers, staggered in front of him but turned quickly away when he saw the knife.

There was no gendarme in sight, as usual, so she hopped quickly over the turnstile and turned left toward the track that would take her downtown, toward the Île de la Cité and the main police station. Behind her, she heard an oath as the much-larger Chechen muscled himself up and over the electric gates.

Two steps at a time, she ran down the stairs to the platform, only to see the red lights of a departing train recede down the tracks ahead. The sign above the platform told her the next wouldn't arrive for two minutes. She calculated quickly that she could run the length of the platform to the complicated system of transfer tunnels that make up the station, but after twenty yards the heel of her left shoe broke. In the few seconds it took to remove both of them, Max caught her arm in a viselike grip.

"End of the line, lady," he gasped. He was panting hard from the run.

As people arrived for the next train they started to gather around the curious sight. Most backed away when they saw the knife in Max's hand — except for one shabbily dressed young man who had been asleep behind the row of chairs lining the station wall. When he saw Max's large knife, he grabbed the canvas backpack he'd been using as a pillow and held it out like a shield. Max took his attention from Aurélie long enough to wave the knife threateningly at the young man, who did not back down but kept pushing the rucksack, clearly ready for a fight. The crowd had grown to a dozen. Aurélie caught a glimpse of one man pressing the emergency phone button on the wall to call the métro police.

Aurélie was strong and in better condition than Max was, from lifting weights and the long runs she and Eddie made frequently along the Seine, but she knew she could not beat him in a knife fight, so she played for time. She grabbed Max's wrist with both hands and pushed the knife away while the young man moved in with his backpack. She flexed her toes and gripped the rubber buttons of the warning strip, pushing hard to keep Max off balance until she felt the cold wind that every arriving train pushes ahead of it, then heard the sound of brakes as the train entered the station. The sound rose an octave as the driver saw the fight and began a full panic stop.

A second before the train passed, she planted her foot behind Max's ankle and pushed him with the last of her strength. He dropped the knife so he could hold her with both hands, but it was too late — by then she had tipped him beyond the point of no return. She released her death grip on his right wrist and he tumbled headlong in front of the hundred-ton train. His anguished scream died abruptly as the first car rolled over him.

The young man grabbed Aurélie tightly around the waist to pull her out of the way, but even with his help they bounced a dozen feet along the side of the slowing train. Aurélie caught a glimpse of passengers holding tight to their seats to avoid joining the standees who had been thrown like dominoes to the floor. And then she and the young man found themselves side by side on the platform, bruised and exhausted but alive.

She turned to look at him. "You are a brave man. Thank you."

"I am a soldier, or at least I was. Where did you learn to fight like that?"

She picked one of the blue plastic chairs lining the station wall and sat down. "It's the second time I've been threatened by a man with a knife," she said. "After the first I swore I'd never be the victim again, so I made my fiancé teach me. He was also a soldier."

"It worked. What did you say to that man just as you pushed him in front of the train?"

"I told him to tell his friends in hell that I sent him, for Édouard. That's who taught me to defend myself."

"He did well. Now I have to go. The police will be here soon and we are not friends. My name is Luc. Luc Chatel. I hope we meet again."

"And I am Aurélie Cabillaud. Please stay. I can just about guarantee the police won't bother you today. Or at least tell me where I can find you to thank you."

"To help a beautiful woman in distress is enough thanks. Now I must go, quickly." He hoisted the backpack to one shoulder and disappeared into the gathering crowd.

∫

Eddie had split off from the police searchers because he expected Aurélie to try to escape and run for the safety of a crowd. He turned right on the bustling Rue Daguerre and walked quickly toward Avenue du Général Leclerc, one of the main routes into central Paris from the southern suburbs.

"Did you see a young woman, blonde, almost as tall as I am?" he asked a woman who stood at the corner trying to sign up blood donors for the Red Cross.

She shook her head, but the American tourist she'd approached spoke up. "I saw her, with a man running after her." Then he switched to English. "Do you speak English? That's all the French I can muster. A really pretty blonde woman ran down the stairs into the métro. There was a big guy running after her. He looked like a Slav of some sort."

"Thanks," Eddie said, and turned quickly toward the métro stairs, just in time to catch a glimpse of Sonny Perry holding the handrail tightly as he limped down, favoring his left leg. He was out of sight before Eddie got to the bottom of the stairs and used his Navigo pass to go through the turnstile.

The train's driver had called the transit police and now stood over Aurélie as she sat in one of the plastic chairs lining the tiled wall of the station, trying to get more details about the body under the train.

As she started to tell the driver the dead man was a kidnapper, Sonny pushed him roughly aside and reached for her arm.

"You're coming with me," he said, pulling her to her feet.

She kicked him again in the thigh, but without her shoes it didn't have the same impact. "No!" She looked back toward the stairway and shouted, "Édouard! Help me!"

Eddie jumped down the last four steps and sprinted toward her. "You're a dead man," he hissed at Sonny, who released Aurélie and reached under his jacket for a small black automatic. Eddie took a final quick step toward him and knocked the gun away before it cleared his waistband. It clattered across the platform and fell onto the tracks, and Sonny turned and scurried as fast as his bruised leg would allow toward the exit at the other end of the station.

Eddie started to run after him but paused to look at Aurélie, then at the mangled body barely visible under the train. He gave up the chase.

Aurélie turned and put her arms around his neck. "Oh, Édouard," she said. "I was frightened." She kissed him, hard.

"I was, too. I'm so sorry this happened because of me. But I'll have him and his boss before this is all over."

"Don't apologize. I'll just have to be more careful. Both of us will."

Philippe and Capt. Alberti arrived at the same time, followed closely by two gendarmes and a police doctor. Aurélie turned from Eddie to embrace her father.

"I'm glad you're safe," Philippe said. He walked to the edge of the platform and looked down at the body. "You handled him really well. I'm proud of you."

Capt. Alberti turned to Eddie and said, "I've put out an alert for the American, but if he gets on a train it will be very hard to catch him. Can you tell me anything more about him?"

"No more than Commissaire Cabillaud can. I've met him before, in Florida. His name is Sonny Perry and he's tied deeply into the Russian mafia and a gold smuggler who may be plotting something very dangerous. We need to find him."

As Capt. Alberti questioned Aurélie, Eddie leaned over the edge of the platform to peer closely at the body, which had come to rest under the middle door of the first car.

"Philippe, come over here," he said urgently, then pointed at the man's ruined face. "I know this man. Jeremy and I saw him at Henri Gascon's cocktail party where we first met Filer. He was standing against a wall watching us. Filer was obviously afraid of him. I'll bet he and the one you arrested threw Filer off the balcony."

"You're probably right," Philippe replied. "This is a very dangerous gang but now we have three of them. With luck we'll get to the head man."

The doctor stepped toward Aurélie and said stiffly, "Madame Cabillaud, it's important that you go to the clinic for a short examination so we can be sure there's no permanent damage."

Eddie thought the doctor's overly formal approach bordered on ridiculous, and wondered how Aurélie would react. Laughter was definitely not what he expected.

She raised her hand to her mouth to cover a smile and stifle a nervous giggle. Eddie felt relief flood over him and he picked up the infectious smile in spite of himself. The doctor looked back and forth at them, confused.

"We'll meet you there," Eddie told him.

A driver had been alerted to wait for them on the street outside the station entrance. As they settled into the back seat he gripped Aurélie tightly and looked into her eyes. "Chérie, are you really OK?"

She raised her skirt. An ugly bruise the size of a man's hand was imprinted on her thigh, and as he saw it his good humor disappeared completely. "The bastards!"

"This is going to be sore, but it was worth it. One of them tried to rape me. I kicked him very hard in the balls and he handled me pretty roughly with his hand down there. I just want to be sure nothing's permanently injured. And I got bounced around pretty good on the side of the train. You'll probably have to live the celibate life for a couple of days."

"That's a small enough price to pay. Was it Sonny?"

"No, the third one, the one who stayed back in the apartment. They called him Jacob. I'll tell you all about it later, but now kiss me."

He did. And he resolved silently that whoever set this up would die. And there was no longer any doubt who set it up.

CHAPTER NINE

Paris, Rue Saint-Roch

A hard rain drummed on the broad living-room windows of the penthouse atop the Hôtel Luxor. Low morning clouds obscured the view of Notre Dame, but Eddie and Aurélie paid no attention — they were deep in conversation, planning the next step.

"I've been cooped up here longer than I can stand it and I feel like my old self, so this afternoon I'm going back to work. Is there anything new I should know?"

Eddie replied, "I'll tell you everything I know, which isn't a hell of a lot. But are you sure you're ready?"

"I think so. I'll probably limp a bit, like I hope Sonny is still limping, but work is what I do. I need to get back to it."

"Well, I won't even try to talk you out of it.

"First of all, Sonny Perry is nowhere to be found. Philippe thinks he got on the 6 train. Somebody who looked a lot like him got off at Montparnasse, then disappeared."

"And how about the Chechen, Jacob, the one who gave me the bruise?"

"Does it still hurt?"

"Just a little, but it's better this morning. Jacob?"

"He's not talking and probably won't. But our witness the taxi driver is pretty sure he was in the car that nearly ran us down, and Philippe is fairly certain he was one of the Chechens who flew in from Moscow just after the FSB agent was killed. The investigating judge will keep him on suspicion of throwing Filer off the balcony, too."

She stood and walked to the fireplace, favoring her sore leg. "There's one other thing we need to talk about, Édouard. We need to do a reset on the deal we made. I know you've always wanted to find and punish the mastermind, and after the last few days I've changed my mind. I agree he should be punished."

"He should be dead. He will be dead." Aurélie could tell he meant every word.

"No argument from me, but that would be very dangerous. However, it's important to you and what's important to you is important to me, so I will release you from your promise not to chase him, on one condition."

"And that is?"

"I want to be involved. In everything. All the time."

He looked at her suspiciously. "I always like having you near me, but this could be dangerous and I have picked up some military skills over the years..."

She held up her hand to stop him. "I can't do close combat like you did with those Germans looking for the painting three years ago, but I did deal with the Chechen kidnapper pretty well, with help from the unknown soldier. I'm strong. I lift weights, I run. I'm in good shape. And I couldn't bear to lose you to something I could try to prevent. I insist on being involved."

"With luck, this will all go without too much drama," Eddie replied. "Philippe and the police will find Sonny and his boss, they'll go to jail for a very long time, and that will be that. The Florida prison will look like a country club next to Santé Prison here, too bad for Sonny." He thought for a few seconds. The sound of the rain grew more intense.

"OK. I'll take that deal. We may not be able to be together all the time, but at the least you'll be involved in all of the decisions and we'll work together when it's not stupid."

∫

By the next morning, all traces of the storm had blown out into the Atlantic and Aurélie suggested they meet Philippe for lunch at the Luxembourg Gardens instead of at the bistro near his office that he'd suggested.

They settled on a secluded bench near the Medici Fountain and Eddie pulled one of the Gardens' signature green metal chairs in front to serve as a table. From a plastic bag he pulled their lunch — a baguette jambon he would share with Aurélie, a roast beef sandwich on Cuban bread for Philippe.

"I just got off the phone with Icky," Philippe told them. "He's really pissed at the Russian restaurateur in Miami. He's going to go down personally and have a little chat.

"Also, Interpol put out a Red Notice for Sonny Perry. I don't know how much good it will do, but we might get lucky."

As they chewed their way through the sandwiches, Philippe recounted some brighter nuggets of information he'd learned since Aurélie's kidnapping.

"I've learned more about the Miami Russian's brother in Nice. He's in pretty much the same racket. I just found out he has some serious tax problems. The fiscs think he's been laundering money for some of his Russian customers, too."

Eddie said, "The tax police aren't something you mess with.

"I thought the Russians preferred Cyprus. It would be a lot safer than running afoul of the French tax authorities."

"Normally Cyprus is where they go, but it's riskier now so they're spreading their bets. Icky has a retired man down there named Walker Evans, who says the Russian restaurant is having a bad time. If the owner thinks he's at risk of a tax fraud charge he might be more reasonable."

"I know Walker," Eddie said. "He went with me on a couple of missions in Kuwait. He's a good man."

Walker Evans was a respected agent who'd retired young and was well known in the restaurants and night clubs of Nice. On a conference call with Icky and Philippe that afternoon he'd told them about Vitaliy Budzivoi's problems and added, "Recessions and financial pressures screw up everybody's usual values. When they were making money, these guys would never think of ratting each other out, but times are different now. I've been in his restaurant quite a few times and it's clear he doesn't have nearly as many customers now as he did two years ago. And some of his competitors say he spends a lot of time badmouthing his brother in Miami. I think we can play them off against each other."

Philippe said, "Our intelligence people are telling me much the same thing. We need to talk to him, and I should do it. Icky, could Walker go with me?"

"Sure, if he wants to. Why not?" Icky replied. "He's on his own now. It'll keep the Agency out of it, at least officially. I'm still having some problems with the congressman who sent Lee Filer to us, so anything we can do to keep this off his radar is a good thing."

"Good. I'll come down tomorrow and we'll pay him a visit."

Icky said, "And I'll make a personal visit to his brother in Miami. But we've already talked to him once, so I think I'd like to wait and see what you develop before I fly down there."

CHAPTER TEN

Côte d'Azur

Philippe and his assistant Gabriel Domingue took a cab to the gleaming seven-story building Walker Evans called home. They had left Paris in the rain, but the clouds had disappeared by the time they touched down at Nice Côte d'Azur airport.

The cab left them on the long curving sidewalk overlooking the wide beach of the Promenade des Anglais, famous throughout the world for its beauty and sophistication. Sunbathers had begun to choose their beach chairs from the tight group set out in military formation in front of the cocktail lounge just below the seawall. The water in September was already too cold for most swimmers, but no one wanted to miss a day in the Mediterranean sunshine.

"Who is this guy?" Gabriel asked, pointing to the condo across the street, its glass facade gleaming in the late-morning sun. "This must be one of the most expensive buildings on the Côte d'Azur. I thought he was a retired spy."

"Walker is one of the golden few who could have done anything he wanted," Philippe told him. "He came from money but couldn't stand his older brother, who ran the family business. They supplied some essential piece of American cars. Walker was a basketball star in college and thought he wanted to be a diplomat, but after a year or two of that he decided he preferred the cloak-and-dagger world and moved over to the CIA. He spent twenty years in some very dangerous places, then one day decided to retire and move to Nice.

"My ex-wife Barbara lives down here. She tells me he's big on the party circuit, which is the reason he knows so much about the man we're going to see today. And as you'll see, he stands out in a crowd."

Gabriel thought he was prepared for anything, but Walker Evans was a surprise.

The oversized mahogany door opened to reveal one of the tallest men Gabriel had ever seen. He had not met Icky Crane, but would have instantly recognized them as the same height: five-foot-nineteen, as Icky waggishly told his friends. The man was huge and 1930s movie-star handsome, with wavy gray hair and a thin aristocratic-looking mustache. In white trousers and a double-breasted blue blazer, he looked the part of a movie producer lording it over the set.

"Philippe, nice to see you again." His voice boomed through the cavernous apartment.

Philippe quickly introduced Gabriel and the three sat down to a view of the Mediterranean that spread before them like an endless blue blanket. Puffy clouds floated in the distance, and a half mile offshore two cigarette boats slalomed around each other. The contrast with the dreary rain of Paris the last two days could not have been more stark.

Walker knew the story, but wanted to be sure Philippe and Gabriel were completely up to date. He asked, "So Icky talked to Boris Budzivoi in Miami, and then he had Raul Gutierrez go at him, too?"

"You probably know better than I do," Philippe said, "but the kidnappers were hiding Aurélie in Boris's apartment. We think it's been a safe house for his crime family for several years, but he's now the owner so he's in a jam and knows it."

"And Aurélie? Is she okay?"

"She's was handled a little roughly but she gave as good as she got — she kicked one of the kidnappers and nearly crippled him, then when the second one tried to cut her throat she pushed him off a métro platform in front of a train. No loss, except for the information we might have had from him. His partner survived, although he's not talking yet. Both of them are Chechens."

"Then he'll never talk," Walker said. "Most of what you hear about the Russian mafia is wrong. It should be called the Chechen mafia. Boris's brother Vitaliy is a sort of ex-officio Chechen, on his mother's side, and I've seen him with some nasty characters. I don't know about

Boris. They're really only half brothers, with the same father. He was a Russian Army officer who got cashiered for stealing, if you can imagine that."

"But we're looking for more than just Aurélie's kidnappers?"

"We are," Philippe said. "Icky has been trying to trace the source of a lot of gold bullion that seems to be coming in from the Balkans and winding up in Germany, around Munich, where the trail goes cold. One of his unofficials got a lead on it last week. We think Aurélie was kidnapped because Eddie Grant was getting too close to some answers, but the odd thing is, he wasn't even looking — and certainly never thought he was at all close.

"You remember the Nazi gold bullion they found in Paris a few years back? There's probably a connection there, because we've never been able to learn who was behind all the murders that seemed related to that case. And the guy who was the lover of the man Eddie killed in Sarasota just escaped from prison in Florida. He's here now, and he's the one who arranged for the safe house and he kidnapped Aurélie at Gare Montparnasse. He's still at large."

"I knew Eddie in Kuwait, and of course his family is well known among the business set here and in Paris."

"Eddie mentioned you worked together, but didn't say much about it."

"Where you have a war you have to have spies. I was working in Riyadh at the time, so it was natural for the Agency to send me up to Kuwait. I helped the Special Forces identify and arrest some of the Kuwaitis who'd decided to cast their lot with Saddam Hussein. I went along once or twice with Eddie — he is very effective. When one of them tried to ambush us, he stood straight up and ended the fight with one shot. I'd never realized how effective buckshot is until I saw that combat shotgun at work. Eddie's only problem is that he's never certain he's up to the job, but I've never seen a case where he wasn't."

Philippe agreed. "I've never had any doubts about him."

"But now the man of the hour is Vitaliy," Walker said. "We can probably drop in on him just as his lunch hour is at its peak. And by the way, this could be a little dangerous. He won't like being pushed into a corner. What do we want to know from him?"

Philippe answered. "We need to ID the mystery man who's bringing the gold into Germany. The evidence we have so far points to an exporter in Munich named Claude Khan, but it's tenuous.

"Whoever this guy is, everyone we've talked to so far is more afraid of him than of the police, but I suspect our Mr. Budzivoi can be convinced that he has more to fear from the French government than from this one unknown man. Just a couple of months ago our interior ministry deported another Russian hoodlum, and he disappeared into Siberia a few days after he got to Moscow. Vitaliy won't want that fate.

"His brother gave Icky's man a name, Alain Alawite. We don't know much about him yet, but we need to at least confirm the name, if we can."

Philippe was grim. "This is going to be the worst day of his life. He's going to talk or the gods of French justice will deal with him, and quickly. Before the sun sets."

"Okay," Walker said. "Then I suggest we get started with a good lunch, then chat with Vitaliy when we're finished. At least he'll get something out of the day that way. I'm buying."

The golden sun helped lift Philippe's mood during the three-block walk to the restaurant. He and Gabriel followed Walker as he turned off the Promenade into a one-lane side street, where the restaurant occupied the ground floor of a discreet stone apartment building. It was marked only with an enameled black plaque marked "Budzivoi" in white letters styled to look vaguely Cyrillic.

Each of the widely spaced tables was covered by a starched white cloth, a small vase of flowers in the center. Fewer than half of them were occupied, a bad sign at the height of the lunch hour. They asked for a banquette on the left, where a complimentary kir appeared quickly.

"Please thank M. Budzivoi for the kir," Walker said to the waiter, "and ask him to visit us when he has a moment."

Vitaliy looked nothing like Raul's description of his brother Boris. He was fifteen years younger and slim, and while no one would call him handsome, he had an air of distinction and competence that surprised Philippe and Gabriel. When he appeared at their table they exchanged surprised looks. Walker, who lunched there frequently, muttered, "I should have warned you" as soon as Vitaliy went back to his office next to the kitchen entrance. "He's not at all like his brother. Much smoother. I think he's more dangerous. Did you see that short finger? He lost the last two knuckles in a knife fight in Moscow."

Veal chops finished and dessert skipped, their waiter — a compactly built young Russian with a military bearing — brought them small fragrant cups of expresso. "Mr. Budzivoi says go right into his office when you're done with the coffee," he said.

When they had finished, Walker looked at his colleagues and asked, "Now?"

"Just one minute," Philippe said. He took out his iPhone and picked a number from the contact list. When it answered, he spoke just long enough to give the time — 2:15 p.m.

"Precaution," he said. "Now we can go."

They knocked on the office door and entered to find Vitaliy frowning at a spreadsheet. "I'm trying to figure out how to stay in business until the economy turns," he said sourly as he closed the laptop and invited them to sit. Philippe and Walker took the two chairs in front of the desk; Gabriel pulled a third from a corner and sat behind them to take notes.

Walker began.

"Vitaliy, there's nothing official about my visit. You know I'm retired. But I thought it might be easier if I came to introduce you to my guests. Commissaire Cabillaud and Officer Domingue are from the Paris criminal police. They are here about a single issue, very tightly focused, that they think you can help them with."

Philippe fired the first shot. "For example, we are not at all interested in things like taxes. I know the fiscs came to see you recently, but we're not here about that."

"I appreciate that," Vitaliy said. "They say you find a tax problem every time you scratch a small businessman, especially a restaurateur, and I'm no exception."

Philippe started slowly. He asked about his brother's apartment, which Vitaliy had once owned himself.

"I sold it to my manager Vladi a few years ago, and he sold it to Boris. You just met Vladi. He doesn't usually wait tables, but one of the waiters called in sick this morning so he's filling in. Vladi was a decorated soldier in the Russian Army before he got kicked out for hitting an officer who insulted his religion. He's a little touchy, but he's a good manager and I was lucky to get him.

"That apartment has been a pretty good income producer, but now Paris is clamping down on short-term rentals so I think he just wanted to be out of it. Anyway, my brother is a bit of a sucker."

"You know about the two Chechens and the American who were in the apartment?"

"I know they exist. I don't know anything else about them."

Philippe unfolded a sheet of paper he'd taken from his jacket pocket and studied it carefully. "Would it surprise you that somebody here called one of them just as the police were moving in?"

"Of course it would surprise me. I have no knowledge of them or of any kidnapping. I hope your daughter wasn't hurt." Vitaliy was still trying to be solicitous, but Philippe could see that he was getting more nervous as it became clear what direction the interview was taking.

"What are you trying to tell me? Do you think I had something to do with that kidnapping? That would be stupid. I know the French government would throw me out of the country in a minute if they thought I was involved in anything like that."

Walker intervened. "Vitaliy, let me tell you a few things that Philippe maybe can't because the prosecutors haven't developed the evidence sufficiently, or maybe they just want to surprise you very early some morning. There are something like 3,000 criminal gangs in Europe, and the people I used to work for know full well you head up one of those. For example, they know about your accounts on Cyprus and the money laundered through them. They know about your cigarette smuggling between Greece and Bulgaria. That's a very nice racket, but nobody but the Greeks care about it right now. Maybe the Germans, a little.

"But listen well to this. They know you've been asked to do a hit on Eddie Grant. They don't know if you ordered the kidnapping, but I can tell you that if this goes any further it will be the end of the line for you in France. And maybe the end of the line period."

"I don't know what you're talking about," Vitaliy said, visibly shaken.

Philippe waved a hand dismissively and looked at his watch. "It's now 2:50 p.m. Just before we came into your office I started a clock. If the three of us don't walk into the préfecture by three-thirty, two things will happen: first, the CRS will pay you a visit, and you know they never come in small numbers; second, anything they find will go directly to the public prosecutor, along with all my records. The tax police will close you down immediately, if there's anything left to close after the CRS finishes its work." It was the threat of the CRS that had the most obvious effect — no one wanted a visit from the dreaded riot police, who always came by the busload and were not known for their subtlety.

"What do you want from me?"

"Only a few things," Philippe responded. "We will act on them, but we will not say where the information came from. It could have been your brother, for example."

"That idiot. He's the reason I'm in this fix. He took it personal when Eddie Grant killed his man Dmitri. And that was stupid."

"Did he arrange for Sonny Perry to break out of jail in Florida?"

"Sure he did, along with a lawyer who does his work. I had nothing to do with that. I heard Sonny came to France, or maybe Germany, but I don't know where he is. I swear that. Boris got him out through Cuba somehow. He has connections there."

"Did you provide the muscle for the kidnapping?"

"Nah. I never heard of those guys. The grapevine says they're Chechens who only got into the country recently. I have no idea how they got here."

"Do you know anybody doing business in Chechnya?"

"Sure I do," Vitaliy said. "But it's a really dangerous game. They still think they're going to break away from Russia and they're true believers — they're just as single-minded as the Arabs. In fact, they get a lot of their money from the Arabs, particularly Saudi Arabia."

Vitaliy turned to Walker. "You know one guy who deals in Chechnya. It's your guy Ahmed, in Munich."

"How do you know him?" Walker asked.

"I don't, but I'm told his washing machines are showing up in strange places."

"Anybody else?"

"Here and there." Then he paused as if to think, and rubbed his temple with the stub of his middle finger.

"There's one man you might look at, but it can't come from me. He'd kill me in a minute if he knew I talked about him."

"We won't tell anybody who doesn't need to know, and we won't tell the prosecutor unless he asks."

"There's a very strange guy in Munich. Moves around a lot, does business in Germany and the Balkans. He's close to Ahmed, too. He's mysterious and has a bunch of names. I know him as Claude Khan, but sometimes he goes by the name Alain Alawite. He's a French-Arab mix, born in Paris during the war, and both of those names are probably made up. But for God's sake don't let him know I told you or I'm dead."

"I appreciate your coming through for us," Philippe said. "Did he set up the kidnapping?"

"Boris told me he did. Boris wanted me to take out Eddie Grant, but only after we kidnapped him and sweated some information out of him. Khan is a big-time goldbug and is looking for hidden Nazi bullion because he thinks the price of gold is about to shoot up. And he thinks this guy Grant knows where a valuable old painting is hidden, or maybe has it himself. I don't know how much manpower he has anymore, 'cause he had to bring in Chechen and American muscle, but I wouldn't want to bet against him. The story is that he used to be connected to the East German government, before the Wall fell. But I didn't have anything to do with setting up the kidnapping or using the apartment. Khan had Sonny Perry go straight to Boris's lawyer in Paris for that."

Philippe knew Vitaliy had already put himself in grave danger, but figured once the dam had burst he should try for more.

"Who here would have made the call to tip off Sonny that the police were closing in? You?"

"Sure not me," Vitaliy replied. "That's a question I can't answer."

"This Khan. Is he in the washing machine business with Ahmed, or what?"

"He buys from Ahmed, but the washing machines are secondary. What he wants is the box. A washing machine is mostly empty space, so he fills some of it with more profitable cargo. I don't know what it is, maybe weapons, maybe drugs, maybe both. Not every trip, and not every box in a shipment, but enough to make good money. And of course he sells the washing machines. But he's more intense about it now. It's like he knows something big is about to happen."

"When did you last hear from Khan?" Philippe asked him.

"Not for a few weeks. When I turned down Boris, I think I burned that bridge, which doesn't bother me. Khan is evil — take that from someone who's met a lot of really bad cases in his day. He's the reason I got a permit to carry a pistol."

∫

An hour later, they sat in Walker Evans's living room huddled around a secure speakerphone. Icky Crane joined the conference call from Washington; Eddie and Aurélie participated from Paris.

"Well, we have a name," Philippe said. "Vitaliy Budzivoi tells us Alain Alawite and Claude Khan are the same man, although he suspects both names are fake. Do they ring a bell?"

Eddie and Icky started talking at the same time. Eddie shut up to give the floor to his friend.

"His brother Boris in Miami gave us the name Alawite," Icky said. "Supposedly he's half French, half Saudi, and lives in and out of Germany. And he likes gold and stolen art. And we're told that Sonny Perry borrowed the apartment where Aurélie was kept, on instructions from Khan. And Khan is the exporter in Munich that Ahmed and Jen Wetzmuller think is smuggling weapons and gold."

Aurélie jumped into the conversation. "Édouard and I heard the same name when we were looking for the Raphael painting. A retired art dealer told us Alain Alawite was a guest at a dinner party to celebrate the wrap of a TV show on art stolen by the Nazis. That old fellow, Jacques something, said he had too much wine and predicted that the painting would be found near Gare Saint-Lazare, which of course it wasn't. But it really got Alawite's attention. He went back to Jacques later for more information, and so did Roy Castor. Eddie's father followed up with Jacques but wasn't able to get anything else from him, either.

"Jacques said the name was a made-up joke. He had no idea what the man's real name was, but thought we should be able to find him. He had some businesses in France but he was a desert Arab. He spoke French like a native, though."

Philippe added, "Vitaliy gave us a lot of general stuff, but not much in the way of specifics. He wants us to think he's an outsider and Boris is the insider working with Khan on the real dangerous stuff. We don't know if that's true or not, but you have enough to catch Boris between a federal arrest and deportation and a Florida prosecution for murder of the prison guards. Icky, can you follow up with him?"

"I can be down there tomorrow, and in the meantime we'll see what we can find out about this guy. Eddie, can you join me?"

"Sure, and I'll bring Paul Fitzhugh along. Aurélie?"

"Can't. I have to earn a living. But thanks for asking."

"And I'll see what we can do to find Claude Khan," Philippe said.

∫

As the taxi pulled up at the airport, Philippe turned to Gabriel and said, "I'm not going back with you. I need to see someone here on a completely private matter, so I'll call you when I'm on the way back."

He gave the driver an address in one of the best neighborhoods of suburban Nice, the home of his former wife Barbara, who'd divorced him thirty years before when Aurélie was a toddler. She abandoned them for a Cypriot shipping executive named Ben Pelonie, a dominating man who had become rich arranging the movement of all sorts of merchandise, most of it legal, between Russia and the Arab countries via the Black Sea. For twenty-five years she had disappeared from his life, for which he had forgiven her, and also from Aurélie's — for which he had not.

The Pelonies had moved back to France, and Nice, five years before. Ben had become a near-recluse because of declining health, but Barbara had swept like a tornado into the social scene of the Côte d'Azur. They lived an opulent lifestyle in their white-columned mansion overlooking the city and the coastline. Ben's close dealings with Russian import-export firms, most of them financed through Cypriot banks, pulled them into the center of the Russian expatriate community, which was growing rapidly as the Russian economy became dominated by the constellation of wealthy businessmen circling around Vladimir Putin. The oligarchs scrambled to find safe-haven footholds in countries where contracts were held sacred and their money was out of easy reach of the Russian government. At the same time, the smaller merchants who felt threatened by the close cooperation between the government and their larger competitors also looked for safe places to put their money and their families. The Mediterranean climate of the Côte d'Azur and the strict financial regulation of the French government met both requirements.

Philippe had seen Barbara only once since their divorce, although he knew Ben had died the year before. Two weeks ago she surprised him with a telephone call, asking him to visit her when he was next in Nice. He had called the day before and arranged to meet her in the late afternoon, planning to take a late flight or the overnight train back to Paris.

From the street, Barbara's house was striking: a façade of six tall white columns with hand-carved Corinthian capitals lined up across a wide porch looking up the wooded valley into the upper hills. But she and her frequent guests preferred her signature view of the Mediterranean from the deck behind the house, which surrounded a fifty-foot pool and connected the main house to a guest house containing two one-bedroom apartments.

Philippe's first impression was that the landscaping was not as pristine as it had been on his one earlier visit. The lawn was manicured, but some of the plantings had weeds around them and several of the boxwood hedges showed signs of their age and needed to be replaced.

He rang the doorbell, expecting a maid to answer, but Barbara opened the door herself. She looked as attractive and fashionable as he remembered. Her figure was almost as slim as she approached sixty as it had been at thirty, and her glossy black hair, now pulled into a severe ponytail, was still one of her best features.

"Thank you for coming, Philippe," she said simply as she stood aside for him to enter the central corridor that led to the pool at the far end. They exchanged bisous gravely.

"I didn't think I would be here so soon, but I have a case that needed attention. I can stay a few hours."

"That will be enough. I just need some advice. But first tell me, how is Aurélie? Lately I've regretted that I'm not part of her life now."

"She's fine, but she had a close call. She was kidnapped a few days ago by a couple of Russians — Chechens, really. She escaped, but it could have turned out badly."

"That's terrible. Was she hurt? Do you know who did it?" Barbara obviously had not lost all her maternal feelings — she was shaken.

"It had to do with the adventure she had three years ago, the matter of the old painting and the Nazi gold. She and her fiancé Eddie found the gold but not the painting.

"In fact, I suspect some of your friends may have been involved. I saw one of them today and I'm pretty certain he knew about it. If not more than knew."

Barbara gasped. "Who?"

"Vitaliy Budzivoi. He and his half brother in Miami, Boris, are what the Americans call persons of interest."

"Vitaliy," she said. "It's funny, or maybe not so funny, but he's part of the reason I need to talk to you. Would you like a coffee, then we can go into the library and talk?"

"Coffee. Yes, please."

Expresso cups in hand, they walked across the central corridor into a room Philippe hadn't seen. It had obviously begun as a library — the walls were lined with books to the ceiling — but it was also a tribute to Ben's hunting prowess. A stuffed leopard and several tigers stood around the walls, evidence of many African safaris. A pair of elephant tusks reaching to Philippe's shoulders bracketed the stone fireplace.

"I had read Ben was a hunter, but this is more than I expected."

"Most of his hunting was done long ago, but he did like to have the reminders around him."

She invited Philippe to sit in an armchair to the right of the unlit fireplace and sank gracefully into its twin on the other side.

"Philippe, I think my problem may be in your line of work. You may have noticed that this house isn't as well kept as it used to be, and if you look carefully in the other rooms you'll find some bare places on the walls where we once had paintings. Ben really wasn't able to keep up with business for his last couple of years, and I found right after the funeral that I was in trouble. He had tax problems, business problems, you name it. He owned quite a bit of commercial real estate in America, and we depended on it for income because he thought it was safer than owning houses. And it was, for a while. Then the recession hit commercial properties and that income has dried up.

"He also had investments in France, which have done better, but there's quite a bit of money in Chez Budzivoi, and Vitaliy isn't able to pay me.

"But here's the problem. My accountant is also Vitaliy's accountant. I'm beginning to think he's not completely honest."

Philippe instantly recognized an opportunity to learn more about Vitaliy and his Mafioso friends, though he had very little sympathy for Barbara's personal financial problems.

"The money Ben put into the restaurant was one of the first investments he made when we moved to Nice," she said.

"So things were good for a couple of years, until the recession hit, and got harder after that?" Philippe asked.

"More or less. Actually, Vitaliy kept up his payments until Ben died, although it must have been difficult for him. He keeps telling me he'll try to send me some money, but I haven't seen anything in a year. As a result, I've had to sell the paintings and my grand piano and cut the staff back to barely enough to keep the house presentable. I may have to sell it."

"That would be a shame. Is Vitaliy the only bad debt?"

"No. When we left Cyprus, Ben sold the business to a man he'd worked with for years. Unfortunately, that man got behind on his payments at the same time as Vitaliy. In a way, he has problems from two sides. His Cyprus business is suffering from the recession and the political crackdowns in Russia, and he's an investor in Vitaliy's restaurant, so he no longer has that cash coming in, either. That's if Vitaliy has quit paying him, too. It's a perfect vicious circle."

Philippe was curious. "Do you think he might be paying the guy in Cyprus but not you?"

"Sure, because he could cause a lot of trouble. He does business with a lot of the people who eat at Chez Budzivoi and, like Vitaliy, he's tied in with some unsavory characters in Russia who could be a real threat. And, to state the obvious, he's a powerful man and I'm a powerless widow."

CHAPTER ELEVEN

Miami

The Air France flight pulled up to its gate at 2 p.m., precisely on time. Eddie had brought Paul Fitzhugh, who ostensibly was the manager of Gran'Langue's buildings but in fact had been Eddie's top sergeant during Desert Storm and had become his willing teammate when his problems turned physical.

Icky waited just outside customs. They followed as he strode quickly through the terminal to the pickup area, where Raul Gutierrez waited in a no-parking zone, chatting with an airport policewoman.

As he drove east on the Dolphin Expressway, Raul briefed them on his conversation with Boris Budzivoi two days before.

"He was nervous as hell, and he tried really hard to make me think he had nothing to do with Sonny Perry's escape, which isn't very likely. With the new material Icky says you have from his brother, it should be pretty easy to make more progress. I think he knows everything you need."

Paul asked him, "His brother is pretty smooth, but I hear Boris is a lot different. Is that so?"

"Boris is an old-school thug. I met a lot of men just like him when I was working in Cuba. I think he's gotten softer, probably just because he's not living in Russia anymore, but he's still a thug. Even has a picture of Putin on his brag wall."

He stopped the car in the loading zone in front of the Golden Samovar and all four went in. The same bartender who'd tried to stop Raul said, "He's not here," before they asked.

"Where is he?" Raul asked.

"I don't know. He didn't come in today, but he doesn't always work the lunch hour."

"When he comes in ask him to call me right away." Raul gave the bartender a card.

Back outside, Icky said, "We shouldn't wait to see if he comes to work tonight. I have his home address — let's go there and talk to him. Somebody else may be looking for him, too."

Boris lived in one of many expensive high-rises on Brickell Avenue, a short drive back to the mainland, all of them with spectacular sunrise views across the sparkling blue waters of the bay.

Raul showed his federal ID to the doorman, who took a key from a safe in the manager's office and led them to a glass-walled elevator for the ride to the fifteenth floor. On the way, he volunteered that they were the second people looking for Boris that day.

"But the first guy already had a key. He had another man with him and said they worked for Mr. Budzivoi and were bringing him some papers to sign. They were there less than a half hour. Big, beefy guys. They could have been the bad guy in a James Bond movie.

"Here we are. Fifteenth floor. You take the key and bring it back to me when you leave, and don't tell anyone I gave it to you. I have to stay on the door." He handed the key to Raul.

"It's a good thing we came," Eddie said. "It doesn't sound like that was a social call."

The doorbell chimed inside, high note, low note. In a few seconds Raul pressed it again. When there was no answer, he pushed the door open slowly and called for Boris, but got no response, so they began to look through the three large bedrooms, one by one.

"I rented a place downtown from a Russian," Raul said. "It had flocked wallpaper and a lot of black-and-red furniture. This guy must have the same interior decorator."

Paul walked down the long hall, opening each door and looking inside. At the second bedroom he stopped and called out, "Here he is! Come here when everything else is clear."

When Eddie arrived he found Paul leaning over Boris's still form, feeling for a pulse in his neck.

"There's a pulse, and it's pretty strong," Paul said. "Help me get him untied. Get a knife from the kitchen."

Icky said, "I'll go get it. I don't think Eddie should be around this guy with a knife in his hand right now."

Boris had been worked over thoroughly. A bloody gash ran from the top of his head to his right ear and there was a deep bruise under his right eye. His wrists and ankles were taped together and he had been gagged with silver duct tape. Paul pulled it slowly away from his mouth, then used the knife to release his wrists and ankles. He choked as Paul carefully pulled a sock from his mouth, then turned to the others. "He's really lucky to be alive."

As they turned him on his back Boris began to stir, then opened his eyes.

"You," he said to Raul. "You're the Fed who came to see me yesterday. What are you doing here?"

Icky stepped up. "We're here saving your life. In an hour you'd have suffocated from that gag, which is probably exactly what was intended. We're also here to ask you some questions.

"Do you want us to call an ambulance? They'll bring the police. Paul, how badly is he hurt?"

"Not too bad," Paul responded. "The cut on his head has stopped bleeding and I can put a bandage on it. The bruise on his face will be ugly for a few days. He'll have some pain, but unless there's something internal he should be OK."

"No...no," Boris said, waving his hands around in confusion. "No police. I know who did this and I'll handle it in my own way. Believe me, I will. Help me up."

Paul took his arm and helped him to a chair in the living room. He walked heavily, slowly — it appeared to Raul he had aged ten years.

"OK," he said. "I understand now that we have to be on the same side of this."

Icky took over the interrogation. Boris was still hazy, but he remembered their telephone conversation, and was clearer about Raul's visit.

"What do you want to know?"

"First we need to get the characters straight," Icky said. "You told my colleague Raul about a man named Alain Alawite, who buys gold and art. Your brother tells us he's also known as Claude Khan. Which is it?"

"I think Khan is his real name," Boris said. "I can't be sure, but I think he took the name Alawite to throw off the French police when he moved back to Europe several years ago. He told me once that his grandfather was a French count and his father a Saudi prince, but I didn't believe him. But I think he's really Khan, not Alawite."

Icky questioned him closely about his conversations with Khan and Vitaliy. Boris told how two of his men had picked up Sonny at a bar in the Miami suburbs. Following a schedule Khan sent by email, Sonny had posed as a tourist from Texas and rented a campsite at Long Key State Park, where he waited until after midnight for the fishing boat that would take him to Cuba. There he caught a plane to Paris to meet Khan.

"The trip to Cuba was nearly a disaster," Boris said. "They got past the U.S. Coast Guard OK, but less than a mile off Matanzas the Cubans stopped them. The fisherman was able to talk his way out of it, with the help of some dollars, and he was finally able to put Sonny ashore in the country not too far from Havana. From there I had a man pick him up.

"Khan had gotten him a passport from Cyprus. He laid low for a day in Havana while they got it all tricked out with his picture, then the next day he got on the plane. I haven't heard anything about him since."

Icky was insistent. "You didn't arrange for the escape from the prison van?"

"No, that wasn't me. Sonny told my guys someone in Jacksonville set it up, and he first heard about it from his lawyer during a visit. Khan's people delivered Sonny to the bar an hour before my guys got there. They drove him to the Keys and then drove back, and that was the end of my involvement. The guys told me Sonny was a nasty piece of work. They considered just throwing him off a bridge."

"And the kidnapping?"

Boris again tried to dodge responsibility. "I didn't know nothing about a kidnapping. Khan just asked if I knew of a safe apartment in Paris he could use and I just gave him the name of my lawyer. The guy I bought it from didn't know if it was rented out or not, and I'd just bought it, so I thought it would be better if the lawyer handled it with Vladi. I didn't ask for any rent.

"I didn't know it was a kidnapping, but I understand it better now. He was really pissed at Mr. Grant here and must have wanted some way to get at him. But you understand that I wouldn't have had any problem with that if I'd known." He glanced nervously at Eddie, who looked at him with a threatening scowl, then back at Icky, looking in vain for support.

"Tell us more about Khan," Icky commanded. "What kind of business is he in?"

"I've only met him once and that was almost ten years ago. He told me he'd been born in Paris during the war, that his father was a Saudi prince and his mother was the daughter of an old French count who wanted the Germans to win. He lived with his mother until he was eighteen, then went to Saudi Arabia. He did a lot of things after that — after all, he's pretty old now so he's had the time — but now he's into gold. He thinks the price is going to jump up real high soon and he's buying all of it he can.

"In fact, he's started a sort of unofficial hedge fund and given some of his friends a chance to buy into it. I even put a little money in."

"A little? How much was that?" Icky asked.

"A couple hundred thousand dollars."

"That must have got his attention."

"Not hardly. He has millions and millions in it now, maybe hundreds of millions, from bankers and politicians and God knows who else, all of it stored in Dubai. He says he'll sell it within a year and we'll make a lot of money. He keeps twenty percent of anything we get over 1,500 dollars an ounce. I also lent some money to that congressman so he could buy in."

"Congressman Tennant? I thought he was swimming in cash."

"Maybe he is and just wanted more of the gold. Maybe he's a true believer like Khan. But I think he was just short of cash. I've lent to him before and he's always been good for it."

Icky looked over at Eddie. His expression said clearly this was significant information.

"When did you first meet Khan?" Icky asked.

"Like I said, ten years or so ago. Somebody offered to sell me some pieces of old gold and I needed a place to sell them. My brother knew a man in Germany and dropped the word, and it wasn't long before Khan gave me a call. As soon as he saw the pictures, he bought. I just sent the pieces FedEx to a place in Germany and in a couple of days the money was in my bank account, like eBay. I sold him a few more things I found."

"Did you buy from Al Sommers in Sarasota?"

"A little. His stuff came to me through my friend Dmitri, who this asshole killed." He pointed weakly toward Eddie, who was standing with Paul against the wall.

"Too bad about your friend," Icky told him, "but for Eddie it was kill or be killed and I don't think he thought about it any more than you would have if you'd been in his situation. Did you sell him any other stuff?"

Boris thought a bit and shook his head to clear it. "Can I have a beer? The refrigerator is around the corner."

"I'll get it," Paul said, and headed toward the kitchen.

"Yeah, I bought a couple of pretty good paintings from a broad up in Sarasota," Boris continued, focused on Icky now. "She got my name from a friend of Al Sommers, another kraut named Kraft. Erich Kraft." He turned to Eddie and said accusingly, "I hear you had something to do with him getting killed, too. What are you, some kind of Dr. Death?"

Eddie crossed the room in two steps and had both hands around Boris's throat before anyone else could move. "You scumbag. Every one of your good friends was involved in killing my father, my wife, and my son, and the way I see it you're a part of the gang. You just might get out of this day with your life, but if it were up to me I'd throw you out the window into the parking lot and break your worthless neck." He pushed Boris away hard, turned on his heel, and walked toward the door, where Paul stood with beer in hand, smiling. No one had lifted a hand to protect Boris. The mobster's expression said he knew he was in the deepest trouble of his life.

Icky asked, "Other than Sonny, have you been in touch with any of the others in Sarasota?"

"Just the broad, Jen something. She came to see me six or eight months later looking for Khan. She said she was moving back to Germany and needed a job, and could I introduce them? She didn't have his name and I didn't give it to her, but I did send him a message about her. I never heard nothing more about it."

They questioned him for another hour while Paul went out for hamburgers. When he returned they took a break, leaving Raul to make certain Boris didn't try to contact anyone outside.

As they sat around the coffee table in the over-decorated living room, Eddie said, "Khan is our man. He has to be the one behind everything that's happened, from my family's death to Aurélie's kidnapping, plus God knows what else."

He shifted his focus to address Icky directly. "Aurélie told you during our conference call yesterday about the art dealer who hired Eric Kraft during the war. Kraft went to Poland and brought him the painting and five crates of gold, which he delivered to a prominent collaborator. We think he kept the gold for himself because we found it hidden in a sub-basement where his house once stood.

"But we learned something else, which matches exactly what Boris just told us. The count had a daughter, who had a son by a Saudi prince who was a sort of unofficial ambassador to Vichy France, although of course he found Paris more congenial. The boy stayed with her until he was eighteen, then he disappeared. I think he's become our man Khan. The age is right.

"There's one area we haven't explored, and that's Khan's past in Germany. We have some indications that he worked for the East German government, but let's try to find out what he did there. Jeremy might be able to help us with that."

Icky handled the questioning when they returned. Boris told them immediately that Khan had worked for the East German government in some capacity.

"From what I heard, everybody there worked for the Stasi, one way or another. It could have been that or it could have been somewhere else. I wouldn't be surprised to learn he was a policeman of some sort."

"Do you know if he worked in Berlin or in West Germany?"

"I don't know. I once heard him say he'd made a lot of money in West Germany. By then there was no West or East Germany anymore, so he could have been talking about the past, or he could have been just using the old term like a lot of Germans do. I just don't know."

"Then let's go back to your other conversations with Khan. Did he ever give you any idea of what else he deals in? Does he sell drugs, for example?"

"I never heard him mention drugs, but he might. He did ask me once if any of my Cuban friends could get Russian anti-aircraft missiles, but that's nothing I've ever done and I told him so."

Icky sat up. "What kind of missiles did he want?"

"Something small, he said. Something that could be handled by one man. I didn't know what he was talking about so I don't know anything more about it."

"And when you wanted to reach him, how did you do it?"

"By email. He used a French Gmail account. The address was odd — au2011. But he always replies by telephone, never email, except for that one time to tell me to pick up Sonny."

Icky and Eddie held a brief closed-door conference in the most distant bedroom and decided Boris had to be held incommunicado at least overnight so he wouldn't have the chance to call any of his confederates. Eddie was especially worried that he might warn his brother.

"It's pretty risky from a legal point of view for us to hold him like this," Icky said. "I don't think he would make an issue of it because it would mean talking about what he told us, but it could be a problem one day. The loan to the congressman is almost sure to make waves. Are you comfortable with this?"

"Sure am," Eddie told him forcefully. "This is the best chance we've ever had to roll up this entire network. It looks like these people intend to be a serious threat to national security, as the politicians never tire of saying, and you know my reasons — this affair has dragged on too long. It weighs on me too much. I have to resolve it, no matter what. Let's find the guy."

Eddie and Paul took a cab back to the airport to catch an overnight flight to Paris. On the way, Eddie called Philippe several times without success and spoke once to Aurélie, who also had no idea where her father was, except that he had flown to Nice and expected to return that night.

"But he said my mother had asked him to see her about some problems she's having with her husband's estate."

"Would he do that? I've never heard him say a good word about her."

"He might," she replied. "He got over the divorce long ago, but he was still angry that she abandoned me. I told him not to worry about it because it doesn't bother me anymore, but I don't think Philippe has that much forgiveness in him. But she was a beautiful and seductive woman, so anything could happen."

CHAPTER TWELVE

Côte d'Azur

A nd so it had. Philippe and Barbara talked about her problems for two hours, which gave him several valuable nuggets of intelligence about Vitaliy Budzivoi's business dealings and Ben's former life in Cyprus. And then she offered to make dinner.

"Something simple, maybe an omelet and green salad? How would that be?"

Against his better judgment he said yes. It wasn't long before he accepted a glass of excellent dry white wine from Switzerland, and in an hour they were in each other's arms in Barbara's large bed. Or rather, he was in her arms as he paid moist attention to her nipples, first the left, then the right, a slow routine he'd performed a thousand times in their three years together, and that had never failed to please.

"Philippe! You remembered! And you haven't lost your touch, even a little bit," she cried once. He was tempted to quiet her but stopped when he realized they were safe from curious ears inside her massive house, unlike the tiny apartment they'd shared during their short time together.

A half hour later he rolled onto his back, exhausted, and went soundly to sleep, forgetting to turn his telephone back on. Nor did he remember when the sun streamed through the window and Barbara woke him with a soft but insistent touch, beginning a second chapter that ended just like the first.

At nine o'clock, he could no longer sleep through the delicious smell of coffee. The unfamiliar bedroom confused him briefly. Barbara must have opened the drapes covering a large window because he had no memory of the broad view over her pool and the hills that rolled down to the sea. He did recall rushing to undress her and leaving their clothes in an untidy mess on a chair next to the window, and there they all remained, hers on the bottom of the pile, his on the top, his underwear hanging from the chair's back.

He looked at his phone on the night table and remembered turning it off at the last minute. He also remembered telling himself he must turn it on in an hour or two.

"*Merde*," he muttered as he saw that he'd received six calls, four from Eddie and two from Aurélie. He decided to start with Eddie's last voicemail and work backward.

"Philippe, it looks like you're in for the night wherever you are, so I'll summarize and we can talk tomorrow. Boris Budzivoi confirmed just about everything his brother gave you, but he added some details.

"Khan gets his messages from a French Gmail account, au2011, which I suppose you could translate into 'gold this year.' Would you start the process of looking at the account? I know the privacy laws make that difficult, but Icky is getting pushback from his people and may not be able to give us much help for a while.

"He's asking them for a full-court press but is afraid he'll get a lot less. There are political forces at work that he hasn't been able to bypass yet.

"In the meantime, I'm going to work another angle. The answer to this whole riddle is buried in the past, and there's nobody I know better at that kind of archaeology than Jeremy Bentham, so I'm going to see him as soon as I get back to Paris."

Eddie would land in a few hours, then go to Jeremy's home near Canal Saint-Martin. Philippe looked out the window again and saw Barbara sitting on the edge of the pool, naked, waving an invitation to join her. Oh well. He could get a plane to Paris in the afternoon. Today would be for exploring memories.

"I'm glad you finally got up. I was starting to get cold out here in my altogether," she told him with a smile as he sat down next to her. His hand moved to her breast as he kissed her. She pressed her hand over his and pushed it down between her legs, then held him.

"Back inside?" she asked after he was fully aroused.

"Right now!" he answered. He stood and pulled her to her feet while she maintained her tight grip.

Later, exhausted, they talked quietly of the past as they lay quietly in the big bed.

"Could we have done that in the water?" she asked.

"Dunno. I never tried it. You were always the swimmer, and Aurélie. I remember our vacations at the beach in Trouville. I would never go into the water, but she loved to splash with you."

"Does she still swim?"

"For an hour at least once a week. She and Eddie run a lot, and they lift weights. She's really fit. That's what got her out of trouble when the Chechens kidnapped her."

"I still can't believe somebody kidnapped my daughter and tried to kill her. Did you catch them?"

"We arrested one, and one escaped. She threw the third one under a métro train, so he won't be a threat to anyone."

"I'm amazed. I couldn't have done that at her age. Young women just weren't that physical."

Philippe was silent for a long moment. "It's why she's still alive."

CHAPTER THIRTEEN

Paris, Canal Saint-Martin

During the long taxi ride from the airport, Eddie's mind wandered back to his first meeting with Jeremy Bentham. He'd been a lost freshman wandering the arid campus of West Plains University in 1984 when he'd found a bench under a pecan tree and collapsed onto it, his large bag of new textbooks beside him. The high, direct sun was unlike anything he'd ever seen in Paris, during September or any other time. It drained away all his energy.

As he read through his list of courses he sensed, rather than saw, a long shadow stop on the gravel walk separating his bench from the manicured boxwood hedges of the central quadrangle.

"Eddie?" The voice sounded like his father's, but couldn't be. His father was in France.

"Eddie? Have I found Eddie Grant?"

He looked up tentatively at the silhouette of a tall man, his face made invisible by the brilliant sunlight behind him.

"Eddie? I'm Jeremy Bentham. I told your father I'd look you up, but I didn't expect to see you so soon."

"Major Bentham!" Eddie jumped to his feet. "I'm supposed to find you and introduce myself, but..."

"Monsieur." The driver had to call him twice. "Monsieur, here is the Impasse Molière. You wanted to come here..."

Eddie paid the driver and patted the head of his large bulldog, which sat drooling on a towel in the passenger seat, then rolled his small carry-on behind him down the patched asphalt sidewalk that led to Number 8.

Years before, when Jeremy and his wife Pat had bought and restored the elegant eighteenth-century townhouse, Canal Saint-Martin had been a dangerous area. As it gentrified, the burglars and pickpockets found better prospects in the 19th and 20th arrondissements and the far side of Montmartre, in the 18th beyond Sacré-Coeur Cathedral.

They had been happy part-time Parisians for years. Retired young from the Army to return to West Plains as chairman of the history department, where he had been ROTC commander during Eddie's first year, Jeremy started a third career as an author. In five years of juggling teaching, research, and writing, he published three well-received books about life and politics in East Germany before and after the fall of the Berlin Wall.

The Benthams resumed their friendship with Eddie's parents, which had begun in the 1970s when Jeremy was a rising young officer and Artie Grant was the dean of American businessmen in Paris. Artie's exploits as an American military spy during World War II were not widely known, but Jeremy's passion was military history and Artie, to him, was the essence of heroism — willing to risk all for the cause he believed in, but not to call attention to himself by boasting about it later. He also admired Margaux, who as a child and then a teenager had followed her father the Résistance leader through the South of France and then to Paris, where he became a prominent minister in the de Gaulle government.

As Pat's health declined their lives shrank. When she could no longer walk the four blocks to their favorite Alsatian restaurant across from the Gare de l'Est, Jeremy resigned his teaching job and turned full time to Paris and his writing. He spent long hours in the old house, staying close to his library and the flower garden. At first, Eddie had the feeling much of his will to live had died with Pat — he'd been a beacon of joie de vivre when they arrived in Paris, and then the beacon became a guttering candle.

That had changed the night he accompanied Eddie and Aurélie to the studios of *France Televisions* for an interview about finding the treasure of Saint-Lazare. Jeremy and the striking blonde interviewer,

Juliette Bertrand, were immediately attracted to each other. She joined them for dinner — Eddie and Aurélie left the restaurant at midnight, but Jeremy and Juliette stayed, until the proprietor finally made them leave, then spent the night at Impasse Molière. A month later she moved in.

Eddie rapped the ancient lion's-head door knocker sharply, twice only as Jeremy had requested of all his friends, and when he heard nothing after thirty seconds — Jeremy was nothing if not prompt — he turned away from the door and pushed open a spring-loaded gate guarding the path to the garden. He found Jeremy sitting on a stool, blissfully hoeing between two rows of marigolds.

"Ah, Eddie," he said with a smile as he sat up. "Come over here and tell me what's up. Is Aurélie with you? And how's the bruise?"

"Bonjour, Jeremy. Aurélie had classes all day today, and my butt is still sore, but it's on the mend. In fact, it survived eight hours in an airplane seat. I just got back from Miami, and I could use your help."

A broad smile crossed Jeremy's face. "Always nice to be needed. Come on inside and let's see what you have. I've done about all I can for these wretched flowers in any case."

He and Eddie had not worked together until Icky asked both of them to attend the banker's cocktail party, but they had known each other so long and shared so many bottles of red wine over Army stories that each knew something of the other's volunteer work.

At one long evening in a neighborhood bistro Jeremy favored and Juliette was slowly coming to accept, Aurélie said she was surprised at how alike the two men were. Both had hair so dark it reflected purple highlights when the light was just right, although Jeremy's was graying at the temples.

"It's my penalty for being twenty years older," he said with a grin. As soon as he retired from the Army, he'd let his hair grow longer and cultivated a luxuriant mustache that had an affinity for drops of wine and miscellaneous debris. Juliette did not approve of the mustache and the hair was a length five years out of fashion, but in public at least she kept her views to herself.

More than once, Eddie and Jeremy had mused about Icky's reasons for keeping their jobs separate, and they had finally concluded it was just the instinctive caution of a seasoned intelligence agent that their known association as friends could threaten their security. They had long ago given up worrying about it and were both surprised that Icky asked them to look at the gold fund together.

Jeremy led the way up a long ramp into the dark house, kept cool by its thick stone walls. He stopped at a bench just inside the door to drop his gardening gloves, then turned left into his library, which he'd converted into a bedroom when Pat could no longer reach the second floor. After he met Juliette, he'd built shelves on three of its walls, all the way to the twelve-foot ceiling. Eddie could see no space for more books, and knew Jeremy had left as many again in the master library upstairs, which he'd turned over to Juliette for a study.

The books were organized by language, English on the left, German on the right, French on the shorter back wall. Military history dominated because the violent torments of twentieth-century Europe had been Jeremy's life. In the center of the U stood a massive oak desk Jeremy had bought at the Porte de Clignacourt flea market to replace the desk he'd left for Juliette upstairs.

Jeremy waved at a leather armchair as he pulled an old-fashioned wooden chair from under his desk and swiveled around to reach into a small refrigerator for an almost-full bottle of brilliant red wine. "Ballon de rouge?"

"Sure."

Jeremy poured a glass for each of them and took a sip. "Well, what is it out of my checkered past you need?"

"Your memory. Paul and I were with Icky in Miami yesterday about the gold, and we ran up against something you may be able to help us with."

He summarized the testimony of the brothers Budzivoi about the mysterious hedge fund manager.

"We've heard a couple of times that he had something to do with East Germany. He was born during the war, so the age could be right. He'd have been in his forties or so when the Wall came down. Could you tap your sources and see if he left a trail? It could be serious, because he once asked for portable anti-aircraft missiles."

Jeremy sat silently through two more sips of the wine. "Not too bad, is it? I get it at Nicolas, down at the corner. Pretty cheap." He took out his handkerchief and mopped up a drop that stuck to his barrel mustache.

Silence again. Then, "Icky told me about Miami but neither of us saw any reason for me to go, and I'll do almost anything these days to avoid airports.

"Manpads. That's serious. They're the terror of civil aviation. Short for Man Portable Air Defense Systems, and that's what they were designed for, but they're spreading all over the Middle East and those folks aren't thinking in terms of defense. They're on the offensive. Manpads have been around for half a century, but lately they've become much more effective. The Afghans used them against Russian helicopters in the '80s, then the Chechens used them with great effectiveness during the Second Chechen War, and now there are thousands of them loose in Libya thanks to the civil war they have going now.

"It was a manpad attack that kicked off the genocide in Rwanda. Did you know that?" He didn't wait for an answer.

"When I was researching my second book, I met some pretty senior people. By then I was a professor at a backwater American college, no longer a two-star. If I'd still been in the Army, they wouldn't have talked to me at all." He grinned. "No offense to your alma mater."

"None taken. It was back in the woods, wasn't it? But it had what I needed, a good ROTC program. How those Texas Baptists do love the military. And they thought you were great."

"I found I could get along with them pretty well as long as we avoided sex and religion." Jeremy put the glass down on his desk, too hard, misjudging the distance. A few drops of the wine splashed out on the polished wood.

"Damn. Angelique will kill me," he said ruefully as he reached for a napkin. Angelique, his housekeeper for years, came in five afternoons a week to clean up and make dinner, which Jeremy and Juliette ate late after her evening newscast.

"Is this guy Khan related to the treasure? If he is, don't I recall a promise to Aurélie you wouldn't chase him?"

"I am certain now he was the man behind it all, including Artie's, Lauren's, and Sam's deaths. And, yes, I did promise to let it lie, but since she was kidnapped she's changed her mind, as long as I keep her involved."

"That's between the two of you," Jeremy said, "but I don't want to be involved in a deception."

"You won't, and I wouldn't ask you to be," Eddie said. "Y'know, I've only killed one person in my life, and it was a boy — that fifteen-year-old in Kuwait who shot Paul. I mean, there's no doubt it was him or me, but I still feel bad about it. Maybe that I'm sorry I had to do it is a better way to put it.

"But if Khan is the man and I get the chance, I'll kill him with my own hands, and damn the consequences."

"I sympathize," Jeremy replied, "but I wouldn't repeat that to anyone else. Whatever it was you said — I've forgotten already."

"I won't repeat it, and you're right, of course. Do you think you can help? It's really important, and not just for historical reasons. I just found out the other day that Jen Wetzmuller is involved in this one, just like last time, and she's afraid Khan is planning something really big and violent."

"Jen Wetzmuller! I thought you left her behind in Florida."

"So did I, but Icky asked me to go talk to Ahmed Matossian and she turned out to be working for him. In fact, talking to her was the entire reason for my visit, but nobody told me until it was too late to turn back."

"Ahmed? Jesus, I haven't thought about him for a long time. He was a good student, but he dropped completely out of sight when he graduated. I've heard a few things about him here and there, but..." Jeremy's voice trailed off.

"He still has his import-export business, and Khan is his best customer," Eddie said. "But now he's concerned about Khan, too."

Jeremy replied, "I don't have to tell you to be a little careful of Ahmed, do I?"

"He's in a dicey business, import-export in the old Soviet bloc," Eddie replied. "I'd be surprised if he's turned, but I know Icky keeps tight limits on him. It would just be prudent not to trust him with the crown jewels."

"Smart. Let me make some calls and see if any of my old contacts are still alive. They were a really odd group, not a few of them dedicated Nazis who turned into enthusiastic police-staters for the other side when they had the chance. Give a man the chance to dominate and control other men and he'll do anything you ask of him. They were a nasty, murderous lot. Come back and see me in three days."

∫

Eddie's overnight case bumped behind him up the low steps to the footbridge crossing Canal Saint-Martin. He stopped for a few minutes to watch a canary-yellow cruise boat pass slowly below, returning the wave from a group of German tourists who blearily saluted him with their beer bottles. At the end of the bridge, a drum circle of a half-dozen men in long dreadlocks hammered out a complex rhythm, attracting a small knot of watchers, some of whom dropped coins into the basket a dour confederate passed among them. Two homeless men picked up their knapsacks and moved away.

His phone chirped. Icky was calling to discuss their next step, and he didn't waste words.

"Bad news. I asked my boss to let me give this the full national security treatment because I'm pretty sure your man Alawite, or Khan, or whatever, is the one moving the gold around, and we think he might be involved in even worse stuff. Unfortunately, we're getting a lot of heat from Dick Tennant, who as I told you is a big supporter when appropriations time comes. We can't prove it, but I think he's dragging his feet because he's afraid it will hurt his investment in the hedge fund. He says I'm chasing shadows, that his brother assures him there's nothing there, and that the French have already looked into it and come up empty. Blah, blah."

"So that's it?"

"I didn't get a flat turndown. My boss wouldn't do that, the risk would be too great that he might be wrong and embarrass the Agency, not to mention himself. He's just slow-walking it. Says he needs more info and that the whole case is speculative. I don't know how speculative it could be when we know the entire Russian mafia is involved, but until I can find something definite to go on I can only keep pushing him."

Eddie was silent for a moment. He let his hand fall to his side, then gazed into the green canopy above the languid water of the canal. To his surprise, he felt a sense of relief flooding in. It was now certain that no one else could solve his problem. It was his alone and, dangerous as it might be, that knowledge gave him a profound sense of purpose.

"I've been thinking," he said. "What could I do to find that something definite?"

"I hoped you'd ask that. Could you do a little traveling? We have some leads, but they will need confirmation."

"Sure. Paul and I can go just about any time."

∫

Jeremy called Icky after Eddie left. There were too many holes in what Eddie knew — Jeremy knew Icky would have been following someone like Alawite, or Khan.

"I'm embarrassed, General," Icky said. He always called Jeremy "General," even though he'd been asked not to. "I should have more information about this guy but I just don't. We don't have the budget to pursue dead-end characters and neither do the Germans, although I've leaned on them about all I can get away with."

"So this is some sort of bureaucratic screw-up?" Jeremy asked.

"I wouldn't say that. We know what we need to do, we just don't have the resources. Those are all going to the Arab world now, not the old Stasi types. Our mutual friend the congressman is a perfect illustration - there's no way we can spend too much on drones for the Middle East, but when it comes to investigating anybody even remotely connected to his brother, he makes it clear our budget screws will be shut down tight if we don't back off."

Jeremy paused. "I can believe that. I knew that guy when he was a twenty-five-year-old jerk from West Texas. His father made some money in the oil patch and he managed to get into cell phones early, but he's still a Johnny one-note. It used to be Communists, now it's Arabs and Democrats.

"I believe you, Icky, mainly because I saw him myself. But please don't lie to me. We're both in the business of lying, but when we start doing it to each other we'll get into trouble, and that's what causes friends to turn on each other." He didn't need to remind Icky that he'd been a West Point classmate of the Director, but the unspoken threat hung in the air. As soon as he hung up, he regretted the harshness of his questions.

∫

Jeremy moved from the swivel chair to the cracked leather armchair Eddie had just vacated, then sat quietly for half an hour, trying to calculate the best way to use his old contacts to help trace the elusive goldbug. He poured another glass of wine, then stepped to the fireproof steel file cabinet in the corner of the room. Distracted, he fumbled the combination the first time, but on the second try it opened smoothly.

The third drawer from the top was labeled *2002* — one year after the grim deaths that had started the long process leading to his meeting today. It was also the year he had retired from the Army, convinced he was unlikely to advance further and dismayed at his government's rush toward an invasion of Iraq and, worse, many of his fellow generals' passive acceptance.

He reached to the back of the drawer and pulled out a dog-eared Moleskine notebook, its black cover pitted and gouged from being thrown in countless suitcases, its elastic band long since torn loose at one end. He turned on a reading light and began searching through the notes he'd made during a three-month reporting trip in Germany.

He remembered an interview with an old agent of the East German state security agency — the then-feared and now-reviled Stasi — who had told him a story of espionage in West Germany during the '70s and '80s. He hadn't used the information in his book because he couldn't find enough documentary confirmation before he ran out of time, but it had sounded legitimate. He'd intended to go back to it for a later book, but Pat fell ill and after she died his agent hadn't been able to find a publisher who thought another book about East German spies would sell.

Here it was, on page seventy-seven, the notes of his interview with Luther Waltraud. He'd interviewed Luther for almost six hours in his studio apartment in a dilapidated part of Frankfurt near the southern railroad station. Luther hadn't been an old man at the time, but his health was failing, and Jeremy wondered if he was even still alive.

Most of Luther's memories were just like those of the other forty or so ex-Stasi agents Jeremy had already met, but he was unusual in that he'd spent the last fifteen years before the Berlin Wall fell living in the West as an undercover agent, and had stayed after the reunification. The moving company he'd started with Stasi capital had turned out to be remarkably successful, so the loss of a tiny pension hadn't been important to him.

Jeremy carefully reread the notes and replayed the conversation in his mind. He recalled the way Old Luther had looked and sounded, the musty smell of the small apartment. He thought of him as Old Luther even though they were almost the same age, but Luther'd had the air and smell of decrepitude about him even then.

"I did what I was told," he'd said. "I did my duty. They told me to spy on my neighbor, I did it. They told me to make a renegade policeman disappear, I did it. They told me to come here and I did it, and I did it so well I couldn't afford to go home. Even if there had been a home to go to."

He'd stumbled into a lucrative source of business. He made friends with the publisher of a small magazine aimed at American enlisted soldiers just at the time the Army made it easier for them to bring their wives and families. While most still lived on the military bases, enough wanted to live "on the economy" to make his business successful, and he quickly became their favored mover. The soldiers were a good source of information, especially the officers, but their real value lay in introducing him to American businessmen, who were full of the economic intelligence he needed to please his masters in Berlin.

"Before long, I knew everything. What big shot for what chemical company was sleeping with someone else's wife; who was stiffing the German government on taxes; all sorts of useful stuff. I passed it back to Berlin and they sent someone to make use of it. For me to do it would have tipped off the mark."

One of the hoods Berlin sent was a young man on the make who especially liked it when he was assigned to turn a secret homosexual. "He was AC-DC himself, in the closet of course, but the job gave him the opportunity to make a lot of contacts, if you know what I mean. He was young and good looking, and he got laid more than anybody else I ever met. He called himself Khan."

Jeremy had asked gently, "What did your masters do with the information he pried out of these businessmen?"

"Not much. You couldn't do anything too overt, but we kept our marks warm by pushing them for small stuff from time to time. Remember, East German intelligence was expecting the Americans to invade any day, and they wanted to have the makings of a fifth column ready to go. At that time, an assignment in Germany was a big deal for a rising American businessman, so if somebody didn't go along he might find himself the subject of all sorts of gossip and be demoted back to the States. That could be a big career setback.

"I think Khan was part Arab or something, and he spoke good German, although he obviously wasn't a native. He also spoke good English, but French was his strong language. Along with Arabic, although there weren't many Arabs here then. Lots of Turks, though, and he could talk to most of them.

"He did the heavy lifting, the really hard cases. The day-to-day stuff was done by a man who worked as a driver for me, a tough guy named Eric Kraft. He'd been a Nazi policeman during the war, so he took to Stasi like a duck takes to water. He got assigned here after I'd turned a few people and Khan had milked them. It was funny — he was married to a German woman for a few years. And at the same time he was having it off with his wife's sister, who still lives way out in the suburbs. Khan was there, too."

Jeremy asked, "Do you have any idea what happened to Khan or the others?"

"Not Khan. He disappeared shortly before the Wall fell. I suspect he's got another identity now, or two or three of them. He was a natural con man, and he was really tight with the Russians, so he might be working for them somewhere, for all I know. Kraft died of cancer not too many years later. His son, who was just like him, disappeared. The wife's sister is still around, last I heard. An old woman puttering around in her garden."

Jeremy sat back. That was Khan, and he was inextricably linked with the Krafts, father and son.

He remembered being convinced that Luther didn't have contact with Khan at the time, but that he might have a friend who would talk, given the right incentive. He was now sure this was the beginning of the conspiracy that led to the murder of Eddie's father, wife, and son in 2001. He sat back, satisfied he understood the history and amazed once again by the long tail evil drags behind it.

∫

Jeremy reached across the big desk for his new HP laptop and searched for Luther's name. Still there, still in the same old building, although he imagined the neighborhood was either much worse or much better than it had been eight years before. An Air France flight would leave for Frankfurt just after 8 p.m., but a train left at seven. The trip would take two hours longer, but skipping the airport chaos at both ends would mean he'd arrive in downtown Frankfurt at about the same time. And he wouldn't have to worry about security.

He picked up the phone to tell Juliette she'd be dining alone, then packed a bag. Almost as an afterthought, he turned back to the study and opened a safe bolted to the floor of a closet. There, wrapped in flannel and carefully tied with twine, lay the Glock 9mm pistol Icky had once sent him via diplomatic pouch. He tucked it into his suitcase with two extra magazines and, an hour and a half after Eddie had left, locked the door behind him and started the short walk to the Gare de l'Est and the Inter-City Express for Frankfurt.

CHAPTER FOURTEEN

Frankfurt

At eight o'clock the next morning, Jeremy found a cab several blocks from Hotel Wilhelm, a renovated hulk used mainly by German businessmen and Eastern European tour groups.

"Frankensteiner Platz, bitte," he told the driver. He got out on the square just across the River Main in Sachsenhausen, where he and Pat had lived happily for a year when he was a young officer a few years out of West Point. The Army's postwar presence was already dwindling and they lived among the Germans, seeing other Americans only when Jeremy worked or they had to appear at Army social events. The experience had solidified his grasp of the German language, which would make it possible for him to do the research he needed to write his books twenty years later.

There was almost no chance he would be followed — who even knew he was in Frankfurt? — but when he left the taxi he started to meander through the neighborhood, headed ultimately toward the railroad station to the south but walking jauntily down one side street and then another, occasionally doubling back to force any tail into view. It was a pleasant walk. Few people were on the streets and the air had the crisp bite that predicted an early winter. He knew that Frankfurt, less than a hundred miles north of Paris but further inland, would soon be overcast and gray while Paris would still have many sunny days ahead before winter set in. It made him anxious to return home.

The drab gray concrete building where Luther lived was part of an identical row built after the war, and reminded Jeremy of a line of sullen gray sentries with their toes lined up along the dirty sidewalk. He walked past it, pausing after twenty yards to survey the street around him in the plate-glass window of a grocery store, then continued to the end of the block and turned the corner. There, he stepped into a doorway to study the list of tenants while watching to see if anyone turned behind him. Clear.

He walked briskly back to Luther's building and ran his finger down six of the doorbell buttons. Someone would always answer a blind buzz with an equally blind push on the door button, as every deliveryman knew.

Luther's studio had once been an attic. Jeremy took the elevator to the fifth floor, the last stop, then walked up one floor and stood listening at the beige steel door. He saw that the lock had been forced since his visit, the damage poorly repaired. When he heard a TV set turned up high he was certain he had found his man, for Luther had complained that he was going deaf.

He rapped sharply, waited a minute, and knocked again. After the second effort he heard a chair scrape on the floor, then the sound of a hacking cough. The door opened slowly.

"Luther! It's nice to see you again," Jeremy pushed the door briskly and stepped inside, closing it quickly behind him. "I want to continue our conversation. Is now a good time?"

He was clearly Old Luther. What hair he had left was now mousy gray, and he was more stooped. He wore an old sweater frayed at the elbows over a dirty blue shirt and dingy brown work pants held up by a worn leather belt now much too long for his shrunken waist.

"I know you," Luther responded, not quickly. "You're that American professor who asked me a lot of questions about my moving business."

Jeremy had not spoken conversational German for more than a year, so he had to think fast.

"That's me. Professor Bentham. Jeremy Bentham. I'm working on another book and found my notes of our conversation. They were interesting, and I thought your story deserved more attention than I was able to give it last time. Can you help me again?"

The old man brightened visibly at the compliment. "Well, come in. Sit down over there." He pointed to a small wooden table. Jeremy pulled out one of the straight chairs and sat down, shifting around until the Glock no longer pressed uncomfortably on the small of his back. Luther sat down opposite him, obviously in pain.

"It's a good thing you came now, Herr Professor. I'm sick, cancer, and the doctors aren't sure I'll make it through the winter. As it is, I can hardly get up and down the stairs. If the health service didn't send someone with food I'd probably starve. I haven't had a visitor in weeks, so you're welcome."

"I'll try not to tire you out. My wife went through the same thing and I remember how hard every day became."

Jeremy went straight to the subject. "I just wanted to talk to you some more about the people you identified as potential Stasi informers and the men Berlin sent to follow up with them. One of them was your driver, Kraft, and the other was the young man you called Khan."

"Kraft was OK. He was one of the true believers, like a lot of the ex-Nazis. He'd been part of the Milice in Vichy France so he knew something about police work, and he was hard and mean. It was dangerous to cross that one. God knows why that woman married him, but she only stayed with him a few years, then chucked him out."

Jeremy asked, "So he handled some of the work and this man Khan from Berlin did the rest?"

"It worked both ways. Khan didn't like to get his hands dirty, so if something rough had to be done he'd bring in Kraft. That only happened once that I can recall, because when he was working he made himself look really evil and got most of what he wanted with pure intimidation. He came across really threatening. It wasn't an act — he made a snake look like a harmless teddy bear.

"He was pretty sure of himself, too. He liked to refer to himself as 'Count Khan,' because his mother was the daughter of a French count. He didn't push that too hard, though. "

Jeremy said, "You gave me a lot of information last time about his time in Stasi. Now I'm trying to find out more about where he came from, and if possible where he went when the Wall came down."

"Three of us got drunk a couple of times and he talked about his childhood in Paris, and said he'd lived in Saudi Arabia a few years after that. He never told us any more about that time. I figured he left under unpleasant circumstances.

"There was a rumor that he still had family somewhere over there. Once or twice I heard him mention a son. I think he lived somewhere in Iraq. That was the only non-communist country to have full relations with the GDR, so it would make sense for his family to be there, especially if he wasn't welcome in Saudi Arabia anymore."

"What kind of work did he do for Stasi when he wasn't helping you?"

"Much the same thing elsewhere. Sometimes I'd need him and find out he was in Vienna or somewhere like that. He went to Hamburg a lot, and I seem to recall that he had business in Munich, as well. Quite a bit of it, in fact. Then he had the same duties we all did in Berlin, like keeping track of deviant citizens."

Jeremy thought a minute, then asked, "Is there anyone still around who might have any idea what happened to Khan after the Wall?"

"A few of us — mainly the ones who got sent out of the GDR to work — used to get together every few years. There hasn't been a reunion for at least five years, and there probably won't be any more. We're all getting too old."

Jeremy pulled the dog-eared Moleskine notebook from his pocket and opened it to the 2002 interview notes.

"You told me that Khan was really tight with the Russians..."

"Sure. Of course, you had to figure that anything Stasi learned would or could go back to the KGB anyway, but the Russians really liked Khan. He was smart and could be charming, and they used him in the same way Stasi did. For them, I think he might have got his hands dirty once or twice. But I didn't get involved with that very much. And I never liked the Russians. Still don't. They all smell of cheap cigarettes."

"Do you think anybody from that time would know more about his work with the Russians? That would add a really interesting chapter to my book."

Luther rose slowly and walked to a chest of drawers standing next to his narrow bed. From the top drawer he took an address book and returned to sit opposite Jeremy.

"Here's one who might still be around. His name was Cate, Albert Cate. When I knew him he was Albrecht, but everything's turned to English these days. He was from Leipzig, and last I heard he was still there." He turned the address book to Jeremy and pointed. Jeremy wrote Cate's address and telephone number in his notebook.

"I'll take the train to Leipzig later today and look for him in the morning. Should I just drop in on him or call ahead?"

"Just drop in, if he's still there. He wasn't very friendly when he was younger, and most of us don't mellow with age. If Khan still has Russian connections, he may know."

Jeremy questioned Luther for another hour, then tore a page from the back of the notebook and wrote his name and cell number on it. He folded the sheet around two 50-euro notes and left it on the table. "A little something from my publisher. Thanks for Cate's information and sharing your memories with me."

At the Sudbahnhof, Jeremy found a taxi and went straight to the Wilhelm. He picked up his overnight bag and crossed the street to the Hertz office in the Hauptbahnhof, where he rented a black Mercedes, the heaviest and fastest car available.

He followed the river for two miles, then merged smoothly into the fast traffic of the A5 autobahn and called Juliette to tell her he would be away another day, but offered only a bare-bones summary of what he was doing. She knew of his informal connection with American intelligence and would have been surprised if a retired general was not still active in his government. But he had assured her early in their relationship that he did very little government work, usually only one assignment every year or so, and they had agreed she would not ask.

The relationship with Icky posed more of a problem. Jeremy had advanced in the military on the basis of skill and resourcefulness, and had retired because he saw other generals passively accept the orders of Defense Department decision makers with little or no military experience but strong political connections to the president. He was glad he'd left before the long disaster of the Iraq War had a chance to unfold just the way he'd warned it might. And he was dismayed to hear that a congressman was preventing Icky from putting enough people on this case, possibly to protect his own financial position. That aspect would have to be dealt with.

Personally, he would be glad to work it as a team with Eddie, but he was becoming more and more concerned that Khan was a serious risk who would need more resources than two unofficial volunteers could bring to bear. Perhaps Luther Waltraud and Albert Cate could provide the ammunition Icky needed to get the Khan problem taken seriously.

He left a message on Icky's voicemail, telling him he would try to see Cate in less than four hours and needed as much information about him as possible.

∫

Jeremy was a half hour away from Cate's address in north Leipzig when his cell phone buzzed. It was Carole Westin, Icky's deputy charged with finding lost money and treasure — and in chasing terrorist financing, which had become her main job.

"Jeremy, would you mind telling me how you got to these two men?" she asked politely. Excessively so, he thought.

"I probably shouldn't, and let you think I'm a genius detective. The truth of it is that I interviewed Old Luther for one of my books but didn't use much of his material. I found the notes recently and went looking for him, and he sent me to Albert Cate. Are they important?"

"They were once. Luther was a double agent in the '80s, or thought he was. He sent back chickenfeed from American businessmen who were working with us, but he brought us some pretty valuable information about Stasi plans to undermine the West German economy. Cate was his control. A thoroughly nasty type, very tight with Russian intelligence."

"That's what Luther told me," Jeremy responded.

"He should know. Both of them were external agents, allowed outside East Germany at a time when that was very rare, and they both reported back to the KGB through a man named Claude Khan. We hadn't looked at Khan until recently, but now we think he's involved in moving bullion from some of the old Soviet republics back into Germany, then on somewhere else."

"Khan. He's the man Eddie Grant is after. I wouldn't be surprised about the gold. He's out pitching for investors in a hedge fund that invests entirely in bullion. He thinks the price is going to rise rapidly sometime soon."

Carole said, "As I think you know, Icky put a man in Khan's group but he died in a fall from a balcony in Paris."

"Lee Filer. I used to watch his TV show from time to time."

"You have odd tastes. Icky thought he would have enough credibility to penetrate the Khan group because of his background as a TV goldbug. Instead, he went silent soon after he arrived in Paris, and the next thing we heard was his obituary.

"Anyway, Cate was basically a Russian hood. Since the Wall fell he's been working for an artists' booking agent, setting up concerts around the old Eastern bloc. He does seem to be pretty good at that job, but we suspect he's taking advantage of the travel to do other things as well. We haven't seen him and Khan in the same place, but then we haven't been looking. Until this hedge fund and the bullion traffic came onto our radar he was a has-been spy, and we didn't have the resources to watch him. I don't think the Germans were watching him, either."

"Is he still involved in anything that would give me leverage?"

"You could act like you know he's still working for the Russians. The Germans wouldn't like that. I think it's true."

∫

Cate's address was a four-story red brick apartment building separated from the street by a narrow front garden. Jeremy checked the occupant directory and found Cate on the third floor, then went to his car. In a few minutes a stocky woman, her gray hair half-covered with a red nylon scarf that was the only flash of color in a drab outfit, walked up to the door and fumbled for the key. As she turned it, Jeremy stepped up to open the door for her, then followed her into a small lobby.

She went into a ground floor apartment while Jeremy walked purposefully up the stairs to the third floor, then to Cate's front door, where he knocked in what he hoped sounded like a neighborly way.

The peephole turned dark, then he heard the sound of locks turning and a chain being removed. The knob turned slowly to reveal a short man, his red hair graying at the temples. His black eyes were fierce and penetrating, a dangerous look the slight smile did nothing to soften.

∫

"Come in, General. I thought you might arrive today," Albert Cate said in perfect English.

He pointed to a tattered brown armchair under a single window facing the street, and took its twin at the other end of a blue velour sofa that had seen its best days before the Berlin Wall fell. A window at the end of the room looked out over an ill-maintained park. Jeremy noticed that Cate had placed him in the full glare of the setting sun. Not bad, he told himself. He's trying for every little advantage he can find.

For the first half hour they danced around each other, each trying to figure out the other's motives.

"I don't believe you're here about another book, Herr Professor," Cate said finally. "I have read all three of your books, and I frankly doubt there would be much interest among American publishers in another one about the old, broken-down Stasi. In fact, I know you started one but couldn't find a publisher. By the way, my favorite was *Berlin Dawn*, but I wish you'd talked to me. I could have helped you."

"I wish I'd met you earlier," Jeremy responded. "You were too good at your job. I didn't even know your name until today. You see, I'm not a spy. I'm a writer, and once I was an Army officer."

"Of some distinction, I hear. When you were stationed in Frankfurt we checked you out carefully and you were obviously marked for greater things. I believe you retired as a major general, and pretty young? Were you pushed out?"

"No, but I would have been eventually. I couldn't see anything good coming from a war of choice in Iraq and sure enough nothing did."

Cate reached to the book-laden table at his left and took a cigar from a humidor. "Do you mind?" he asked Jeremy. "Havana. Hard to get in the States, I hear."

"I hear that too. Please go ahead."

"So you're looking for information about Claude Khan. Luther tells me your questions are more about what he's doing these days than about his past."

"That's true, but I'm interested in his past as well. I am planning another book, but as you've certainly figured out this visit is also an effort to help a friend."

"As it turns out, I know quite a bit about Khan. As Luther no doubt told you, we worked together in Berlin. We were Stasi, but we also worked for the KGB. I almost said 'with,' but we were colonials and they didn't think of us as equals in any way. I was senior by just a little bit, but Claude was very talented and the KGB types liked him. We got along well, so much so that we stayed in touch after reunification."

"I was told Khan left Germany."

"You have to remember he'd left France when he turned eighteen, then Saudi Arabia a few years later. He had no national loyalties. But he had to leave Germany. He'd been involved in some very wet stuff for the KGB, and the CIA was on his trail. He got out just a few days before he'd have been snatched."

"Someone turned on him?"

"Oh, yes. Not everybody liked Claude. I always suspected it was Luther but he denied it. It could have been any of a dozen people. It might even have been me. Our Claude can be charming but that's not his natural personality. He's really a dangerous and untrustworthy man, as I have learned."

"Would you tell me more about that?"

"Of course. When Luther said you were coming to talk about Khan, I cancelled a dinner date. I know some things you need to know, and I know your reputation and that you'll whisper the information in the correct ear.

"But first I have a question for you. I've been reading European and American history quite a lot lately, and I remembered your name as I was going through a book on the American Revolution. There was an English philosopher, a very prominent one whose thoughts influence American society even today. His name was also Jeremy Bentham. Was he an ancestor?"

Jeremy laughed, short and humorless, eager to get Cate back on track.

"That Jeremy Bentham, the original, was my great-something. At a distance of fifteen generations it's hard to be sure but yes, he was my ancestor."

"A very unusual man."

"He was like a lot of wealthy and educated eighteenth-century men. His interests were boundless. He was very interested in happiness, which we seem to have learned far beyond reason. But he's best remembered now for his will."

"Remind me, please, Herr Professor."

"He directed that his body be dissected publicly, before an invited audience, and that afterward his skeleton be stuffed with straw, dressed in his clothes, and displayed with his mummified head on top.

"The head didn't work out and was replaced with a wax copy, but the entire assembly is still on display at a university in London. He called it his auto-icon."

Cate leaned back and dragged on the Havana. "Fascinating. Are there others like you?"

"You mean with the same name? There must be, but I haven't met them."

It was then that Jeremy noticed the bulge under Cate's sweater — he too had armed himself, not knowing whether to expect friend or foe.

"Claude left Germany early in 1989," Cate began, apparently satisfied with Jeremy's answers. "The Wall hadn't fallen yet but from the inside, and looking at what was happening in Russia, it was obvious the DDR was going to be history. You wrote well about that period, so there's nothing I can tell you.

"He'd had a good career in Stasi since he joined us around 1970, but as I said he'd made a lot of enemies, some of them powerful. He couldn't go back to Saudi Arabia so he moved to Kuwait. He'd made some money and kept it in Switzerland — hell, so did I. How do you think I can live here? He used it to buy an oil brokerage company and started making even more money. He'd always been fond of Saddam Hussein, so he got a reputation as a collaborator. You know the story of Operation Desert Storm..."

"I was there," Jeremy interjected.

"Claude was part of the collateral damage. When the American soldiers came to arrest him they killed his only child, a boy of about fifteen who'd lived in Kuwait and Iraq all his life. It infuriated him."

The last tumbler clicked into place. Jeremy recalled the time a small group of Special Forces soldiers had been sent to arrest an Iraqi spy at his palatial home at the edge of Kuwait City.

The man had just opened the door when his teenage son dashed down the stairs firing wildly with a Kalashnikov. It was bad luck that one bullet struck Paul Fitzhugh a glancing blow on the top of his head, a wound that was nearly fatal. Paul's commander stepped in front of him and killed the boy with one blast from a twelve-gauge combat shotgun.

That commander was Eddie Grant.

"That explains a lot," Jeremy said. "He didn't go by Khan then?"

"No, he used another name. I knew it once. Anyway, the Kuwaitis kept him in prison for a year, then kicked him out of the country. Even though he'd managed to get a great deal of money out to Switzerland, he still wanted more. So he came back to Germany and went into business. By then, everything was peace and sweetness between East and West and no one had much interest in an old Stasi agent."

"What did he do?"

"Little of everything. Real estate, a chain of restaurants, some stuff that wasn't entirely legal. In fact, he pretty much decided to live on the edge, to make as much as he could as fast as he could. He told me one time he'd found a new opportunity in Eastern Europe and was exporting washing machines there — he'd bought into a business in Munich. If I know Claude, washing machines weren't all he was exporting."

"Drugs?"

"Almost certainly. And cigarettes coming back the other way. But I wouldn't be talking to you about either of those. No, he was looking for weapons, and he found them. He wanted to be the biggest weapons dealer in Europe. I don't know if he's accomplished that, but I do know he furnished a lot of the small arms the Chechens used in their failed efforts to get free of the Russians. He still sells them some things, even though their best source is now in the Middle East.

"Do you have time to hear the whole story, or at least as much of it as I know? It will help get you inside Khan's head and, unless I miss my guess, that's where you need to be."

"I have the time," Jeremy said quietly. "Please tell me."

∫

Cate paused long enough to take two puffs on the cigar while he gazed out the window, then began to tell his story.

"When we worked together at Stasi, I learned I couldn't trust him. No one with any sense would trust him, but I recently let my own greed get in the way of good sense.

"I hadn't heard from Claude for several years. Then, a few months ago, he turned up at my front door just the way you did — he followed someone into the building, then came up the stairs and knocked. I was expecting a delivery and didn't look through the Judas hole, so you can imagine my surprise when it wasn't the FedEx man but Claude, as well turned out as ever in a brown suit, complete with silk tie and shined shoes. He never wears anything but brown.

"He told me how he and his hedge fund investors are going to make millions in the gold market. Its price now is almost as high as it's ever been, but he believes it will go much higher because it responds to fear, like a herd of sheep threatened by the distant howl of a wolf, and he was sure something was about to happen that would cause a great deal of fear. In fact, he's going to make it happen."

"Did he say what?" Jeremy asked.

Cate ignored the question. "He knew I'd maintained sources in the Russian security services. He and I shared the duties of telling our Russian masters what we were up to, or of following their orders when they wanted something specific done. And he was right, I did and do still have several contacts among the old KGB staff. Not the current president, unfortunately." He looked directly at Jeremy.

"Claude wanted something very special, something that's been hard to get because it is so dangerous. He said he had an order for 500 units of a very specific type of weapon. He did not tell me who his customer was, but I surmised it was the Chechens."

"And what was that weapon?"

"Anti-aircraft missiles. Manpads, or Man Portable Air Defense Systems. They are potentially the most destructive weapons short of nuclear weapons because they can shoot down airliners. They've already been used, if not terribly successfully — the poor desert Arabs have turned out to be bad shots, but with training the door will open wide and we'll see the monster.

"Imagine the reaction if someone shot down two or three large airliners just as they were landing or taking off at JFK or Charles de Gaulle? It would be chaos, 9/11 all over again.

"Manpads haven't been much in the news lately because they're so tightly controlled. The first exception was Afghanistan, where both the Russians and Americans left them behind. But now there's a huge new source just coming available, and that's where Khan wanted to go fishing for them."

"And that is...?"

"Libya," Cate replied. "Khadafy had tens of thousands of manpads. Most of them were Russian, some were Chinese, and a few were American. All were stored in his weapons bunkers, most of which have now been overrun by the rebels. It still isn't all that easy to get working models, but it can be done. I learned how to do it."

"Was this what you told Khan?"

"Yes. I got in contact with an old source who is now a senior agent in the FSB. Other than the name change, everything is still pretty much the same as it was in the KGB. He didn't want to tell me but he owed me a favor, so when I pressed he gave me the name of a renegade Saudi who is advising the rebels in Benghazi. He said Khan should take a suitcase full of dollars and go see this Saudi."

"Did Khan do that?"

"I don't know. The son of a bitch promised me five percent of his hedge fund if I made the introduction, but he reneged and left me only a thousand euros. I think he probably went around me to make the deal. It wouldn't have been hard, since I stupidly gave him the name of my source."

"Five percent could be a big kiss. Did he go to Benghazi?"

"Not necessary. The Saudi had already smuggled hundreds of missiles out of Benghazi through the Egyptian desert. They were in a warehouse in Cyprus and could be picked up by a smuggler's boat. Those are all over that end of the Med."

Jeremy crossed his fingers and asked boldly, "Who is your source?"

"I don't really want to get him in trouble, but you may need to talk to him. He's in Munich now, on vacation visiting his wife's sister…"

"Gregor Ashkenazi," Jeremy interjected.

"You know him?"

"Never met him, but I know he's dead. Someone put a bomb in his car and set it off while he and his wife were on the way to the airport."

"Then I think you may have a bigger problem than even I thought."

"Do you know where Khan is right now? He didn't show up for a sales party in Paris a few days ago."

"A week ago he told me he was going to Cyprus. That was when he told me I'd only get the miserable thousand euros."

"That must have pissed you off. Tell me, do you know where he can be found in Paris? We know about the house near Munich, but he must have some kind of base of operations there."

"I don't know where it is, but I know who might know. He has an old friend who operates a sort of Asian general store for the tourists. It's more of a hobby, really, but she keeps just enough stuff on the shelves to attract a few visitors. I used to call and leave messages with her if I wanted to reach Claude, but that's been a while.

"She won't talk to you if you just barge in, so I'll give you an introduction." He took a business card from his wallet and tore it in half. "She knows this card. It's her own. You take the half with the address and I'll mail her the other half. She likes to be called Madame Nguyen."

CHAPTER FIFTEEN

Paris, Rue Saint-Roch

The next day started with an early-morning phone call from Icky — very early. Even for morning runners like Eddie and Aurélie, 4 a.m. was early.

"Sorry, old boy. I hope I didn't catch you two at an awkward moment." Icky chuckled. "I heard from Jeremy. He managed to pin down a couple of our man Khan's old acquaintances from the Stasi. It seems Khan stiffed one of them out of a lot of money, or the possibility of a lot of money, and hell hath no wrath, et cetera, et cetera.

"Anyway, Khan went to Cyprus a week ago. Fortunately, we have a couple of reliable people there who work in shipping, and they picked up on Sonny Perry three days ago. Khan's tough to find because he blends into the background almost anywhere, especially in the Med, but Sonny might as well have been wearing cowboy boots with blue stars on them."

Eddie, annoyed, interrupted him. "So you want me to go to Cyprus?"

"Nothing that easy, old sport. Sonny and a couple of local nasties pulled a bunch of wooden boxes out of a remote warehouse one day, and six hours ago they put twenty-five German refrigerators on a tramp steamer heading up the Aegean. It stops at two or three places, but the odds are Sonny and his refrigerators will go all the way to the end of the line, in Alexandropoulos. That's the closest port to the Black Sea."

"And I should go to Alexandropoulos?"

"Didn't I just say that? Can you take Paul? Call me when you have your flight planned and I'll try to find a contact there for you. It shouldn't be too hard. With the recession, Greece is in a terrible mess and I suspect policemen are cheaper than they've been in a long time."

Icky turned very serious.

"Eddie, Jeremy talked to a man he thinks is pretty close to Khan, even though they're on the outs right now. What he learned makes him think we're dealing with a problem much more serious than a freelancer who wants to trade Kalashnikovs for gold bullion, although we know Khan has done that. You remember the term 'manpads,' don't you?"

"Hell, yes. You and I saw portable anti-aircraft missiles all over the place during Desert Storm. I think you even went out to rescue the pilot of an F-16 who got hit by a Strela and the infantry company that was attached to us for a week shot down a bunch of Iraqi helicopters."

"Well, Jeremy's source says he's looking for manpads, a lot of them. Khadafy had thousands of them when his revolution started, and we've started to pick up their trail outside of Libya. If our man in Cyprus is right, and the wooden crates Sonny picked up are anti-aircraft missiles, then he's dealing in them by the hundreds. It would be bad enough if he were to sell them to the Chechens, but think what the consequences would be if he sold them to Al Qaeda or decided to use a few himself."

Eddie paused for an instant. "That would sure bump the price of gold."

∫

"What now?" Aurélie asked sleepily from the other side of the bed after Eddie hung up.

"Greece. They found Sonny on a boat from Cyprus. Most likely it's smuggling weapons of some sort from Libya. Icky's afraid it might be anti-aircraft missiles."

"When do you have to leave?"

"Soon."

"Define soon."

"I don't think a half hour will make much difference," he said, throwing back the covers and sliding close to her.

"I hoped you'd say that," she said as she sat up and began to pull her nightgown over her head. "Now kiss me. Then give me something to remember you by while you're running around Greece."

CHAPTER SIXTEEN

Alexandropolis, Greece

Fourteen hours later, Eddie and Paul checked into Hotel Topkapi, a block from the broad but eerily deserted port of Alexandropoulos. Their room on the top floor had a sunny balcony with a view of the port and the sea to the south.

"Icky told me Sonny's on a little freighter called the *Agios Daphne*, or *Saint Daphne*. It's riding high in the water, not carrying much cargo, so they may have chartered it. His source didn't know what it's carrying other than Sonny and his refrigerators," Eddie said.

Paul plugged his laptop into the hotel's Ethernet port. "The wiring here looks pre-war, although I'm not sure which war. I sure as hell hope this works."

In a minute he had found one of the marine traffic sites that follow ships using the Automated Identification System. "Here it is," he shouted to Eddie, who was on the balcony scanning the southern horizon with binoculars. "They're too far away to see now, but they're about to pass a whole fleet of ships waiting to enter the Dardanelles."

Eddie came into the room and studied the screen closely. It showed a chart of the coastline and islands to the south of their hotel, with a dense cluster of red and green icons spread across the center of the screen. Paul pointed to one of the small green shapes, the only one that did not seem to be lined up to enter the Dardanelles.

"She's green, which indicates a cargo ship. Tankers are red, and the blue ones are high-speed ships, usually ferries. Sonny and his pals are just picking their way through the traffic jam, and when that's done they should have clear sailing all the way to our port."

Eddie said, "He could turn toward Istanbul, but Icky thinks he'll land here and take the cargo overland to the Port of Burgas, in Bulgaria. To get past Istanbul he might have to deal with the Turkish Navy, and I doubt he wants to take that chance. And we know Khan has used Burgas before, so he probably has the port guards in his pocket. If the ship stays on that course, when will it arrive?"

"They're only sixty or seventy miles away, so if they're making six knots — call it nine or ten hours. We'll need to check during the night to make sure we don't miss them when they arrive. If they turn off the AIS transponder, we'll have to watch for them the old-fashioned way."

"How does that thing work?" Eddie asked.

"Sort of like the way airliners report their location, except it mainly uses ground stations along the coastlines. Each ship transmits a position and the AIS system retransmits it to other ships, and of course to the web. It's reduced collisions a lot, especially in crowded areas like the mouth of the Dardanelles. If we could see it, it would look like a ship parking lot. A lot of the goods shipped to Russia and Eastern Europe go through there."

Eddie picked up his phone. "Time to call Icky's contact here. He'll have a package for us." The man on the other end answered quickly. Eddie gave only his name, then a password. Then, "Hotel Topkapi."

He listened for a minute, then put the phone back in his pocket and said, "Icky's friend is Mr. Smith. No kidding, he said Smith."

"Sure," Paul responded with a grin.

"We're to meet him in an hour at the open-air vegetable market near the lighthouse. He'll be wearing blue slacks and a green shirt and carrying a French bag filled with vegetables. We're supposed to pick up a local newspaper and fold it to show the picture of the soccer team. And put a thousand euros inside it."

"Jesus! What did Icky buy from the guy?"

"Two 9mm Glocks."

∫

They changed quickly into dark trousers and knit shirts — what Paul called their "cat-burglar outfits" — and set out to survey the downtown area. They ambled along the waterfront for a half mile, then settled into a sidewalk cafe in the shadow of the lighthouse guarding the port.

The kiosk in front of the hotel had only one copy of the newspaper showing the soccer team, and Eddie snatched it as a short, mustachioed man dressed like a working fisherman looked at him balefully from a few yards away, then turned to find a copy at another kiosk. As they walked back down the waterfront, Eddie carefully removed from his pocket a package of ten 100-euro notes folded inside a single sheet of paper and slipped it inside the newspaper, which he folded in quarters and held with the picture visible.

Their contact was late. They walked down both rows of stalls and found no one who vaguely fit the description until he came puffing up behind them, pushing his way through the thin crowd. His left hand held a heavy bag of vegetables, which he quickly offered to Eddie, who gave him the newspaper. The handover took no more than three or four seconds.

After wandering through the market for another few minutes, they turned away and found a sidewalk café near their hotel. Eddie carefully put the bag of vegetables between them and ordered a retsina. Paul ordered coffee.

∫

Paul recognized Eddie's mood from their days together in Desert Storm. He was always calm, but in the hours before action he became Buddha-like, tranquil and unruffled.

Eddie called up a guidebook on his iPhone. "Y'know, this place is a lot closer to Istanbul than it is to Athens — you can see it in the name of our hotel. The Greeks have fought with their neighbors over it for a long time. Its last occupier was Bulgaria.

"The Orient Express used to stop here, but now it's mainly European groups and people traveling on the cheap."

They had taken a table as far from the other tourists as they could, but Eddie still looked around carefully. He started to pull his chair closer to Paul, but thought better of it when the steel leg scraped harshly on the red tile floor, so he leaned across the table.

"Even though Icky is pretty sure where they're going to go, we'll still have to follow them. We don't know if they'll go directly to Burgas or stop somewhere on the way, or they could go somewhere else entirely," he said.

He opened the map on his iPhone. "They'll probably want to get out of Greece as soon as they can, so my guess is they'll follow the mountain highway due north. The Bulgarian border is closer that way. The risk of the bigger highway is that it runs very close to the Turkish border for almost the whole way. I could be wrong, but I think they'll avoid that in favor of the less-busy route."

"Makes sense to me," Paul responded. "We should go now and rent two cars, so we can switch off following them. Just in case. The Avis office is just the other side of the lighthouse. Then let's come back here for dinner — I just saw a grilled red mullet go by and it looked delicious."

∫

The green icon inched its way up the screen. Paul looked out the sliding door and said to Eddie, "There's no need to watch yet. They're still a long way out. Why don't we set two-hour watches? I'll take the first one."

Grumbling, Eddie went to bed fully dressed. Paul pulled his laptop as close to the door as its cable would allow. He wrote down the latitude and longitude of the *Agios Daphne*, then clicked to see its statistics and picture.

He saw a creaky old freighter that had been active in the Aegean at least since World War II. At one hundred feet long, it was large enough to carry cargo among the islands, and with its shallow draft it could go into small ports where larger freighters would risk running aground. Icky had told them its crew consisted of the owner and his son, aided by an engine-room mechanic who had been on the ship for five years. The owner knew he should retire and turn it over to his son, but would not give it up and insisted on taking only those trips his declining strength would allow. This included a once-a-week circuit among a half-dozen islands, but did not usually include Alexandropoulos.

When it was his turn to stand watch again, the ship was noticeably closer to the port.

"I bet Sonny is on the bridge goading him to speed it up. Maybe they have an appointment?"

"I'd be surprised if customs was open at 4 a.m. here, but maybe they set something up in advance. When it's an hour out, let's go down and watch from the street," Eddie said.

"I checked the weather, and sunrise won't be until almost seven. Sonny probably wants to get the boxes unloaded and on a truck while it's still dark."

∫

At five-thirty Paul announced, "They're about an hour out." Eddie jumped up and turned his binoculars toward the sea.

"There she is, just on the horizon. And she has deck lights on, too. Of course, the whole ruse depends on making everyone think it's just an average day's charter trip. Let's go. I paid the hotel bill when we checked in."

During their walk down the waterfront, they had decided the best place to watch the *Agios Daphne* arrive would be from the littered but deserted parking lot that adjoined the main wharf. They left their cars parked on the street and walked across the lot to a sandy berm and settled in behind it, out of sight from the wharf and separated from it by a rusty fence. Streetlights a hundred feet away cast a dim glow.

They waited as the old steel freighter, once painted a bright blue and white but now faded and rusting, picked its way between the arms of the seawall and turned toward the wharf nearest them. At the same time, a box truck painted with the name of a shipping firm drove on to the wharf and stopped.

∫

Two bulky stevedores stepped out of the cab and walked to the back of the truck. The taller one pushed roughly on the overhead door. It opened with a clatter.

The main wharf lights had been turned off, but by the early glow of sunrise Eddie could see the two men reach into the truck, pull out beach chairs, and sit facing the sea. A lighter flared as the taller one lit both their cigarettes, then pointed toward the south, the lighter still burning in his hand. The sound of their conversation carried on the still night air, unintelligible.

As the ship inched toward the wharf, the two men moved to its bow and stern to wait for the crew to throw out the monkey's fist at the end of the thin rope tied to the heavy mooring lines.

"No Sonny," Paul whispered.

"The two guys with the mooring lines must be the owner's son and the engine-room man," Eddie said. "I suspect Sonny wants to stay out of sight as much as he can."

∫

As soon as the ship was tied fast to the dock, the two seamen walked quickly to a midships crane. A motor hummed, and a large pallet carrying four boxes rose over the side, then swung out and dropped gently to the dock. The stevedores unhooked the cables quickly and the crane returned to the ship, only to appear a few minutes later with another pallet of the refrigerators.

"Just like Icky said," Eddie murmured. "Refrigerator boxes. There should be twenty-five of them."

The truck crew rolled the boxes quickly one by one to the hydraulic lift on the back of the truck and up into its dark body. Within thirty minutes, all twenty-five boxes had disappeared and the stevedores moved again to the bow and stern and prepared to release the lines. It was only then that the ship's gangway came out and Sonny Perry walked quickly down it. He moved directly to the truck's cab and sat inside.

"He doesn't think there's anybody watching, but he's taking no chances," Paul said. "He'd shit himself if he knew we were this close."

The burbling sound of the freighter's revving engine carried across the wharf as it backed slowly away from the dock, then turned to head out to sea again. Eddie stayed to make certain it left, while Paul followed the truck out onto the beach road, headlights dark until he was out of sight of the ship. As they expected, it turned left — toward the shorter route to Bulgaria.

Eddie followed ten minutes later, when the ship was safely in the open sea. He noticed that it turned to the right, down the coast toward its home port of Thessaloniki. Before he left, he sent a quick text to Icky.

∫

Paul and Eddie followed the truck in near silence for more than two hours, until Eddie's phone chirped.

"They've stopped for gas on the bypass around Haskovo," Paul told him. "I've gone on past the station. Why don't you stop at the intersection just after you get on the bypass and watch for them. They're in the only gas station. Then you follow and I'll pull in behind you."

"Will do," Eddie responded. In a few minutes, he found a wide shoulder on the bypass about a hundred yards from the gas station and pulled over to watch as the driver topped off the right-hand diesel tank. He walked to the small guard's shack to pay his bill while the shorter man slid into the driver's seat. When both were back in the truck, it pulled out slowly. Eddie waited two minutes and pulled out on the highway behind it.

"We're about halfway to Burgas now. He will have to take the A-1 from here," he told Paul.

In a few minutes, they were on the main east-west autoroute, following one of dozens of Greek and Bulgarian trucks that carried cargo to and from the bustling port, one of the busiest on the Black Sea. Eddie felt comfortable enough with the crowd to move closer to the truck, just in case it took a detour. It might, he thought, because Icky had not been able to determine what ship would be used to carry the missiles from Burgas to their final target, which he believed would be somewhere on the Russian coast at the other end of the inland ocean.

CHAPTER SEVENTEEN

Burgas, Bulgaria

There was no detour. The truck drove straight to the heart of the Port of Burgas. It slowed at the gate for a perfunctory security check, then stopped at a steel warehouse separated by twenty yards of dusty concrete from an aging freighter that loomed over the dock, its deck alive with seamen rapidly stowing bags of vegetables in its holds.

Eddie pulled off the road behind a stand of trees. Through his binoculars, he could clearly see Sonny emerge from the truck and open an overhead door. After that, the loading process they had seen in Alexandropoulos was reversed. Sonny counted carefully to be certain all twenty-five boxes were unloaded, and in less than a half hour all were stored. Then he peeled a stack of green 100-euro notes from a roll and gave them to the drivers.

The taller driver threw his arms into the air, then went to the cab and returned with a paper. He pointed forcefully at it, then Sonny took the roll of bills out and peeled off several more, after which the three shook hands and the truck headed back toward the autoroute. Sonny went back into the warehouse and closed its door from the inside.

Eddie's phone vibrated and he heard Paul chuckle. "Icky said Khan tried to stiff one of his old Stasi colleagues, now Sonny tries to stiff a poor Greek truck driver — the guy who could send him straight to jail if he got pissed off enough. It's beginning to look like this is the gang that couldn't shoot straight."

"Maybe," Eddie replied. "But does it seem strange to you that Sonny was alone with the shipment? Would you put that much trust in this guy?"

"Yeah, I thought of that. I've been watching your back, but I don't see anything yet. Let's wait and see. After all, one Chechen is dead and one is in jail, so Khan may be short-handed."

Paul had found a sheltered spot on the other side of the broad concrete loading area, which held only a half-dozen steel shipping containers spread about at random. From there he could see the warehouse entrance clearly, and could watch Eddie and the road approaching him from behind.

They waited, grateful that the temperature had dropped ten degrees during their drive north. The sun crawled past its zenith and headed down toward the horizon.

"Sonny must be the only guy less comfortable than us," Eddie told him during one of their infrequent phone calls. "It must be hot in that steel building, and I don't see any sign of AC. If he leaves, we need to go in and look it over."

"Roger," Paul responded.

In late afternoon, a Burgas taxi drove past Eddie's car and stopped at the warehouse. The driver honked twice. Sonny came out, looked carefully around him, and got in the back seat. Eddie made a note of its license tag and the name of the cab company, then called Icky, asking him to find out the destination.

In half an hour the response came back. The cab had gone straight to Burgas airport. Sonny had paid the driver and gone into the arrivals terminal.

"He's picking up somebody," Eddie told Paul. "This is the only chance we'll get."

"Where should we leave the cars?"

"I'll move mine to the parking lot across the street, because it's a little exposed here. You'll be OK right where you are. It looks like the side door has a standard Yale lock. Can you handle that?"

"Usually it only takes a credit card, but even if it's protected I can probably pick it. Sometimes you can just turn the knob hard enough and it will open. And we need to stay out of sight of that old Victory ship at the dock. It's Russian, so I wouldn't be surprised if it's the way the missiles are going to get to Chechnya."

Paul had the door standing open when Eddie arrived. "Credit card worked," he said.

Inside, they blinked as their eyes adjusted to the dim glow of a frosted yellow skylight, which was almost obscured by bird droppings. The warehouse was empty except for the refrigerator boxes standing in a disorganized jumble near the overhead door.

"We need to open one of those boxes and be sure we're following missiles and not refrigerators," Eddie told Paul urgently. "Let's pick one from the other side. Maybe it will be less obvious one of those has been moved."

A mezzanine ran across the far third of the building eight feet off the stained concrete floor. They chose one of the cartons just out of its shadow and turned it carefully on its side. A tool bench under the back wall yielded a pair of pliers that Paul used to pry three heavy copper staples out of the cardboard top.

Inside they found four wooden crates, and pulled out one. It had been painted — "probably in that Cypriot warehouse," Eddie said — and had no visible identification markings. They carefully pried off the top, and inside lay two five-foot fiberglass tubes.

"Jesus," Eddie said. "These are the SA-7s, one of the older Russian manpads, but still very, very dangerous."

They recorded the serial number of each missile, and Eddie photographed them with his iPhone. Then they re-closed the crate and slid it quickly back into the refrigerator carton. When they had heaved it upright again, they chose another one and opened it — it also contained the four wooden crates, each containing two SA-7 missiles.

"I'll close this one and get the staples put back as close as possible to the way they looked. You'd better get on the horn with Icky," Paul said.

"In a minute. What I'm trying to figure out now is, where's the rest of it? These are the tip of the spear, but without gripstocks they're useless as shoulder-mounted weapons. The Libyans used them as vehicle mounts, but the Chechens will want the full portable capability. Where are the gripstocks?"

"Explain?"

"The missiles are dangerous enough by themselves, but to be used by one man they require a separate device, the gripstock, which includes the actual trigger mechanism and some of the control circuits, plus the battery. Normally there would be one gripstock for every six or eight missiles, but Icky told me the Russians were pretty reluctant to give many of them to the Arab countries. They have to be here somewhere."

"Well, we can't really afford to open all these cartons," Paul replied. "Sonny or the Chechens would see immediately they'd been tampered with."

"You're right. So we have to stay here until we know where the gripstocks are. It won't be fun and it might be dangerous, but I can't see any other way to find out."

"Okay. I'll run up to the mezzanine and book us a couple of rooms."

"Very funny."

In two minutes Paul called softly to Eddie. "I think I found a way. Come take a look."

The mezzanine had a floor of soft wood planks, and a large stack of boxes covered by a grimy canvas tarp stood next to the wall. Paul had flipped the tarp back so he could survey the boxes.

"Cigarettes. We've stumbled into a smuggler's warehouse. Remember Ahmed said Khan smuggled cigarettes out of Greece? It's a big business here, and there's a ready market for cut-rate smokes among the Eastern European immigrants working in Germany and France. This must be where he stashes them.

"We can move the boxes around and make a sort of dark cubbyhole to hide in. I'll cut a hole in the floor so we can see what's going on below."

"What if they decide to take a load of cigarettes back to Munich with them?" Eddie asked.

"Then we're screwed unless we can scurry over to that little closet in the corner. We can't use it now because there's no way we could see the missiles downstairs, but with a few seconds' notice we might be able to squeeze in."

In fifteen minutes they had rearranged the cigarette boxes to open a sizeable hiding place in the center. They spread the tarp to be sure the front was covered, then went inside to try it. Paul took out a penknife and started to widen the crack between two floorboards.

"Tight, but it will work as long as we're quiet. It's a good thing the sun is about to set. It would be hot as hell if we have to get in there before sundown," Paul said. Both looked up at the dingy skylight, which was already beginning to darken in the late afternoon.

Eddie said, "You watch the ship and I'll watch the approach. If what we hear about Khan is true, he'll do this deal only in exchange for bullion, which will be heavy. Sonny will probably come back with a truck."

Paul moved to the port side of the building and found an old bucket, which he upended as a seat so he could watch the Victory ship through a narrow crack in the steel wall. "These pants have had it anyway," he said wryly.

"How much gold will he get, d'ya think?" Paul asked in a hoarse whisper.

"Let's figure." Eddie took out his iPhone and fired up the calculator. "There are twenty-five boxes, each with eight missiles, so that's 200 missiles. Icky told me last week the market price for illegal manpads is about 30,000 dollars each."

"That much?"

"They're a lot cheaper if you can buy them legally, or if you can just steal them from Khadafy's inventory, but these went through a middleman, maybe more than one. For now let's figure 30,000 dollars times 200 missiles, which is 6 million dollars.

"The gold we found behind Saint-Lazare station was in crates of 25 kilos, which is about 880 ounces. The last gold price I saw was 1,700 dollars an ounce, so they'd need 3,500 ounces or four cases and change, by the time you add in some bribes. The gold they'll get will weigh about what one crate of missiles does."

"They'll be able to ship it back in the trunk of their car."

Eddie said, "I'm guessing that's exactly what they will do, and it's probably why Icky has lost track of so much gold around Munich. One person driving a car or van across EU borders, with basically no customs inspections, could move a lot of it over time.

"It's scary, but it probably means Khan has sold a lot more manpads across the Black Sea. I can't see him taking this risk for 6 million dollars, when he wants to own hundreds of millions in gold. Or maybe these guys are regular customers. Jeremy said he was looking for 500 missiles."

"It sounds like a hell of a lot to me," Paul said, "but I understand what you're saying. The world of bankers and terrorists isn't bothered by a lot of zeroes. For that matter, you see money a lot differently from the way I do."

"Sorry. Can't help that. It came with the family. Sometimes it's not all that great."

After an hour, Eddie whispered urgently, "Red Alert! There's a van backing up to the door."

They scurried into the hidden cave among the boxes of cigarettes and took up positions at the narrow slots they had gouged in the wood floor. Underneath the tarp, it was blacker than a moonless night in the deep woods.

The overhead door rattled and shook as it opened, and then a figure walked backward into the warehouse. Eddie poked Paul's shoulder when he saw in the dim light from outside that it was Sonny, carrying a Kalashnikov rifle slung over his right shoulder. Eddie hadn't seen one of those since Desert Storm. It was a Kalashnikov that had dealt Paul the grievous head wound that nearly killed him, but in the end led to his joining Eddie's business.

An old windowless van backed slowly through the door. As Sonny directed with hand signals, the driver steered it around the refrigerator boxes and stopped, then Sonny closed the door and returned to open its twin on the other side, facing the port. A shorter man stepped out of the driver's side of the van and took the Kalashnikov, then backed away to cover the door.

"No trust there," Eddie mumbled almost soundlessly.

As the door slowly opened they could see the feet of two people, a large handcart between them. On the cart were stacked five cases similar to the ones containing the missiles, but shorter.

With the door fully open, Eddie and Paul saw two men who looked remarkably like the Chechens who had kidnapped Aurélie in Paris. Then the short man with the rifle moved to meet them in the dim light spilling over from the ship's loading operation. They could see clearly he was wearing brown slacks and a brown jacket. Even though a hat covered his face, Eddie touched Paul's shoulder again and whispered excitedly, "Khan!" Paul grunted. They'd found their target.

Khan shook hands with the two men as though they were old friends. Eddie was certain he had made this transaction before, perhaps several times. Behind them waited three burly sailors, each with a handcart. Two were empty, but the third carried four small white crates.

The man with the first handcart rolled it through the door and Khan signaled with a wave of his hand that he should put it behind the truck. Khan selected a crate from the center of the stack, then handed the rifle to Sonny and set about opening it. Eddie saw the dull gleam of gold bullion as the lid came off, then Khan carefully removed twenty-five one-kilo bars, one at a time, counting as he stacked them to one side.

"This is the moment I always look forward to," they heard him tell Sonny. "Did you ever see anything more beautiful? I never have understood why anybody would want to use anything else for money."

Sonny stammered and said, "Maybe because paper is a lot easier to carry? This stuff is a backbreaker."

Khan was silent as he refilled the crate and fastened the lid, then signaled to the incoming sailors that they could take all but one of the refrigerator boxes. The last box went into the van, the gold crates beside it.

When the last of the large cartons had been rolled to the ship, Khan reached into the truck to pull out a large suitcase, more like a traveling salesman's large sample case, and handed it to the last sailor. "The gripstocks," Eddie whispered.

Sonny went to the door chain and pulled it hand over hand until the door was closed and the warehouse dark. Khan lit a flashlight and looked into the back of the van.

"Let's get on the road now. It's a long drive but we can cover a lot of ground tonight."

Sonny responded. "OK, but let's take some cigarettes." Eddie and Paul froze and prepared to scuttle to the closet.

Khan paused a few seconds, then replied. "Not tonight. Cigarettes are so important to customs that it's too risky. If we get inspected now we just have a refrigerator and a few old wooden boxes. Leave the cigarettes and I'll have the others include them on their next trip."

Eddie relaxed. If what he'd heard about Khan was true Sonny would not challenge him which he didn't. He heard Sonny grumble a bit, then ask, "You want to drive first?"

"You start," Khan responded. "My back hurts and I need to rest for a couple of hours. Let's get out of here."

The door opened, then closed. Eddie moved back to his wall to watch them drive away then said, "Let's get after it. I'm parked closer so I'll go first. We'll do it the way we did coming from Alexandropoulos."

∫

Without German license plates, the van would have been indistinguishable from dozens of other old white trucks on the road that night. Eddie followed it through downtown Burgas and out Stambolov Boulevard to the A1 autoroute that winds down the length of Bulgaria into Serbia and, beyond the Balkans, to any of the Western European nations.

I'd bet anything he's headed to Munich, Eddie told himself. And I bet he and Sonny are going to switch off driving and go straight through, bad back or not.

He called Paul. "When we get to the first rest stop we need to ditch one car and drive together. They'll probably drive nonstop, and neither of us will be worth a damn if we drive eighteen hours. We'll call the rental company and tell them where to find the car."

"They won't be happy," Paul replied.

"Is there a choice? I can't think of one."

"Me either. I suggest we keep your car. It might go a little faster."

Eddie had rented the largest car in the small fleet at Alexandropoulos, a Renault Megane. It was roomy enough for one of them to sleep in the back seat, and it had a powerful engine. He was glad to have a car more powerful than the van they were chasing.

At the rest stop, Paul threw his bag behind the Megane's back seat and left his car in a remote corner of the lot. Eddie filled his tank, then bought two coffees at the sleepy concession stand. He was the only customer and had trouble extricating himself from a conversation with the waiter, who had lived for a year in Marseille and was anxious to practice his French.

∫

Two hours later, they saw the van pull off and stop at another rest stop. "Probably changing drivers," Paul said. "How do you think we should handle it?"

"If we pull in the same rest stop more than once or twice they'll get very suspicious, so we'd better go on beyond it and wait for them to pass us again. There's probably a bridge or a maintenance turnout we can use."

In five minutes they found a hidden parking place twenty yards off the road and sheltered by trees. When the van passed them a few minutes later, they waited for four cars to pass, then pulled back into the light traffic behind it.

∫

In Zagreb, they turned east toward Slovenia and Austria. As the miles rolled by it became more and more clear the truck was headed toward southern Germany.

Paul looked at his watch. "We've been chasing these guys fifteen hours. They must be as tired as we are."

"It's just a few hours to Munich, and they'll want to get there after dark. Jen said Khan had a house out in the country, so they might go there, or they may have a place to stash the missiles somewhere else."

"Or at Ahmed's place," Paul said drily.

"Jeremy knows something about Ahmed," Eddie replied. "Or at least he has strong suspicions. But I can't see Ahmed throwing in entirely with the other side."

"A lot of people drown one step at a time. First they're in the shallows where they think it's safe, then they take a wrong step and the bottom drops out from under them. If Khan got him into arms smuggling a little at a time, he could be in so deep now he can't get out," Paul replied. "Just one man's theory."

Eddie drove in troubled silence for another mile before he answered. "Is that what you think happened to Jen, too?"

"I think Jen was beyond help when I met her. I'm sorry about that, because I know you were close to her, but she'd already been seduced by something. My guess is it was the money Al Sommers held out to her. We now know — or we're pretty sure — Khan was already the brains behind that group. The Mafioso in Miami didn't know what an important piece of news it was when he said he'd bought things from Jen. Her business was about to fail and she was afraid of going to jail for stealing customers' money. Whatever the cause, she was never what we thought she was."

Eddie replied, "I know you're right, but I hate to admit it. For now, we have to treat both of them as part of the other side. But neither of them was involved in the death of my family. Khan was, and for that he will pay."

∫

Three hours later to the minute, the truck turned off toward a large gas station. "We'd better take a chance and follow them this time," Eddie said. "They could head cross-country from here and we might never find them, especially now that it's dark."

They chose a parking place surrounded by a hundred cars, in front of a small restaurant. They watched Sonny gas the truck and move it to the far end of the service plaza, where the overhead lights were barely bright enough for them to see. After ten minutes, a black Mercedes sedan stopped behind the truck. A large man got out of the passenger seat and opened the back door, where he stood and waited until the diminutive Khan left the truck and walked to the open door.

Khan finished a one-sided conversation with a dismissive wave of his hand and sat down in the back seat of the Mercedes. The large man closed the door and walked toward the driver's window of the van while the Mercedes drove away — but headed toward the country, not the autobahn.

Meanwhile, the large man was in an arm-waving argument with Sonny. It ended only when he finally made an angry "move over" sign to Sonny, then opened the door and sat in the driver's seat.

"Wonder what that was about?" Eddie mused. "Anyway, I got the number of the Mercedes. It's a Paris plate. You take over driving and I'll tell both Icky and Philippe. Neither will want to share it with the other."

He stood near the edge of the pale yellow circle for a full minute, listening for any sounds that would announce a lookout, or even a roving night watchman. He heard only the scratch of boxes being pulled across the steel floor of the van — the hard wooden scrape of the crates containing the gold. He counted two of those, which meant part of the gold was destined to go elsewhere. The two pulled from the van sounded heavy and full, so most of it was to be left here.

Gingerly, he stepped into the bushes to send Paul a quick text about the divided cargo, then he crept further along the fence until he could see the van in the dim light thrown by a high fixture at the other end of the building, plus a narrow band visible at the bottom of the door, which had just closed with a loud metallic clatter. At that moment, the van's engine started and it drove toward him. He threw himself quickly into the bushes and stood rigid, wishing he'd blackened his face. His cat-burglar outfit wouldn't be easy to see — although if anyone gets close they'll smell it, he said ruefully to himself. There had been no change of clothes on the long chase from Greece.

There was still work to do. He badly needed to know what Sonny had left behind in Ahmed's warehouse, and the only way to do that was to find a way to look inside.

First, he called Paul and told him to follow the van. Then he crept quietly around the warehouse to the back side, which another chain-link fence separated from a dense grove of trees and underbrush.

He didn't want to turn on his phone's flashlight, so he stood in the dark shadow of the building until he could just make out the shape of an empty wooden box, which he carefully moved to the wall under a tiny pinhole of light. By standing on the box and stretching as high as he could reach, he was able to peer through the hole — as long as he held fast to a drainpipe. The box teetered dangerously.

The refrigerator carton was nowhere in sight, although there was a corner of the warehouse he could not see. That might be important, he told himself. Maybe they need them sooner than we think.

Startled, he turned at the sound of something scuttling near the end of the building. He saw nothing. Squirrels or rats, he told himself, then turned back to search for the two crates of gold he expected to find. Their fresh white paint stood out on the far side of the room, waiting for Khan's next messenger to pick them up and deliver them — where? Paris? Dubai? Riyadh?

CHAPTER EIGHTEEN

Munich

In less than fifteen minutes, the van took the exit Eddie remembered from his visit to Ahmed. They followed, and it soon became clear Ahmed's warehouse was the destination this time as well.

"Let's drive past. Maybe we'll be less obvious," Paul told Eddie.

"We're going to stick out anyway," Eddie replied. "There's only one entrance and this place probably doesn't get a lot of traffic at night. But you're right — that's what we have to do." He looked closely for Jen's BMW but her place was empty, as was Ahmed's next to it.

A quarter-mile beyond it, they parked behind another small industrial building.

"We have to find out what they're leaving here and what they're taking with them," Eddie said urgently. "I'm going to walk back and take a look. Wait ten minutes and follow me, but stay on the north side of the road. We don't want them to see either of us, but we sure as hell don't want them to catch both of us."

A fence lined with dense, thorny bushes separated Ahmed's warehouse complex from the two-lane street. Eddie pressed as close as he could, but stayed on the sidewalk where his soft-soled shoes made almost no sound.

He walked as silently as he could toward the one dim streetlight he needed to pass. It's a damned good thing we have clouds tonight, he told himself. A bright moon would make this nearly impossible.

Satisfied, he edged backward from the wall. Before he could step down, he heard a quick movement to his right and felt a hard hand on his back, pressing him firmly against the steel wall. At the same time, he felt a sting in his right thigh, followed by an intense burning pain. The hand pressed hard until the tiny light coming through the hole grayed into darkness. He fell heavily from the box, but felt nothing.

∫

Paul had rushed back to the car. He waited as the van passed him, then sat down and checked his phone for a map of the industrial park. It was odd — the van was driving away from the park's only entrance. He decided to wait with his lights off even though there was some risk there might be a second, unmapped exit that Sonny could use to get away.

With his window down, he heard the truck's engine stop and idle in the distance, then after a minute reverse and head back. The driver had chosen the wrong direction.

Paul waited as the truck rolled slowly past him. He expected it to drive through the gate of the industrial park, but to his surprise it turned back toward the warehouse.

Alarmed, Paul moved urgently to the fence on the other side of the street and carefully parted the bushes. The view was less than perfect — the warehouse next to Ahmed's blocked his view of all but the cab of the van, and that was in deep shadow.

He heard footsteps and Sonny's twanging West Texas voice, followed by the guttural voice of the Chechen, but could not make out their words. Something heavy fell into the back of the truck, then the doors slammed closed and it rolled away from the building, this time taking the correct turn toward the exit.

Paul had to make a split-second decision. Instinct told him to follow the truck. He would have Icky send help to search the warehouse, but if it was Eddie who'd been dumped in the van, chasing it might be the only way to save him. If he could be saved.

∫

The van steered a steady path up the autobahn. Paul fell back a half mile, even though he was certain Sonny knew he was being followed and was planning to draw him into a trap. He would have to be alert.

After five minutes the truck turned down a two-lane road. High rain clouds covered the half moon, leaving the countryside shrouded in darkness. An occasional break let him see that he was in the midst of farmland that appeared to stretch for miles in every direction.

In an effort to convince Sonny he wasn't being followed, he rounded a curve in full view, then slowed to a stop and turned around, hoping they would think he was giving up the chase. He drove back around the curve, turned off his lights and stopped, then turned to resume the pursuit, this time with only the intermittent moonlight to guide him. It was dangerous, he told himself, but might enable him to get a little closer.

Twenty minutes later, a dim street light barely visible in the distance announced a small village. As he entered it, Sonny tried his own trick. Halfway down the main street, the van's lights went out and it disappeared. Paul pulled over to the shoulder and got out to look toward the spot where the van had been. He focused intently on the crossroads in the middle distance — he was pretty sure he'd seen the truck turn left, but he could barely make out the dim line of the intersecting road as it left the village behind the single row of houses that lined the street on that side.

After ten minutes, he finally saw the van creep slowly down the road.

"You think you can slip away like that, you bastard?" he muttered. "But the big question is, are both of you in the truck or are you trying the same trick again? Let's find out."

He started to put the car in gear, but paused to turn to the back seat and open his small brown canvas suitcase. He first put on a latex glove he'd tucked into the corner, then pulled out the Glock 9mm automatic Icky had sent to them in Alexandropoulos. Then he removed its twin from Eddie's suitcase, as well. Probably better not to tempt fate where the German police are concerned, he reasoned.

He tucked one pistol into his waistband, then drove slowly down the street, straining to catch a glimpse of any movement that might signal an ambush. A half block before the intersection, he found what he was looking for — a narrow opening between two houses that ran all the way to the field behind.

With the car still moving at near-idle speed, he opened the door quietly and stepped out, gun in hand, then crouched and scurried between the houses. He got to the edge of the field just as the silence of the night was split by the harsh sound of rifle fire, followed instantly by glass shattering.

Sonny's goddam Kalashnikov, he thought as he crouched behind a low stone fence and scuttled toward the noise. Another burst rang out, closer.

Paul stuck his head out from behind the fence and saw the Chechen, rifle at the ready, move slowly toward the ruined car. He stepped quickly into the street and took up a two-handed combat position, then shouted, "Achtung!"

The Chechen was quick, Paul had to give him that. He turned and squeezed off a single shot. It went wild, pinging off the second floor of a stone house. But his next effort was too late. Before he had a chance to level his rifle and fire again, Paul squeezed off three rounds in quick succession, two of which struck home in the man's chest. He fell instantly.

Gun at the ready, Paul ran to the still body. The man was dead, no doubt about it. Paul quickly tucked Eddie's gun into the Chechen's waistband, then dropped his own a few steps away. He wadded the glove into a small ball and pushed it into the car's gasoline fill tube. It disappeared into the tank, where he hoped it would dissolve before the police thought to search there, if they ever did.

Then, as lights began to flick on in the surrounding houses, he sat down in the ruined car, picked up a shard of the shattered glass, and slashed at his face and arm.

Lights came on in more windows around the intersection, but he heard no doors opening. No surprise. He laid down on the seat and began to stab fiercely at his iPhone, composing a short status message to both Icky and Philippe. He sent it, then deleted it from the phone.

∫

A door opened. Paul heard the sound of tentative steps, first from the right, then the left. Brave men, he told himself. They have no idea what's going on in this car but they're coming out to see.

Paul started to moan, then sat up just as a beefy farmer shone a light on him. Another beam came from the other side, and Paul noticed both of the men were also carrying shotguns at the ready.

"My wife has called the police and an ambulance," the first said. "Are you hurt badly?"

Paul struggled to recall the German he had learned years before.

"I am bleeding some, but at least I am alive."

One of the farmers pulled the door open and bent to help Paul step unsteadily into the bright circle of light. A small crowd had gathered —

Paul thought almost all of the men of the village must be there, or gathered in a group around the body lying in the street nearby. One of them had carefully cleared the rifle and moved it to the side, where it lay alongside the two Glocks.

∫

Sonny had injected Eddie with a medium dose of propofol, a quick-acting anesthetic, then followed it with another injection of Sublimaze and Valium — the first to keep him asleep, the second to relax his muscles so he would be weak and uncoordinated if he awakened.

Khan had given him strict instructions on how to administer the shots and made him practice on a thick steak. Over the course of an hour he'd broken three needles and nearly given up in frustration, but Khan had made him repeat it over and over until he could do it smoothly and flawlessly.

"This stuff is so much better than the Russian swill we had in the Stasi," Khan told him. "The old anesthetics were crude — even ether was better. And you could never predict how long the guy would be out, or even if he'd wake up.

"Grant will start coming around in an hour, so you have to be at the house before it wears off. I don't want him to have any idea of where he is or how long he's been out. Once he understands and accepts that he's totally in my control, that's when I'll get the answers I want."

Sonny had told the trigger-happy Chechen just to wait and watch to see if anybody was following them. But no, he had to shoot up a car passing by. Well, he could walk the two miles to the house — Sonny wasn't going back now, not after all that gunfire. The street would be full of neighbors and pretty soon the place would be crawling with cops. The Chechen's paranoia had cost them time they could not afford and now he had less than fifteen minutes to get that bastard Grant into the snug basement cell Khan kept for special cases. And Eddie Grant was a very special case. Sonny's main hope was that he'd be given the honor of executing him when Khan had finished his questioning, although he knew his chances were not good — Khan liked to do that part of the job himself.

A few minutes later, he turned down a gravel lane. There was no gate — "a gate tells people you have something to hide," Khan had told him, but Sonny knew the underground sensors had set off a quiet chime in the house.

The gravel road swept around to the left of the old stone house. Sonny followed it slowly up a gradual incline, then drove through the open gate in a fence that disappeared into the hardwood forest behind.

He stopped to close and lock the gate behind him, then drove to a bulkhead door, the universal basement entrance. Next to it, an old coal chute had been welded shut, and the fill cap for a fuel-oil nozzle had been cut into its center. A dim yellow bulb provided weak light.

Sonny backed up to the door. Khan's waiting driver stooped to pull it open, then opened the wide back doors of the van. A few yards away Claude Khan himself, dapper as always in brown slacks and pullover, waited.

"Where's your helper?" he asked.

"I left him to watch a car that was following, but instead of watching he shot it up. I couldn't go back — the place will be all cops by now. I imagine he'll turn up here pretty soon."

Khan seemed unconcerned. "Whatever. We'll need him later, though."

He nodded toward Eddie, who lay still on the steel floor of the van. "You two get this piece of crap down the stairs. I'll show you where to put him."

He ducked down the stairs and turned on an overhead light, then unlocked the door to a room that appeared to be a closet, except that the door was steel and an inch thick.

"The SS built this little interrogation room here in the late '30s, a dozen years after a banker built the hunting lodge. He was a Jew, so in exchange for the house and a lot of other property, they let him leave for England. An SS general used it all through the war."

The room was dim and dank, with a strong smell of mildew from the moisture seeping through the old and porous stone walls. There was no light fixture in the cell, but at the top of two walls small windows of thick glass had replaced the concrete. They were dirty from decades of neglect but admitted enough light to provide meager illumination.

Khan pointed to a thin straw mattress on the floor. "Put him there, and watch his head. He's no good to us dead, at least not yet."

He bent over Eddie's still body.

"Good. He's still breathing. The propofol has already worn off, but the Sublimaze will keep him under longer." He took out a small case and withdrew a syringe. "I'll boost it now, because I want him to sleep at least twelve hours before I question him. He won't know how long he's been out, but he will have a sense that it's been a long time."

∫

Cold. Eddie's first dim thought was of the cold. He felt like he'd been locked in a refrigerator for days. He struggled to figure out where he was, but his last memory was the hard hand at his back and the painful stab in his thigh. He tried to move, to run, to walk, or even to simply shift his leg but found he could not. His body refused to obey his mind.

Slowly, he became conscious of voices around him, close to him — first the twang he recognized as Sonny Perry, then a high, reedy voice with an accent. It was a strange one he did not know — the mastermind? Then he felt a needle's sharp prick in his arm and in a few seconds all went dark again.

∫

Later. An unknown time later, a minute, ten minutes, an eternity? A bright light blinded him. He was awake but not really awake, able to move at a glacial pace and think even more slowly, but he knew he was seated in a chair, arms stretched behind him and secured by something. Maybe handcuffs, he thought. More comfortable than the flexcuffs he'd had to wear in Sarasota.

From behind the light the reedy voice came again. It brought back in a flash his college history professor imitating Lincoln's high tenor, but Lincoln hadn't had a German accent. Now it was clear to him. He was dealing with Erich Kraft's German boss, the ex-Stasi man. Claude Khan himself. Defeating his minions had been tough enough. Dealing with an experienced Stasi operative trained by the KGB would be next to impossible. In fact, it might be impossible.

"Eddie, I have only one question. When you answer it, you can go home to your beautiful blonde bride. If you don't answer it, your body will rot somewhere in the forest behind this house and be eaten by the wild boars, and your beautiful bride will soon not be beautiful anymore.

"Where is the painting? Answer that and go free."

In the silence that followed, Eddie willed himself to wake up fully. He focused his mind on the background noises — a slow drip somewhere nearby, which he hadn't heard until the door opened, so it must be outside this dingy cell. The scurrying sound of a small animal, which he hoped would remain outside.

"Where is the painting?"

The low sound of wind moving across a loosely sealed opening, perhaps a door not completely closed or leaking from age.

He looked around within the narrow circle of light cast by the bright reflector bulb positioned only two feet from his face and saw that the floor was beaten dirt. He could take in just a small section of the wall and make it out as roughly cut stone. He saw the corner of a thin straw mattress and realized that was where he had been dumped. A pool of vomit, only partially dried, had trickled from the mattress down to his feet.

Was this what it had been like for his father on the last day of his life, when some of the same people had grilled him harshly, then when they didn't get the answer they wanted pulled a plastic bag over his head? He knew the level of depravity that confronted him, an advantage Artie hadn't had, and he told himself he must — must — seize the slightest opportunity. And he must be ruthless about it.

Sensation returned. It was clear he'd soiled his pants, which meant he'd been out for hours. In a short while it would smell really foul in here, then he realized the thought meant he was returning to consciousness. Important not to let his questioner know.

"Painting." He mumbled, half intentionally, half because he was still semi-conscious.

"The painting," the reedy voice responded. He knows what the anesthetic does, so he'll be patient, Eddie told himself. I can use that.

"The Raphael. You found the gold in Paris, but not the Raphael. Where is it?"

"No idea," Eddie responded, trying to sound groggier than he was. "Can't think." The voice was full of menace, but at the same time had a seductive layer. Eddie could understand how Khan had been able to draw people so easily into his plots.

"You'd better think, and quick." Then, to someone else in the room, "Take away the chair and chain him to the wall. Give him some water. I don't have time to wait now. We'll try again when I get back." A chair scraped. He heard steps as his questioner walked away.

"Get up," Sonny said roughly. "You're filthy. I'm not going to touch you. Get up!"

Eddie struggled to his feet as Sonny walked around behind him and threaded something between his wrists. He heard the chain scrape across the floor, then the metallic sound of a padlock against an iron ring.

"I can't do anything with my arms behind me," Eddie told him.

"Tough shit." Then a pause for reflection. "I'm sure as hell not going to feed you." He called out the door and another man came through it carrying a pistol in his hand.

"Watch him while I move the cuffs to the front so he can feed himself," Sonny told the armed man. He unlocked Eddie's right hand and re-locked it in front, the chain still in place.

"Now bring some water, then lock the place up, then you can start for Paris. We don't want to keep the boss waiting," Sonny told the third man, who less than a minute later returned with a large pail of water. Eddie briefly considered asking for a cup, but thought better of it as the two men pushed the door closed behind them and bolted it, leaving him in dim twilight. He strained to follow their path across the dirt floor, then counted as they climbed twelve steps. The stairs resonated gently, like new wood. At the top they opened a door, stepped through, and closed it behind them. A key turned and the room was silent.

∫

When I get back. What did Khan mean? How long would he be gone?

Eddie knew he was near the end of the line. Sonny was working with the group that had killed his father, and he had made very clear in Sarasota that he'd love to do the same to Eddie. But he was not a brave man — Eddie had seen that when he'd surrendered to sheriff's deputies with no hint of a fight. So first priority had to be getting out of the handcuffs so he could deal with the weak link.

He was confident he had some time, enough for his focus to return. He began by searching the part of the room he could reach at the end of his chain.

"I feel like that organ grinder's monkey performing for the tourists at Sacré-Coeur," he said wryly to himself as he got on his hands and knees and started patting his way around the earthen floor. "At least the monkey had strangers watching out for him."

He was looking for a piece of wire to use as a lever on the handcuff lock, but ultimately had to admit failure and give up.

"Still too woozy to do this right. I'll try again in an hour."

He awoke to the sound of the door opening. The bright light came on and his heart sank. He had counted on having more time before the next interrogation. It would be tougher than the first.

Good luck, sort of. It was Sonny with lunch.

"Don't get up, asshole," the twanging voice said. "I'm just bringing you something to eat. It's a couple of German sausages and some bread."

He put a paper bag on the floor next to the water bucket. "You still have plenty of water, I see."

Eddie asked him, "How long will I be here?"

"Until the boss says you can go."

"If I tell him where to find the painting, will he let me go?"

"He said he would, and he's always kept his word with me. I wouldn't."

"How long have I been here?"

"It's nine-thirty Friday morning. You figure it out."

The door slammed and Eddie heard the bolt slide home. He had been a prisoner less than twelve hours, but it felt like twelve days. All at once he was overcome with fatigue. He laid down. Just for a minute, he told himself.

CHAPTER NINETEEN

Munich

That half day had been frantic around Ahmed Matossian's warehouse. When Icky received Paul's message, he called Ahmed in to search for Eddie, with no luck. All they found was an overturned box in the narrow walkway behind the building and, as Ahmed told Icky, "That could have been there, just like that, for a year. It's at least that long since I've been back there."

There did appear to be the sign of something heavy dropped next to the box, but the dirt was packed very hard and the sign was vague at best.

When Jen Wetzmuller arrived at nine, Ahmed intercepted her at the front door and drew her into the conference room where he and Eddie had questioned her.

"Jen, there's some chance that Eddie was kidnapped last night, here."

"What? And nobody called me?"

"Icky and I talked about it, but didn't think there was much you could do then. As it turned out, we found nothing, but Paul's car got shot up and he's in the hospital. I have a contact at the hospital who told me he's not hurt badly, but the police are questioning him and showing no signs of letting him leave. Obviously we can't go in and ask him about it now."

"What were they doing there?"

"They followed Khan and Sonny Perry from Bulgaria. Icky says they watched Sonny unload some boxes here. I went into Khan's area and looked, and there are two crates that could be gold bars. In fact, I'm pretty sure that's what they are. That means they took two more gold crates and a refrigerator carton full of missiles on somewhere else."

Jen asked, "So what do we do now? Shouldn't we call the police?"

"Icky says wait. When Paul gets out we can talk to him in more detail and maybe do something with what he knows. If it's an ordinary kidnapping we'll hear from someone today or tomorrow, though. Eddie is a rich guy. It may be just something for ransom."

"You know that's not likely," she said. "But OK. I have a client appointment in an hour, so I'll catch up here and then head out for that. But I'll only keep it if you promise to text me the minute you have any news."

She spent twenty minutes watching the clock, then left, telling Ahmed, "I have my appointment, then lunch, then another appointment, so I will be late if I get back at all."

She could sense him watching her as she backed her BMW convertible out of its space and headed for the highway into downtown Munich. But as soon as she was out of sight, she pulled into a parking lot and dialed the number Icky had told her never to use except in an emergency.

He answered after one ring. "I wondered how long it would take you to call."

"Ahmed, the jerk, didn't tell me until now. You could have called me."

"I thought about it, but you couldn't have done anything then," Icky said. "What do you think?"

"What do I think?" She was incredulous. "What do I think? I think Claude Khan snatched Eddie. There's something big in the air. This has to be the start of it. That, or Claude just saw the opportunity to squeeze Eddie about that damned painting, and took it."

"That's pretty much what I think, too. Do you have any ideas?"

"Sure I do. I'm going to go out there and get him back. It's Friday and Claude sort of expects me on Friday. I'll just be a little early — I usually go after work. I'll tell him I had an appointment north of town and decided to drop in."

"It will be dangerous. Better take your gun." She had a Glock 9mm like the ones Icky had sent Eddie and Paul in Greece, and knew how to use it.

"It would be worse if they found it," she said. "The problem will be finding Eddie, if he's there. That old house was used by an SS general all through the war, and he built in some special features, or so Claude told me. There's supposed to be an interrogation room in the basement, and God knows what else is hidden there."

"Jeremy is already on his way from Paris and Walker from Nice. They should be there in a couple of hours and will meet you at Ahmed's whenever you say."

"Not Ahmed's. Tell them to wait for me near a little park two miles west of Claude's house. There's a place where you can pull off the road for a picnic."

"OK. If Paul gets away from the hospital, I'll send him out there too, but I wouldn't count on it. And please be careful."

"I promise you I will get him out. And then I will kick ass."

∫

Jen was surprised to see only one car, a BMW like hers but smaller, in the parking area at the front door. Khan's large Mercedes sedan was nowhere to be seen, which probably meant both he and his driver were away and her odds would be more even.

She sat for a minute to collect her thoughts, her mind racing as she struggled to pull together some sort of plan. She had no idea at all how she was going to get Eddie out of the house. The back entrance to the basement would be best, if he were in fact held in the old interrogation room. She briefly considered moving her car closer to it, but abandoned the idea as soon as she realized it would tip off anyone in the house about her intentions.

Nothing to do but go in the front door like I always do and brazen it out, she finally decided. She touched the pistol, snug in its holster under her seat, then decided once again it would be better to go in unarmed.

She raised the BMW's top and locked the doors as she always did when she arrived for the weekend, just in case someone was watching from an upper window. Then she straightened up, smoothed her blue skirt with one hand, and walked to the front door, hoping she showed more confidence than she felt.

Inside, the house was still. She walked from the entrance hall into the living room and stood under the stuffed head of an unfortunate alpine ibex that had walked into the sights of some previous owner. She shuddered, as she always did, at the Bavarian hunting-lodge feel of the place, with its dark green walls, hunting scenes, and looming overstuffed furniture.

"Claude?" she called. She didn't really expect a reply, but was suddenly concerned that without Khan or one of his men, she might not be able to find the basement keys she would need.

At last she heard the sound of a footstep on the bare wooden floor of the upstairs corridor, muffled, like someone barefoot or wearing soft-soled shoes.

"Claude, is that you?"

She licked her lips and wiped her clammy hands on her skirt. For the first time, she was terrified.

A figure came slowly out of the second-floor darkness into the dim light of the living room, and she stifled a gasp when she recognized Sonny Perry. The thought of being alone in the house with him frightened her, but it was likely he was the only person there so he suddenly became her only hope.

"Sonny. I heard you were out of jail, but I didn't know you were here. Where's Claude?"

"Gone to Paris. He'll be back in a couple of days."

"I didn't know he was leaving today."

"That's probably because the boss didn't think you needed to know." His voice was low, dangerous. "I've been looking forward to this for a long time, since you helped that asshole Grant kill my friend Dmitri." He had obviously been stoking his own anger since their last meeting three years before.

"In the first place, I had nothing to do with that. In the second, I haven't seen Eddie Grant for three years and probably won't ever see him again."

"Bullshit. You saw him a week ago. And he was in your pants all the time he was in Sarasota. So I decided if I ever got you alone, I'd get some of the same."

"What? You don't even like women."

"I don't like you. Women I can take or leave, but you I'm going to take. And you'll never breathe a word of it to the boss if you want to keep breathing."

Jen wasn't sure what to think. Sonny had been openly if not flamboyantly gay in Sarasota; she had never even seen him look at a woman. But now he was planning to get even with Eddie by raping her. It's a gruesome thought, she told herself, but he has the keys. And how did he know she'd seen Eddie?

He lunged at her and grasped her left arm with a hard grip. She was able to twist away, but the evasion made him angrier. He slapped her hard across the face, then reached into his pocket and pulled out a small silver automatic.

"Don't screw around with me, bitch. You're stronger than I thought, but I spent a lot of time behind bars with nothing to do but lift weights, so I can handle you or any other pissant woman. And I have this." He pointed the gun at her head.

"Kill me and Claude will put your head on the fencepost outside," she told him. "Put the gun away and I'll go upstairs with you. I've always said if something like this happened I wasn't going to get hurt in the process."

He paid no attention but continued to talk, his voice venomous. "You know where this started? It was when Mr. Bigshot killed Khan's boy that night in Kuwait. Khan swore then he'd get even and now he's going to. And so am I.

"And this is where he's wanted to do it all along, in that little room downstairs. Something comes over him when he's there. I think he believes he's the SS general who used it during the war. He's going to really enjoy stringing your boy up on piano wire."

Her legs felt weak. It took all the effort she could force to pull herself up the first two steps as Sonny's news sank in. Khan, her friend and sometimes lover, was completely crazy. He had no plans to release Eddie — just as Sonny had no plans to release her.

Think fast, she told herself. Her step steadied as she began to run through the possible ways she could escape. By the time she approached the second floor, she was back in control.

"I suppose you want the big bedroom? That way you can think you're as good as Claude. You're not, but you can think that."

He punched her in the back, hard enough to push her to her knees. Her legs caught the top step and she fell face down on the wood floor. At the last second, she caught herself with one arm.

He waited as she pulled herself upright, then grunted and waved the pistol toward the master bedroom at the end of the hall, its windows overlooking acres of farmland that stretched away to a hardwood forest. It was the room she and Claude used when she visited him, so she knew it well.

She walked ahead of Sonny into the room and opened the bathroom door.

"If we're going to do this, let's do it right," she said, and began to unbutton her blouse.

"Stay out of the bathroom."

"I'm just going to hang my clothes on the door. Put yours on the chair."

He sat down in the chair and started to take off his cowboy boots, but found he could not with the pistol in his hand. He set it down beside him in the seat. He watched closely as Jen hung the white blouse on a hook inside the bathroom door, then stepped out of her slim skirt.

Next she reached behind her to unclip her bra, and hung it carefully on the door. Then, as the last act, she stepped out of her panties.

"So now you see what you want?" She was taunting him, raising her arms over her head just to watch his eyes follow her breasts. "I'm surprised. You really are a man. Now let's see what you can do."

"You'll see soon enough." He stepped close to her and she turned her head away from his rank breath, redolent of last night's beer. He put the muzzle of the little gun in her navel and twisted it, then began to trace a line down. She froze.

"You'd better stop. If you cut me up down there this won't go the way you want." The gun's motion stopped, then he jerked it away. She stifled a whimper of pain.

She lay down on the far side of the bed and patted the space next to her. But by then he was so aroused he jumped immediately on top of her, forcing her legs apart.

"Not so fast, buster. Women need a little time to get ready. Just take it slow and easy."

For a minute he moved slowly against her. Then, as he tried to separate her legs fully she went rigid. "What was that?"

"What was what?" he asked, disoriented.

"Outside the door. I heard a sound. I thought no one else was here."

As she pointed toward the door, his head — and the pistol — turned to follow her finger. At that moment, she strained to reach the crystal lamp on the night table, gripped its heavy base firmly and hit the back of his head as hard as she could. She heard the sickening sound of Sonny's skull being crushed and felt the gush of warm blood from the gaping wound the sharp edge had opened. He made one panicked effort to turn the pistol but she caught it with her other hand. She heard a single low moan, and then his full weight dropped on her.

She took the gun from his hand and passed it over his body to her right hand, then lay still to be sure he was immobile. His blood dripped across her neck and breasts and onto the elaborate floral bedspread that Khan had chosen himself. Yellow flowers on a brown field.

Dead weight. This certainly gives it new meaning, she thought, grateful to be alive, and a little surprised.

∫

Jen carefully disentangled herself from the still body and pushed it away from her, then carefully left the bed, turning so she could watch Sonny the entire time. She backed into the bathroom and wet a small towel to wash some of the blood from her face, then returned to the room and sat in the chair to watch for several minutes.

She checked his pulse. Nothing. She lifted his head carefully, holding only the hair, and saw that she had hit him so hard brains were spilling out of the wound.

"Bastard's dead, and good riddance," she said out loud.

Then she went into the bathroom and took a hot shower, washing herself carefully from head to toe to remove the final traces of Sonny Perry.

Back in the bedroom, she dried carefully and then dressed. The pistol went into her purse to be disposed of later. She threw both towels on the bed with Sonny, then looked through his clothes for the keys she would need to search the basement. Nothing. Just one keyring, from a car-rental company. The other BMW, she thought.

"Where do you keep the keys to a basement?" she asked herself, surprised to hear herself talking aloud. She was certain she was alone in the house, if she didn't count the corpse, but even so she admonished herself to keep it quiet.

She walked carefully down the stairs. The basement door was on the back side of the kitchen — a solid wooden door of the type a Bavarian carpenter would have built a hundred years ago, with a brass lock that looked much newer. They'd known they'd be using this, so they got the lock upgraded, she thought, then began looking in the area for a key.

She found it in less than a minute, in a balky drawer just across the narrow hallway from the door, attached to a key fob of the sort car dealers give away at trade shows. The shiny new key fit perfectly. A larger key and a tiny one she recognized as a handcuff key shared the ring, so she dropped the entire set into her pocket and started down the wooden stairs, leaving the door open behind her. She found a light switch at the head of the stairs and turned it on, washing the room in a dim yellow glow.

The interrogation room was obvious. It had been built much later than the house, with two walls of poured concrete that jutted out of the old stone foundation walls in one corner.

She went straight to the steel door and tried the other large key. It did not fit. Then she began to look around and found an even larger one hanging on a nail cast into the wall, just around the corner from the door. Perfect — a key from the '30s. It had to be the one.

She turned it carefully, then pulled the door open slowly. When the crack was an inch wide she stopped and said gently, "Eddie?" No reply.

The interior was so dark she could see nothing, so she moved Khan's interrogation lamp to the door. There lay Eddie Grant, asleep and unaware.

ʃ

She walked slowly into the room and knelt by his side.

"Eddie? It's Jen. Can you talk to me?"

He groaned and turned slowly on his back, and she was flooded with relief.

"Eddie. You're alive!" Without realizing it, she had begun to weep. She quickly caught herself — she had to move. Despite what Sonny had said, she had no idea how long Khan would be away, and couldn't risk meeting him just yet. Sonny's word was not something to be trusted.

She wiped her eyes on her sleeve and looked to see how Eddie was shackled. She used the handcuff key she'd found to unlock them, which released the chain. He moaned in gratitude and rubbed his wrists.

"Jen? How did you find me?" His voice was thick, and the words came slowly. She helped him sit up, but he promptly fell back again. "They doped me."

"I knew something was coming, but I didn't know they would stoop to this," she replied. "Just wait here and gather your energy a couple of minutes. I need to clear up a couple of loose ends."

She paused for a few seconds to look around the room and cringed when she saw the iron rings spaced around the walls, plus the long I-beam stretching across the room near the ceiling. It was too high for her to reach — about eight feet off the floor and more than strong enough to hold a man's weight. So Sonny's threat about hanging hadn't been an idle one. She suddenly felt better about her plan.

She ran quickly up the stairs to the basement's outside door, then moved her car from the front and parked it carefully so she could help Eddie into the back seat. It was clear he wouldn't be able to do it on his own power.

Back in the basement, she looked around for the tools she expected to find in any large house with grounds to maintain. In a far corner she found an old lawn mower, and next to it her goal: a gasoline can. She shook it — it was half full.

She carried it back up the stairs to the bedroom where she'd left Sonny's body. He hadn't moved, would never move again.

A computer that fit the description of Filer's laptop lay on Khan's small desk in the corner. She zipped it quickly into a brown leather case that sat on the floor nearby, then took it into the hall.

Next she poured the contents of the gasoline can over Sonny's body and the bed, took out a long wooden kitchen match, and scratched it on the marble sill of the bathroom door.

She threw it on the bed and darted quickly into the hallway, closing the door behind her as the flames leapt up toward the ceiling. Then she ran downstairs and out the front door to move her car around to the basement entrance.

When she got back to the interrogation cell, Eddie was sitting up with his head in his hands.

Again she knelt in front of him. "Eddie, look at me! Focus!" She took his chin in her hand and turned his face to her. "We're leaving right away. I have one more thing to do, but I'll be back in a couple of minutes and we'll go."

The gasoline had been sitting next to two white wooden cases. She had hefted one of them and decided from its size and weight that it probably was an old German gold crate, recently repainted. Each would be worth a million dollars, easy.

She dragged one part-way across the packed dirt floor to the stairs, then picked it up and carried it slowly up to her car, where she put it in the trunk. She repeated the process for the second.

Then she went back for Eddie. He was more alert, but still sitting where she'd left him.

"I'm pretty strong but I can't take your whole weight, Eddie. You have to help me help you. Now I'll lift you as much as I can, and you have to try hard, too."

"I'll give it all I've got, but I'm really weak." At least his mind was working better, she thought with relief.

She went behind him and put her arms under his and tried to lift. He was able to get up on one knee, then groaned and stopped.

She went around in front and tried again. With both arms around him in a tight bear hug, she was able to lift him to his feet. Then she put one of his arms around her shoulder and held tight to his body with both arms. Together they shuffled slowly toward the next and more difficult task — getting an almost-unconscious Eddie up the stairs.

It did not go well. She had to climb a step, then support much of his weight as he struggled to pull himself up next to her. Again and again they repeated the same clumsy dance until they finally were in the open air next to her car. She helped him lie down in the back seat, put the computer on the floor next to him, and drove back through the gate, locking it carefully behind her to slow the fire trucks a minute or two. Then, she headed out toward the country road where she would meet Jeremy and Walker.

From across the field, she watched in the mirror as traces of the fire licked at the roof of the house. She turned toward Eddie and said, "The last and final end of Sonny Perry. Good riddance." He did not respond.

∫

When she reached the end of Khan's long driveway she turned east, away from Jeremy and Walker. A mile down the road, she stopped at a small bridge and tossed Sonny's silver pistol into the fast-moving stream below, then turned the BMW around and headed for her rendezvous.

Ten minutes later, she found them waiting in a farmer's driveway. They helped Eddie move from her car to the large Mercedes Jeremy had rented in Frankfurt. He was more alert, but weak and limp and needed to lie down. She went back for the computer and put it in their car. "This will probably tell most of the story," she told them. "I think it belonged to that TV goldbug Claude hired to help him. It may tell you what he wanted to say to Icky but couldn't."

"Icky wants us to drive straight through to Paris, using roads without tolls to avoid as many cameras as we can," Jeremy said. "What will you do?"

"I don't know," Jen answered. "Probably go back home, see my aunt, go to work tomorrow."

Eddie's eyes were open but he was still groggy, though the anesthetic was wearing off quickly.

"No, no. You can't. Khan will know you were in the house. Follow us to Paris. First take the gold out of your car and leave it in the grass. There may be a bomb."

"How the hell...?" she asked.

"I listened while Sonny dragged them to his van, and again when you moved them in the basement. They're the same weight now, but when Sonny loaded them one was much lighter than the other. Just a hunch."

"That bastard!" Jen muttered. She started to get out of the car again.

"Wait!" Eddie said. "Walker, how would it be fused?"

"When we were in Kuwait, the Iraqis would use a timer that activated when the box was moved. It would go off a set time after it started."

Jeremy added, "That's still the best way to do it if you can't send it a signal, and we're pretty sure none of Khan's men are left around here. Is that right?"

"I'll go move them," Walker said, but as he opened the door Eddie called him back.

"There's not enough time. It could go off any second. Jen, get in here with me now. Jeremy, let's get away."

Jen waffled. "But I need my car. I can't just leave a BMW in the German countryside."

"Icky will see that you get a new one, and if he doesn't I'll buy you whatever you want. Please get in here right now."

He struggled to push the door open and she sat down reluctantly. Eddie reached across her to close it. "Now let's get the hell away from here. It's eight hours to Paris and we need to get started."

Jeremy started the engine again and pulled out into the narrow road. Less than thirty seconds later, the bomb went off with a roar. The car shuddered from the shock wave and Jen looked out the rear window just in time to see a spray of gold bars rise in graceful arcs. Most fell in the tall grass, but a few landed in the roadway and sparkled in the sunlight. The BMW erupted in flames.

"Too close," she said. "But the firefighters will get a surprise when they get here."

Eddie lapsed again into exhausted silence as Jeremy retraced the country roads, heading for an autobahn entrance well away from Munich. That way, he said, they would reduce the chance of encountering the firefighters or police investigating the explosion.

Walker looked over his shoulder into the back seat. "That bomb was designed to kill both of you. It was Khan's last booby trap, and with a little luck he will think you were in the car and got blown up trying to escape."

He quit talking when he realized neither of them was listening. Eddie, exhausted, had laid his head in her lap and gone to sleep. She placed her hand gently on his cheek and as he felt her touch he pressed his face to her breast. Walker heard her say softly, "The way things used to be."

∫

Paul finally talked his way out of the hospital. The doctors were satisfied that he had no serious injury, but were both suspicious and fascinated when they discovered the titanium plate in the top of his skull, his souvenir from Desert Storm.

To shoot up a foreigner's car in the middle of the night, and with a machine gun at that, was very big news in the German countryside. A senior detective Paul's age took the case, and they quickly bonded over tales of their military days. The detective was still pretty certain he didn't know the whole truth, but he was willing to give a fellow sergeant the benefit of his lingering doubt. In the end he assigned a fresh-faced young detective to drive Paul to Munich's main railway station, where he could catch a train to Paris in two hours.

The police had kept his iPhone, so he bought a telephone card and went in search of a public phone. He found a short row of them on a lower level and called Icky.

"I'm out," he said without identifying himself.

"Where are you?"

"Payphone in the basement of the Hauptbahnhof."

"I know the place. Wait at the hotel across the street. Someone will be there in less than an hour."

"Good. I'll get lunch. The hospital food was worse than I remember at Walter Reed."

Icky made a mirthless sound that Paul interpreted as a chuckle and the line went dead.

He had a well-known weakness for street food. A hundred yards from the station he stopped at a carryout stand called the Golden Stag, where he ordered a weisswurst with fries, which he daubed with the curry-infused ketchup meant for the sausage.

A second wurst finished, he walked to the small family-run hotel across the street and found a leather sofa with a view of the front door. He dropped his jacket on the seat to mark his place, then went to the gift shop to ask for the *International Herald Tribune.* It was sold out, so he took the one remaining copy of *Le Monde,* not his favorite Paris newspaper, but it would have to do.

In ten minutes, Ahmed walked through the door and stood blinking in the dim light, then sat down at the other end of the sofa. He placed a cheap briefcase on the floor between them.

"Our friend asked me to bring this to you," he said, speaking softly. "Burner phone."

"What's happening?"

"Eddie's safe, and should be almost back to Paris by now. I haven't heard from Jen Wetzmuller, but she might be with them."

"I need to get there too," Paul said. He had no idea what had happened to Jen. "The police think I'm taking the train and might be watching. If I walk over to the station, would you pick me up at a side entrance and take me to the airport? I can get another car there."

"I can do better than that. I'll pick you up, then I'll get out at a subway station and you take my car."

A half hour later, Paul was turning onto the autobahn toward Paris. He quickly dialed the same number he'd reached from the railway station.

"On the way."

"The others are only a couple of hours out," Icky told him. "Contact them as you get closer."

"Are they all there? I heard we were missing one."

"Nope. And FYI, that one is one of us. Has been since before her father was killed."

"I'll be damned." It was all Paul could think of to say.

Hôtel-Dieu

This is the first time I've held a council of war in a hospital," Philippe said to the group. But he and Icky had decided Eddie must be involved, even though he was still groggy, and the chief neurologist Dr. Santange had been just as insistent that Eddie could not leave until the effects of the unknown anesthetic had been diagnosed — it could be something harmless, or it could be something with long-term ill effects.

As midnight approached, Philippe finally gave in. "OK," he said. "Where's your conference room? Roll him in there where he can listen and that's where we'll meet."

The meeting had started by the time Aurélie arrived. She was not surprised to see Philippe at the head of the table, but she was astounded to find Jen at the other end. She ignored both to run to Eddie's side. He smiled as she leaned in to kiss him.

"Glad to see you again," he said hoarsely.

"Oh, Eddie," she said, then kissed him again, then stopped as she realized she had begun to cry and her tears were falling on his face. "Sorry," she said, as she used her sleeve to dry them.

"What's going on there?" Icky's peremptory voice came from the speakerphone in the center of the table. "We need to get this show on the road."

Philippe responded to him. "Just stand by a minute, Icky. Aurélie just arrived and is saying hello to Eddie."

"Sorry," he said. "Aurélie, whenever you're ready."

Aurélie briefly embraced her father, then turned to look for a seat. Jen asked Paul to move down one place to make room for her. Jen broke the uncomfortable silence by walking quickly to Aurélie and embracing her warmly. "Eddie will be fine. He'll go back to sleep in a minute or two."

Dr. Santange, who had been standing nearby watching, said, "I know he looks pretty sick now, but we think the anesthetics were just that and there should be no serious after-effects. You should be able to take him home tomorrow."

Icky's voice boomed again from the speaker in the center of the table. "We may have a bad situation here and we need to get on it. Is everybody there now? I want to answer everbody's unspoken question.

"Jen Wetzmuller has been working with me for more than four years. She can tell you more when things calm down, but it's enough to say that my people got wind of Al Sommers's interest in the Raphael painting and needed someone who could get close to him, in a white van. We had good information that he was one end of a stolen-goods pipeline that stretched to Paris.

"I called Roy Castor for ideas and he suggested his daughter, who already owned an art gallery. That put her in a perfect position to keep an eye on Sommers and his buddies. We were after the foreigners, since we can't do domestic law enforcement, so Jen also reported to the Sarasota sheriff's office. She did a great job at considerable risk and personal sacrifice.

"After Roy died, she spent a while in our training program in Virginia, then set out to find Claude Khan in Europe. She's been working him since. We're almost there now, so let's figure out a way to close the trap."

The room was silent. Paul looked first at Jen, then at Eddie, guilt written on his face. Eddie appeared to be asleep.

Aurélie immediately understood the magnitude of what she'd heard. Eddie had rejected Jen because of her cover story, not because of who she really was.

Philippe broke the silence. "We know Khan left Munich, and Eddie heard him say he was going to Paris. We think the missiles are close to him. If your goal is to splash an Airbus or two, where do you do it? At an airport, of course. But which airport? And when?"

Jeremy spoke up. "I have one possible lead. Albert Cate gave me an introduction to a woman who was Khan's friend and may still be. He says she runs a sort of Asian goods general store, one of several on Avenue du Général Leclerc. It's not too far from where the kidnappers took Aurélie."

Philippe nodded. "We've had patrol officers watching it from time to time since you called me, but they haven't seen anyone who looks like Khan. But a lot of those old buildings are connected through their basements, so it would just be blind luck if we saw him."

Jeremy said, "Tomorrow is Saturday. Let's pay a call on her as soon as she opens."

"That might be too late." Icky's voice boomed, too loud, and Jen reached to turn down the volume. "Philippe, with all the records you guys keep on everybody, can't you find out where to find this woman tonight, and go see her? Khan doesn't seem to leave joy in his wake, so maybe she would even talk to you."

"I think that's a better idea. I'll find her." Philippe's fingers flew across the iPhone screen as he texted his request to the préfecture.

"Here's why we need to move now," Icky said. "My guys have been filtering through the airline schedules, looking for targets that might interest somebody who wanted to do something really spectacular, a sort of 9/11 all over again.

"The shrinks tell us the most damaging way to cripple the aviation system would be to shoot down both a Boeing and an Airbus, one American, one European. The Airbus would make the Europeans mad as hell, but there's the risk some of our less broad-minded congressmen might not care quite so much about a French airplane, so you'd also need a Boeing to focus their attention.

"A little after 5 p.m., a 747 to Los Angeles and a 380 to Singapore are scheduled to leave. They are both usually on time and use the parallel runways a few minutes apart, or less. And that happens only one time during the week. Saturday."

Jen spoke for everyone in the room when she asked, "So you think tomorrow's the day?"

"It could be. The longer he's on the loose in Paris, the riskier it is for him. I think you should plan on tomorrow."

Phillipe added, "We have a lookout notice in force but I'm not hopeful we'll find him. We don't know what car he's driving or where he stays. We have plainclothes officers on the Chechen lawyer's office."

"The banker, too," Eddie croaked from his bed. "Watch Henri Gascon."

"Would he dare go there?" Philippe asked. "Maybe so. I'll put him on the list, but he's a pretty sensitive subject with the politicians."

His iPhone chirped and he quickly read a message on the screen. "We got around Filer's security. They'll look through it as quickly as they can. Jeremy and Walker, can you come with me to find the store owner? The rest of you, go home and get some sleep. Eddie will have to stay here at least tonight."

Dr. Santange nodded.

As the group broke up, Aurélie leaned toward Jen and said, "Come stay with me tonight. I want to know what's happened to Eddie the last few days."

Jen hesitated. She couldn't tell if it was a tentative act of friendship or just a search for information. She decided on the spur of the moment trust was the best approach and replied, "That would be nice. I could sure use a shower."

Philippe had a police driver drop him off at the préfecture and take Aurélie and Jen to the Hotel Luxor. Jeremy and Walker agreed to meet him a half hour later at the préfecture, a short walk from the hospital. Paul, exhausted after the loss of a night's sleep and all the attention in the German hospital, went home to bed, with a stern admonishment that the others should call him the minute anything new developed.

CHAPTER TWENTY-ONE

Paris, Rue Saint-Roch

Y'know," Jen mused, "I sat in this chair the first time I was ever in this apartment, three years ago when I brought my father's letter to Eddie. And he sat where you are now."

She reached for another of the small open-faced ham sandwiches Aurélie had made on thin slices of rye bread. They were well into their second glasses of good Burgundy and feeling relaxed. Aurélie was finding, to her surprise, that she liked Jen — and, to her surprise, Jen didn't seem to have designs on Eddie.

"The shower was great. I needed just an ordinary bath right now. The last shower I took, this morning, I had to wash Sonny Perry's blood off me."

"You killed him?" Aurélie was incredulous.

"Not much choice. He made it very clear to me that neither Eddie nor I would survive the day. He was trying to rape me, so I grabbed the handiest weapon I could reach, a heavy crystal table lamp. I diverted him by making him think I'd heard a noise outside the door. When he pointed the gun away from me, I hit him."

"I'm surprised you have an appetite after that," Aurélie said.

"I didn't, but it's been a long day and we still have work to do."

"I was curious about tonight, at the meeting. I pretty much expected to find you in handcuffs, or at least under serious suspicion, but it looked to me like you were running the meeting." She took another sip.

"And now everybody knows I'm not what I seem," Jen responded. "Icky says I can tell the story to close friends who might think my behavior has been strange, which God knows it has been. It will be dangerous if we don't catch Khan, but the risk to me will be the least of our problems, far behind shooting down a couple of jetliners."

"So you're working with Icky?"

Jen giggled. "I've been what he calls an 'unofficial' since at least a year before I came here with the letter. But now Icky says he has some other work for me to do. That's something I really shouldn't tell you, but you deserve to know. I'll move to Washington when we get Khan."

"But... I thought you were in trouble in Sarasota."

"We went to a lot of effort to make it look that way," Jen responded. "The police helped. They put out the word I was under suspicion for stealing customer money, then said I'd given up everything I had to settle the case and moved away. That's the only way I was able to make contact with Khan. I had to act like I was on the run from Sarasota and needed a job in Germany."

"So you didn't have to pay customers or anything like that?"

"No, thank God, or I'd really be broke now. Icky handled transferring my money and my inheritance to a bank in Austria, where it sits to this day. I had to convince Khan I was really poor, so I haven't been able to touch it or the salary the Agency pays me. I'll be glad when this sham is over and done with."

"So you're not just a volunteer, but a paid agent?"

"I suppose so. I went through some very tough training in Virginia and the Everglades before they would let me chase Khan.

"You know, the CIA has almost lost the art of human intelligence, of getting close to the enemy. We would never have unmasked Khan with drones, but I was able to work my way into his inner circle because I developed a human relationship with him. I feel pretty good about that, and so do Icky and some of his friends who are trying to push the Agency back toward its roots."

Aurélie sat back, amazed. She knew Eddie would be even more amazed, and disappointed as well that the true story had been kept from him. He would also feel guilty because he'd told Aurélie how angry he'd been at Jen for being so close to Sonny and Al Sommers and Khan's other co-conspirators. And now it had turned out to be a show — although Aurélie could understand why Icky held the secret so tightly. Eddie probably would understand eventually, but he would never be happy about it.

CHAPTER TWENTY-TWO

Paris, Place Denfert-Rochereau

"Fortunately for us, Filer wasn't very creative about his main password, so maybe he was sloppy with his email as well," Philippe said. He and Walker waited in a borrowed conference room at the préfecture for the name and address of the shop owner, and hoped for more results from the computer wizards. "If that's the case we may get a shortcut; if not, it's more detective work for us."

In a few minutes, a uniformed woman came into the borrowed conference room and handed him a sheet of paper. "Monsieur le commissaire, here is the address you requested." Phillippe thanked her briefly, then turned his attention to the page.

"*Merde!*" he said. "This whole affair is taking place in one neighborhood. The owner lives above her store, in the same building.

"We already have officers in street clothes watching it, so we won't need anyone else. Let's go see what she has to say."

Place Denfert-Rochereau was only a short drive past the Sorbonne on the Left Bank, and late at night there was hardly any traffic. Philippe's driver had them in front of the old apartment building in less than fifteen minutes. He didn't need his blue light, but he used it anyway.

While Philippe crossed the street to brief the detective sitting on a bench trying to look like one of the neighborhood's homeless men, Jeremy looked around the street. It was still busy despite the hour — he counted three open restaurants, including one next door, where a waiter was stacking chairs in preparation for mopping the floor, but customers still sat at the tables with their final expressos of the evening. The sidewalk tables had already been pushed back into a military line against the glass.

The Asian Market — that was the store's name, in English — was tightly closed, a steel grate rolled down in front of the display window. In the dim night lighting, Jeremy could make out the small tables, chairs, suitcases, and other inexpensive imports that would be set out haphazardly on the sidewalk when the store opened the next morning. There was a cash register to his right just inside the door, and halfway back he could see the top of a spiral stair leading to the basement.

Philippe returned and called all three of them together into a huddle. "Good news and bad news. We got into Filer's Gmail. The wizards haven't read everything yet, but they did find one draft that hadn't been sent. It didn't have a recipient on it, but it sounds like it must have been for Icky.

"It says Khan was after airliners, and as we suspected he thought a big catastrophe would bump the price of gold. And he listed the same two flights Icky told us about, the ones that will leave Charles de Gaulle around five o'clock, but no date.

"And he said he was pretty sure Henri the banker is in on the whole thing and isn't just a passive investor. He was less sure about his congressman brother, but very suspicious."

"Wow," said Jeremy. "I guess we better get to work. What floor does this woman live on?"

"Fifth. Almost at the top," Philippe said. "Let's get going."

He used his master key to bypass the digital lock on the building door, then pressed the stairway light button in the small lobby. Most old Paris apartment buildings, especially the small ones, do not have elevators, and this was no exception.

There were two apartment doors on the fifth floor, both "blindée," or armored, which the French insurance companies require. A small nametag on one identified the resident as A. Nyugen. "Refugee from Vietnam," Walker muttered as he read it.

Philippe pressed the bell once. The chime echoed through the interior. When there was no response, he pressed it again, twice this time, and in a few seconds they were rewarded by the sound of soft shoes shuffling across the wooden floor.

"Who is it?" a small voice called.

"Police, Madame Nguyen, and we need to speak to you urgently. Please open the door." Philippe tried to be polite until he knew how she would respond to their questions.

They heard the sound of locks opening, and then the door opened a crack, as far as its security chain would allow.

"May I see your papers?" Philippe held out his identity card to her, just as the stairwell light went off. Jeremy pressed the button to light it again.

Madame Nguyen appeared satisfied. She released the chain and opened the door wide, inviting them to enter and follow her to the living room. The walls of the hallway were covered with Asian paintings and prints, and two small tables held brass and stone statuary. Walker, who had his own collection of Asian art, was certain none of it had ever been on sale in her shop.

Madame Nguyen had pulled on a flowing blue kimono decorated with embroidered poppies. The dress and her gray hair, plus her faded but unmistakable beauty, made a striking impression. She also spoke impeccable French, and Philippe complimented her on it.

"Young man, do not confuse the way I look with my identity. I am as French as you are. My father was a consular official in Hanoi until we had to leave. I have probably lived in Paris longer than you. As you can see, I am quite old. There's no hiding that simple fact."

"You wear your years very lightly, Madame," Philippe responded. "And thank you for seeing us this late at night. I am Commissaire Cabillaud, and these two American gentlemen are helping me. May I introduce M. Evans and General Bentham?"

"Are you a real general?" she asked, turning to Jeremy.

"Yes, Madame, I am," he said. "And I have a question for you." He took from his wallet the half of the card Cate had given him in Leipzig.

"Are you familiar with this card?"

"Yes, of course. The other half came in the mail from my friend Albert in Germany, and he told me I should help the person who brought its match. I will help you any way I can."

Philippe turned his iPhone toward her and asked, "Do you know this man?"

She looked at the screen, then at Philippe. "Of course. That's Claude. He and Albert used to work together in Germany, and from time to time they would come to see me here. That is before I was reduced to running a store."

"Have you seen Claude recently?" Walker asked the question.

"It has been some time. We do not visit as much as we used to, mainly because of my age. I don't think he finds me as attractive as he once did. He does honor his promises, however." A note of bitterness had crept into her voice, and all three men noticed it.

"What sort of promises has he made to you?" Philippe asked.

"Oh, he pays the rent on my store. In exchange for that, he can use the apartment in the basement. He has not been there in months, but I believe one of his associates visited last week. I can't be sure."

Philippe asked, "You don't see them come through the store?"

"There's no need for that. You see, the apartment was a hiding place for the Resistance during the war, and they built a separate entrance through the back door of the building two doors down, facing the back courtyard, and another through the basement next door, which leads to the catacombs. I never see Claude or his guests unless they make a point of coming to see me." Her expression told them plainly that she was not happy about the situation.

"Do you have any way to reach him?"

"I have a telephone number for somewhere in Germany, but the last time I tried it no longer worked. I can leave a message for him at the storage box down the street, but there's no way of knowing how soon he will see it."

Philippe asked gently, "Madame Nguyen, it sounds as if your relationship with Claude was once more than just a commercial relationship. Could you tell me more about it? It could be important."

"We were lovers for many years, even during the time I was married. When it began I was young and beautiful and we had a wonderful time. He said he was a businessman from West Germany. I soon learned he was an East German spy, but the war was long over and I didn't care. I saw him once a month for thirty years until he tired of me. He still paid the rent and I let him use the apartment, but now I sense he's involved in something new — something darker.

"All his visitors recently have been Russians. Not Moscow Russians, business types, but country Russians. I think most of them are from Chechnya, and they are very rough people. He is up to something very bad now, and I don't want to be part of it."

"What do you base this feeling on?"

"Good information. My friend Albert in Leipzig told me to stay away from Claude because he is about to get into serious trouble, or cause serious trouble for someone else. In either case, I want nothing more to do with him."

"From where do you know Albert?" It seemed natural for Jeremy to pose the question.

"He was the husband I told you about."

Philippe left the room to call for reinforcements, including a policewoman to sit with Madame Nguyen. He believed her story, but would not take the chance that she might change her mind and try to warn Khan, so someone would have to keep her away from the telephone.

During his absence, Jeremy and Walker had continued to get information from her. They were reasonably certain her memory was sound — in fact, she seemed sharp and focused. Walker, who had recruited many agents during his clandestine years, was satisfied she was the spy's worst nightmare, the woman scorned, and was determined to say anything she could to make trouble for Khan, without being overt about it.

∫

"Yes, of course," Madame Nguyen said when Philippe asked her to take them to Khan's apartment. She took a ring of keys from a hook behind the front door, then led then down the stairs to the narrow entrance corridor. They went out a back door to a paved courtyard facing a small but elegant house that looked like it belonged in a much more prominent neighborhood. "That house was made from stone quarried just under our feet," she said. "The mayor of the *arrondissement* lives there. It's close to the city hall and it's quiet, but I don't think he has any idea a German spy has been going in and out past his front door."

A dozen paces to the left, she stopped at an unmarked service door and entered a code on the keypad. Inside, in the dim night light of the service corridor, they could just make out a door painted the same color as the wall — not exactly a secret entrance, but one that would not be obvious to a searcher who wasn't looking for it.

It opened smoothly toward them. Madame Nguyen reached inside to turn on the light but Philippe put out his hand and whispered, "Let's use my flashlight."

In its beam, they saw an old but brightly whitewashed stairway leading down to the building's storage cave, where the residents kept all the accumulated belongings they could not cram into their small closets.

Philippe asked Walker to remain with Madame Nguyen, then led Jeremy down to the cave. It was lined on both sides with storage rooms crudely assembled from unpainted wood, each with an apartment number and a padlock.

"Number four left, that's the number, and here's her *cave*," Philippe muttered, more to himself than to Jeremy. He selected a small key from the ring she had given him and tried the padlock. No fit. His fingers searched for another one and found it. This one turned smoothly in the lock.

The old hinges on the door squealed as he pulled it open to reveal a room the size of a walk-in closet, lined with unpainted shelves overflowing with the detritus of an old woman's household — a rusty iron, two dusty fans, an old vacuum cleaner, and hundreds of books, many of them turning brown with age.

"We're looking for a semi-hidden door behind one of these old bookcases," Philippe told Jeremy. "During the war it was even better hidden, but Mrs. Nguyen told me Khan had an entire layer of stone removed to make it easier to get in and out.

"You start to the left and I'll start on the right. Let's take a little of this junk off each of these shelves until we find it."

After no more than five minutes Jeremy said quietly, "Here it is." He had removed a plastic sack containing sheets and towels, which had hidden the edge of a door painted carefully to resemble the stone wall.

Together they removed everything from the shelves that blocked the door, then the shelves themselves, and Philippe opened it with the largest key on the ring Madame Nguyen had given him.

"Somebody went to a hell of a lot of work to make this hidey-hole," Jeremy said admiringly as he looked through the door. A corridor led to the right, then down another flight of stairs, at the bottom of which was a small lobby with a half inch of water standing in it.

"Go back and get her," Philippe said. "It will be better if she calls when we open the door."

Madame Nguyen walked slowly down the stairs, then nodded when Philippe asked if she was ready. He turned the key, trying not to act in a surreptitious way, and touched her on the shoulder.

"Claude?" she called out. "Claude, are you in there?"

Silence. Philippe urged her to step back up on the stairs and drew his pistol. Jeremy already had his in hand and led the way as they pressed in.

Empty, as she had predicted. They found a minuscule two-bedroom apartment laid out much like Khan's house near Munich, with one bedroom for the master of the house and another with four bunks for the staff. All the beds were made and it appeared no one had been there for weeks. The refrigerator was empty and had been turned off.

"This is really tight," Jeremy said. "It wouldn't be pleasant to spend much time down here. The bunkroom reminds me of the way sailors live aboard ship."

"Let's look for cameras, just in case," Philippe said. "I'd hate to have them show up outside if they're watching." But a ten-minute examination of corners, bookcases, and the small recesses that make up every very old stone house turned up nothing. Nor were there intrusion detectors on the door.

"They plan to be away a while," Philippe said after the search. He asked Walker and Madame Nguyen to come in and asked her to see if anything seemed out of place.

"This is always how it looks. If he is coming and will arrive late, I put a little food in the refrigerator sometimes, but his people handle the laundry and the housekeeping. This is cleaner than usual, though."

Philippe asked her, "May our forensic investigators come in and search? They'll do their best not to harm anything." He was being polite. Within two hours the investigators would have the apartment and everything around it torn down to its basic structure. If there was anything to find, they would find it.

"If they're careful, of course. Now would you like me to show you the storage lockers? You might find something interesting there."

∫

They retraced their steps to the courtyard outside the mayor's house, but she led them to the left into another courtyard. Behind a medical clinic stood a small building whose facade seemed to consist entirely of steel doors. Ahead, through a broad arch supporting the building above, they could see Avenue du Général Leclerc, with the last restaurant closing up across the street.

"First let's see if our reinforcements are here," Philippe said as he walked through the arch.

In less than a minute he returned, but not with the police officers Jeremy and Walker had expected. Behind him came Aurélie and Jen, one walking on each side of Eddie, not exactly supporting him but offering encouragement and stability.

"What the hell?" Jeremy said. "Eddie, I thought you were supposed to be in the hospital until morning."

Eddie's voice was much stronger than it had been a few hours earlier. "Too much to do, so I called Aurélie and asked her to come get me."

"We've found his safe house," Philippe told the three. "Thanks to Madame Nguyen, we know Khan hasn't been in it for several weeks, and it certainly doesn't look lived in. Now we're going to check out a storage locker he keeps here."

Madame Nguyen acknowledged the newcomers with a nod. "The manager of this place lives in the old concierge's apartment in the basement of that medical office." She took Philippe's arm and pulled him toward a staircase leading down to what looked like a service entrance.

"He won't be happy to be yanked out of bed after midnight," Jeremy said.

Eddie replied, "Tough. If he can help us find what we're looking for, Philippe can pin a medal on him."

He turned to Aurélie and said with a grin, "I think she likes Philippe."

"All the old ladies like Philippe. The great surprise of my teenage years was to learn that my friends' mothers all thought he was the sexiest man alive."

In ten minutes Philippe came back with the manager, a short man with disheveled brown hair who brought with him the unmistakable aroma of cheap wine, and a great deal of it.

"I can't let you in Mr. Khan's locker until he gives permission," he protested.

"Good. We'll take you to a holding cell at the préfecture and maybe let you call him in two or three days. In the meantime, my men will break the locks on every one of these doors until we find what we're looking for."

The manager shrugged as if to say, "So what?" He walked around the corner of the building and pointed at two storage units with rolling overhead doors. "These are the ones," he said. "I do not have the keys."

"We have our own keys," Philippe responded, then waved at a beefy policeman who had been waiting under the arch that led out to the street. The policeman walked quickly to the first of the doors, and Jeremy noticed for the first time that he was carrying a large bolt cutter. He made quick work of the two padlocks and pushed both doors up with a clatter.

Philippe's flashlight probed the corners of the first locker, picking out a large shape at the back.

"The refrigerator case," Eddie said.

"He buys those from me," Jen said. "Why would he have one of them here?"

"When I saw it last it didn't contain a refrigerator, but eight Russian anti-aircraft missiles called manpads. Let's look at it, but I think I know what we'll find."

Philippe and Jeremy tipped the carton on its side. It was lighter than it had been in Bulgaria, and two of the four crates of missiles were missing.

"So now we know four missiles are in the wild somewhere," Eddie said.

Madame Nguyen said, "He had an old VW camping bus in the other locker, but it's not there now. The manager told me he came in to get it just today. I guess that's really yesterday, since it's already Saturday. He thought it was odd, because Claude usually sends one of his Russians, but this time he came along himself."

Philippe turned to the manager. "I want the license plate number of that VW."

He stammered and hesitated. "I don't think I have it."

"You know you're required to. Go get it for us." He jerked his head toward the office, then signaled the beefy policeman to go with him.

"If we get that number, we'll query all the speed and red-light cameras in the area. I'll start a watch on the airport, but they've probably exchanged it for something else so that will be a long shot. And much as I hate to do it, I'll wake up the prefect and ask him to get the Army involved. We need to find him, if possible without shutting down the airport, because that would just tell him to try again another day."

After a tense five minutes, the manager returned carrying a slip of paper. He handed it to Philippe.

"A Munich plate," Philippe said to the policeman. "Find out whose it is, then wait for my orders."

CHAPTER TWENTY-THREE

Charles De Gaulle Airport

Claude Khan had driven the rattly old VW Vanagon away from the storage locker only a few hours before Philippe arrived with Madame Nguyen and his small crew of volunteers. He turned down Boulevard Arago and passed the hulking stone walls of Santé Prison on his way to Gare de Lyon, twenty minutes away on the Right Bank, where he would meet his most important confederate: the manager of Vitaliy Budzivoi's restaurant in Nice.

An offer of 5,000 euros had persuaded Vladi to take three days off from his job managing Chez Budzivoi. Khan threw in a round-trip ticket on the TGV, first class, and was waiting at the station when his train arrived. They shook hands then walked quickly to the camper, which Khan had parked in an underground garage a block away.

They sat briefly in the van as Khan briefed him.

"I know you've done this before," he said. "I haven't. Tell me — is it hard to do?"

"It's not hard if you pay attention. Are you going to shoot?"

"Not me. I can't sit still long enough. Bad back. It will be an American named Sonny Perry, who is supposed to be here some time overnight and will meet us at the airport. I think he was in the Army, but he probably hasn't used this kind of missile" — he pointed with his thumb at the crates in the back of the van.

"So you have four missiles plus the gripstocks. That's good. A man can get off two shots and still get away, but that's all. What is our escape plan?"

"We're going to get another van," Khan told him. "You'll park it at the hotel and use it to get away. There will be no record of it, it won't be hot, and you can drive it straight back to Nice."

"OK. I'll burn it in the slums. That happens there all the time."

Khan and Vladi worked their way south around Place d'Italie shortly before the rush hour began. They passed Santé Prison, then turned south toward the Porte d'Orléans. A few miles outside the city proper, they pulled into a dilapidated used-car lot that specialized in renting vans and light trucks to contractors long on cash but short on legal identity papers.

The owner was a Syrian, still young, who already had the air of a seedy small-time merchant. Khan accepted his first price for the three-day rental of a five-year-old Ford van. It had once been white, but now was pocked with the colorful stigmata of uncounted fender-benders.

"It isn't pretty but it runs good, so long as you don't load it down too much," the Syrian said confidently. "What are you planning to carry in it?"

"Just a few hundred pounds, mostly machinery parts," Khan told him. "It will all be around Paris, no long highway driving."

"OK, then. Just bring it back by this time Monday." He made a copy of Khan's driver's license and took his cell phone number.

"If anything goes wrong I can always talk to Hamid's friends, eh?" he said with a grin. Hamid was — had been — the owner of a small restaurant near Montmartre, but was now serving fifteen years in Santé for beheading Erich Kraft. Khan jumped at the mention of Hamid, because he planned a visit to the man's restaurant, the Café Stop, later in the day. It was an unpleasant surprise to learn his connection to Hamid was so widely known.

Vladi drove the van, and Khan followed in the VW. They stopped at the edge of a quiet park a mile away to move one crate of missiles and one of the gripstocks from the VW into the van, then separated. Vladi pulled the Ford onto the *périphérique,* the crowded beltway built on the route of the city's protective walls, while Khan headed back toward the city and pulled into an underground parking garage. He left the VW in the most remote spot he could find.

Then he walked quickly to the métro stop a hundred yards away. A half hour later, he walked out of the Barbès-Rochechouart station at the foot of Montmartre. Five hundred yards uphill, past the row of sidewalk cafés occupied by Maghrebien men sipping small cups of aromatic coffee — there was not a glass of wine to be seen — he stepped through the door of the Café Stop.

Café Stop had been left in the care of Hamid's cousin Jamal. Khan suspected Jamal wasn't a real cousin, just a trusted member of the same tribe.

"Claude! You're here at just the right time," Jamal said jovially as he emerged from the kitchen door at the back of the small room, wiping soapy water on his dirty apron. "Let's go upstairs."

On the floor above, as is usual for many Parisian shops and restaurants, an apartment served as the office. In this case, it also served as a meeting place for Khan's old network of Middle Eastern friends, although it had been inactive since Hamid's arrest three years before. It was Khan who'd given Hamid the order to remove Erich Kraft's head in a way that would send a visible signal to any other members of the group who might have thoughts of failure.

"Were you able to put the deal together?" Khan asked.

"Sure. You want the Lincoln for a couple of days. My contact is in that business. He has one that's just a couple of years old that he rents out to the other *noirs* in his neighborhood up in the *banlieu*. He wants a thousand euros for three days. All the paperwork is current, so you'll have no trouble if the police stop you."

"That's kind of expensive, isn't it?"

"He suspects we're not renting it for a wedding."

Jamal served as an informal leasing agent for the car among the North Africans, whose reluctance to mix with the black sub-Saharan Africans gave the transaction a margin of safety. Who would connect a Lincoln rented in Montmartre with an owner in the suburban slums? And Jamal had an additional layer of security because nothing on paper connected the deal to him.

"It's high but that's OK this time. Where do I find it?" Khan asked.

"It's in the Chateau Rouge garage. Second level down, turn right when you come out of the stairs and go to the end of the row. It's the second car from the end."

He took Khan's ten crisp 100-euro notes and gave him the key and a parking ticket.

"Just leave it at the same place, with the key under the seat. We'll pick it up in three days, same time." When Khan was safely out the door he counted the bills into equal batches: half for the car, half for him.

Khan covered the two blocks quickly. In forty-five minutes, he was back at the parking garage at Porte d'Orléans, where he switched the missiles to the capacious trunk of the Lincoln, then locked the VW and left. He would have no need for it again. If the police should trace it to the garage, to make things a little harder for them he tossed the keys into a trash bin as soon as he left the exit ramp. They landed in a farrago of fast-food wrappers and sank out of sight.

As he headed onto the beltway toward the airport, he picked up his cell phone and tried once again to reach Sonny Perry. The call went immediately to voicemail, just like the other dozen times he'd tried. It was clear something was wrong, and it was the worst possible time for problems.

His original plan had been straightforward. Sonny would go to the airport and shoot down at least one airliner, then escape. Vladi would try to do the same at the other end of the runway. Khan had decided not to wait for the two massive airliners leaving at the same time. For one thing, they might not take off close enough together. For another, the missiles were old, and there was a good chance one of them would fail. Hell, there was a chance two or more of them would fail. For all the thousands of missiles Khadafy had left behind, the Qaeda boys had only been successful with a few. In many cases they hadn't fired at all, and in others they had missed their targets. In a few cases they were defeated by anti-missile laser systems being installed on more and more new aircraft.

But all that aside, what he planned should be easy, if no one was expecting it. Just in case that snake Filer had been able to get the word out about the two airplanes, Khan would throw up another roadblock by moving up the schedule. He'd told Vladi to take his shot at 2 p.m. precisely, and Sonny would follow his lead.

By the time Khan took the off-ramp for De Gaulle airport, Vladi had safely checked into his room on the top floor of a new Hotel Quick a half mile from the west end of the CDG runways. It was five stories tall, with the flat roof he needed, and stood almost alone in a field that until a year or two before had been farmland.

He found a parking place close to the front door, then told the desk clerk he'd be there for three days.

From the parking lot, he watched carefully as planes took off from the parallel runways. Planes leaving the runways on the north side of the terminal were lower because those runways extended closer to the hotel. Because they took off further away from him, planes from the southern runways had more time to climb, but would still be in range of his missiles. They were rated for use against any airplane flying under 10,000 feet, and they weren't nearly that high when they passed over the hotel.

CHAPTER TWENTY-FOUR

Hotel Rouge

The sun was still half-visible above the horizon as Khan drove into the parking lot of a six-story chain hotel, the Rouge, at the other end of the runways. He'd avoided making a reservation so there could be no trace of a call from him, and he was confident the Lincoln was anonymous enough to buy him at least a few hours.

He checked in using a Bulgarian passport — fake, but good fake, converted from one left behind by a sailor who had fallen overboard one night when the Black Sea was at its roughest. Khan had been accompanying a load of land mines and small-arms ammunition into Chechnya at the time, and saw an opportunity.

Khan had spent a lifetime absorbing the spy's essential knowledge of how to take advantage of the smallest opportunity. The sailor had the bad luck to match his age and size, which meant that only the picture would have to be changed — the description could remain. A knock on the head with a sand-filled sock, a push over the rail, a little work by an expensive forger in Paris and Khan had one more name to add to his gallery of identities.

∫

While the police were breaking into his storage lockers, Khan was sound asleep in his top-floor room, the remains of a room-service dinner resting outside his door.

His alarm went off at 2 a.m. He awakened instantly, pulled on his shoes, and took the elevator to the lobby, where he retrieved a luggage cart and went to the Lincoln.

There, he carefully removed the missiles from their wooden crate and wrapped them in a blanket he'd laid on the cart. The heavy cylindrical batteries and the single gripstock went into a large canvas tote, which he set on the cart before retracing his steps and, with a sigh of relief, locking the door behind him. The missiles slid smoothly under the bed and the tote went into the closet. He returned the luggage cart to the lobby, then drove the Lincoln to the other end of the airport and left it at the Marriott. He caught a cab to Terminal 2A, then walked to Terminal 2E and took another cab back to his own hotel. The police never found out about the deception.

∫

The missiles would do him no good in his room, so he walked as quietly as he could up the stairs to the rooftop door. He had cased it a month before, so he was confident his skills were up to the job, but it took longer than he expected to pick the lock. He'd have to allow time for that when he returned for the main event.

He blocked the door open, then went back to his room for the delicate next step. He carried one missile wrapped in a blanket up the stairs and out the door. By the light of the red aircraft warning lights, he saw an air-conditioning duct that ran around the perimeter about a foot off the roof. He tucked the first missile under it, then returned for the second. He stood back and looked carefully — in the dim light they were almost invisible. He couldn't be sure how hard it would be to see them in the daytime, but he'd picked the best available hiding place and it would have to do.

Damn Sonny! With the missiles hidden the pressure was off for a while, so he gave in to his rage about Sonny's failure to show up on time. He'd been unreliable all along, but Khan recalled what had attracted them to each other. They were kindred souls — both were killers through and through.

Back in his room, he put his phone on the night table and opened a bottle of mineral water from the minibar. He plumped his pillow and sat back to watch an old American movie on the large TV. It would be a long night, but he was keyed up for the challenge. Two planes in one day! It would force the price of gold to stratospheric heights and ensure the success of his hedge fund. He would be set for life and no one would ever again ignore Claude Khan.

CHAPTER TWENTY-FIVE

Hotel Quick

At the Hotel Quick, Vladi had to be more creative. He wasn't a lock picker, so he would have to find his way to the roof by guile or by force, and he decided after a close look at the lock on the roof door that guile would be the better choice.

The way to the roof was through a small brick house containing elevator machinery and a large air-conditioning unit protected only by a thin door, which he was able to force open easily. Behind one of the big and noisy fans, he found an air-intake grill large enough for him to get out to the roof deck. He would be able to remove its metal screws in a few minutes.

He had moved his missiles to his room in much the same way Khan had. Now he wrapped them in a blanket and hid them on the floor behind the main air handler in the air-conditioning room. He took a screwdriver from the tote bag he'd used to bring up the gripstock and unscrewed all but two of the screws around the air grill. He was ready to go, and went back to his room to wait.

∫

Philippe's search of the traffic cameras had turned up a picture of the VW van hurrying through a red light as it made a right turn on the way to rent the Ford van. A flying squad of plainclothes officers, in teams of two, canvassed every car dealer along the decaying industrial strip, and it wasn't long before they stopped at the Syrian's small lot.

He wasn't communicative at all, at least until the smaller of the two policemen made clear they were on the trail of a serious criminal, that they would certainly catch him, and that anyone who tried to cover for him would be in deep *merde*.

It helped that the smaller policeman was from Syrian stock, too. He spoke vaguely of the need for French citizens to protect their country, whether they were born there as he was or had immigrated. But the flights of patriotic fervor — if he'd had a flag he would have wrapped himself in it — paled next to the pure unveiled threat visible in his dark eyes.

Well yes, he did now remember that beat-up VW van, the dealer said. Just yesterday a short man dressed all in brown came in driving it and rented a five-year-old Ford van in much the same condition. With him was a large man with no neck. They spoke Russian to each other. He knew because he had worked for one of the many Russian military bases in Syria before he was able to escape to *la belle France*, for which he and his family would be eternally grateful. He produced the copy of Khan's driver's license, which the policemen photographed and sent immediately to Philippe.

The minute Philippe learned the VW was Khan's, he placed an urgent call to the *préfet de police* — the chief of police. *Monsieur le préfet*, as he was addressed by everyone from rookie policemen to the President of the Republic, had been Philippe's friend for the entire thirty years they had been on the force together. The prefect had so much trust in Philippe, in fact, that he'd been heard to say Philippe would have been the better man for his job, and would have been appointed if he'd had a better political touch. That is, if he'd romanced the politicians as well as he did the women.

Philippe told him quickly that he planned to open the special situations war room deep under the préfecture, a step that was taken only in cases of extreme urgency. He also intended to ask the Army to participate from the outset, because their equipment and possibly their soldiers would be needed. Armed soldiers in groups of three already patrolled all the airport terminals and would be useful eyes and ears if Khan planned any action within the airport itself. Philippe thought that not very likely, but he had to consider the possibility.

By 11 a.m., the Army had flown two Tiger attack helicopters to a remote maintenance hangar. Their support crews and extra ammunition would arrive in an hour.

Police in unmarked cars flooded the streets around the airport, focusing on the small towns clustered within a few miles of the runways.

The first few hours were fruitless, but that changed at noon when two traffic policemen driving a small Peugeot spotted the white van at the Hotel Quick. They drove past without stopping, as they'd been instructed, then called the operations center. Philippe's assistant Gabriel had taken responsibility for the location tracker, a wall of plasma screens showing the map of Greater Paris with every police car represented by a colored icon indicating its capabilities. It told him the two officers who'd spotted the van carried only sidearms, but less than a half mile away were two more carrying automatic weapons. He told all four to meet in a grocery store parking lot around a corner and out of sight of the Quick, then a few minutes later sent them to the hotel, with reinforcements to follow.

Philippe called Walker, who was pacing anxiously around a police substation in the airport, and offered him the chance to go along. He jumped at it and immediately caught a taxi to the Quick. The lieutenant in charge paired him with two experienced officers who were about to begin searching the top floor.

Six floors over their heads, Vladi wiped his room for fingerprints and any other signs of his presence then walked, with more confidence than he felt, up the stairs to the air-conditioning room.

Vladi had avoided listing the van on his room registration, however, which made the room-to-room search much tougher, but a painstaking comparison of the guest list against cars registered led them tentatively to Vladi.

The desk clerk remembered a hulking man who hadn't arrived on the shuttle, and who spoke French with a pronounced Russian accent.

It was a combination of pick-and-shovel detective work and twenty-first-century traffic monitoring that exposed him.

CHAPTER TWENTY-SIX

Hotel Quick

Vladi locked the door behind him and quickly removed the two remaining screws holding the grill, but left it in place while he listened to the pace and flow of takeoffs. Khan had told him to stay hidden until just before he took his shot to avoid the people who would certainly be watching the rooftops, including the crews of planes taking off.

Once he was confident there was a steady pattern of takeoffs, he pushed the two missiles and the tote bag onto the gravel roof and scrambled out after them.

A large air handler sat at each end of the roof. Vladi chose the one facing the door to the stairway and moved the missiles behind it. It gave him some cover from anyone who came through the door, while a low parapet offered some protection against being seen from the ground.

He fitted the gripstock to the first missile and carefully laid it within easy reach.

He sat back against the hot metal wall of the air handler, already wishing he'd brought a bottle of water — the sun was broiling, even on a cool September day. He took off his jacket and folded it into a cushion, then settled back to wait. The compact Beretta Khan had given him cut into his back, so he tucked it in the front of his belt. That was better.

Moving the show up to 2 p.m. had been good idea on Khan's part, Vladi thought. The longer they waited, the greater the chance something would go wrong, and he knew from his experience in the Russian Army that something — either a small something or a very large one — was bound to go wrong.

In fact, that something had already started. The police were spreading quickly through the hotel, clearing the rooms.

Each team of two carried a list of residents, and any they found in their rooms were asked to move to the lobby, but weren't allowed to leave the building.

The officers assigned to Vladi's floor reasoned that their target must be in his room because his van was in the parking lot. When there was no response to their knock, the backup man brought his rifle to the ready position and stood back. His partner carefully slid the card key through its slot, then pushed the door open. Both moved briskly into the room. Walker followed close behind.

"This is it," the man with the rifle said to his partner. "He's on the roof. Sound the alarm and let's get up there before he has time to do anything."

The roof door was locked. When they called back to the command post in the lobby, they learned that no one who had a key was working that day.

"You'll have to do it by force," the lieutenant in the lobby told them.

"What we need is a crowbar. Let's look around. Maybe there's something in one of the other rooms up here," the policeman with the rifle said. He put his hand on the door to the air-conditioning room and tried to turn the knob.

"Locked. But it's a light door. I bet we can kick it in."

"Let me," Walker said. "I'm heavier." He and the larger of the two policemen stood together with their backs against the wall opposite and waited for a departing plane to pass, hoping it would mask the sound they had to make. At the moment an Airbus roared overhead, they kicked the door as close to the lock as they could. It didn't yield the first time, but they quickly kicked it a second time and it flew open with a loud clatter.

Vladi heard the second kick and knew his time was up. He reached for the missile, intending to shoot at the Airbus that had just passed, but it got away before he could ready the missile. He immediately started scanning the runways for another candidate and saw a double-deck

A380 was second in line. It was a much heavier plane than the small A320 that had just passed, so would have to roll much further on the runway and would be at lower altitude when it passed him.

He held his breath as an American Airlines 777 taxied slowly into takeoff position, then waited. It was only a half minute or so, but seemed like hours to him.

The policemen, meanwhile, had crawled out of the mechanical room and crouched close to the brick wall as they surveyed the roof. Finally, one of them pointed at the tip of the missile's launch tube, which had just appeared above the air handler.

"He's behind an air handler on the east end of the building," one of them whispered into his microphone. "We're going to take him but you'd better launch the Tigers just in case."

The 777 disappeared into the distance, then the lumbering A380 began its roll. The policemen had a glimpse of part of the departure runway. One of them nudged the other and said, "They told us the target would be a big one, and that's the biggest. We need to move now."

The Chechen screwed the missile's battery into the gripstock and brought it to his shoulder. As the A380 left the ground. The policemen heard the high whistle that told them the missile's infrared tracking system had locked onto the target, and that the launch signal could come at any second. The missile would not launch until it was firmly locked onto the hot exhaust of the four huge jet engines.

The missile continued to whistle as the huge airplane rose higher. As it began its right turn, an instant before the missile would launch, each of the policemen fired a single shot.

One fired high, the other low. Vladi was barely visible above the air handler and the high bullet missed, but the low one tore into the sheet metal, passed through it, and struck him in the back, a painful but not fatal wound. He jerked and the missile lost its lock on the A380's hot exhaust. The whistle died.

Vladi put the missile on the roof as quickly as he could and pulled the Beretta from his waistband. He had the advantage of some protection, and they had none. As Walker and the two policemen tried to scramble behind the brick elevator house, Vladi fired four quick rounds. The heavy 9mm bullet struck one policeman squarely in the back of the head, killing him instantly. Another found Walker's shoulder, knocking him to the ground and sending his gun skittering across the gravel roof, but he was able to scramble behind the corner of the building with the second policeman.

Vladi felt his back. The bullet had opened a deep gash that was bleeding profusely, so he took the brown jacket and tied it as tightly as he could around the wound, then picked up the missile again.

By this time, the air traffic controllers had stopped all takeoffs from the airport and dispatched the planes back to the terminals, although several were still trying to turn around. The Chechen thought about trying to hit one of them on the ground, but the missile would not give him the launch signal. He took it off his shoulder and sat down to press the jacket firmly into his wound and missed the approach of the first Tiger, which roared overhead no more than fifty feet above him.

As it moved away, he picked up the missile and quickly tried to aim it. The Strela has a minimum range of 800 meters, and as the helicopter moved beyond that he heard the now-familiar whistle as he pulled back on the trigger. In less than a second it changed tone to the launch signal, and the missile ignited.

Its launch charge kicked it out of the tube, then the main solid-propellant rocket motor ignited, pushing it quickly to twice the speed of sound. It overtook the helicopter, whose crew started too late to release decoy flares.

The five-pound warhead exploded on the right-side engine exhaust. The helicopter shuddered and the engine burst into flames, then its pilot managed to get it under control and turned it back toward the airport, seeking the safety of his own base and its firefighting equipment, but made it only as far as the boundary fence, where it banked heavily to the left and, as it lost lift, fell to the ground. In a few seconds the entire helicopter was engulfed in flames. Neither of the crew escaped.

The two men flying the second Tiger had seen the entire drama. They'd been briefed that their target had two missiles, and they watched with cold-blooded fury as the man on the roof rushed to switch the gripstock from the first tube to the second. They knew they had only seconds to stop him, but they also knew they must keep their engine exhausts pointed away from him — modern manpads can fire head-on at their targets, but the old Russian ones must find the heat signature of an engine exhaust.

The pilot decided a direct approach was best and flew straight at the building. As it grew larger and larger in his windshield, the weapons officer behind armed the heavy anti-tank cannon in the chin turret. He put the crosshairs of the sight monitor directly on Vladi's chest and watched him pull the missile's trigger. It was an exercise in futility — the missile would not fire, but the helicopter could, and one burst of fewer than ten shells shattered the missile, shredded the air handler, and spread parts of Vladi's body across the roof. The last bullet passed through the elevator house and landed between Walker and the surviving policeman, who were lying pressed into the rough surface of the roof.

∫

Khan knew there was a chance, although he thought it was a small one, that the van would be found — but he thought there was zero chance the Lincoln would be discovered. What he didn't know was that Jamal held him personally responsible for the heavy sentence his uncle Hamid had received for killing Erich Kraft, and he saw a way to get in the good graces of the police. So he called them.

A man he knew was a terrorist, Jamal reported, had taken his car by force. "Terrorist" was the magic word. Within five minutes, Gabriel had dispatched two cars from the war room and sent Khan's picture to their phones. He alerted Philippe, who headed immediately for the Café Stop.

The four plainclothes officers arrived first, and by the time Philippe arrived they had confirmed it was Khan who took the car.

"How do you know this man Khan?" Philippe asked him.

"Hamid, my uncle, told me about him. He's the reason Hamid is in Santé for fifteen years."

At first Phillippe thought Jamal was a willing partner in Khan's plot, but as he probed further he became convinced that Jamal simply was on a vendetta against Khan — his own holy war. Probably for good reason, Philippe told himself.

He had Gabriel give the car's description and license number to the police around the airport, and within a half hour they spotted it in the parking lot of a Marriott Hotel a half mile from the Hotel Quick. But their search of the hotel's records found no mention of it.

"He's not in the Marriott," Philippe said. "Where is he? The car is a ruse, for sure. Keep the last Tiger up so it can watch the rooftops, and alert the control tower, too. They can see a lot of the buildings."

CHAPTER TWENTY-SEVEN

Gare du Nord

K han had found it easier to pick the lock on the roof door the second time.

He pulled the manpads from under the duct and carried them to a corner of the roof. If someone spotted him from the air, he would just be a workman doing maintenance, nothing to worry about.

He spread the blanket on the gravel roof, then laid out the two missiles. He installed the gripstock on one and set it down carefully next to the battery unit. Then he leaned back to wait for Vladi to make the first move.

He had a good view of the left runway, which they'd agreed would be his target. He watched as plane after plane took off, then sat up as he saw an A380 roll into takeoff position.

In the distance he heard what sounded like shots, perhaps from a handgun, and then he saw a Tiger helicopter take off, then a few seconds later he saw the telltale corkscrew smoke trail as Vladi's missile caught the Tiger in the exhaust.

"Shit!" Khan said out loud. "Now we have to do this all over again."

The A380 had been the last plane to take off or land, so it was apparent there would be no more opportunities.

He knew an aerial search of his and every other rooftop would follow and briefly considered trying to shoot down a police helicopter, but decided this would not be his day for martyrdom. That could come later, after he sold the gold.

∫

Game over, at least for now. He re-wrapped the missiles and slid them back under the air-conditioning duct, then walked down to his room.

Try once, try again, he told himself ruefully. At least he had four more missiles.

Khan was confident he'd thrown the police off the track by moving his car to the other end of the airport, near Vladi. For now they would focus on that area, but soon they would start paying close attention to every person in or around the airport. His best hope of escape would be to melt into the crowds. He would become just one among the million passengers passing through De Gaulle airport that day.

He could walk to the terminal in fifteen minutes, but a single man taking a stroll would look odd and probably invite questioning.

Instead, he joined the small knot of travelers waiting in the lobby for the airport shuttle. He took the last seat in the blue van, and in ten minutes got off at Terminal 2E with two other men.

The terminal was completely packed. Luggage trolleys stacked high with suitcases and cardboard boxes blocked the aisles and tired children wailed, even though outgoing flights had only been stopped for a half hour.

He worked his way slowly through the throng toward the rail station at the east end of the terminal. From there he could take the RER's busy Line B through the poor suburbs into downtown Paris. It was possible there would be identity checks, but he had his Bulgarian passport and had changed from his customary brown clothing into a red shirt with gray trousers and sweater. He would be almost invisible in the crowd.

It was bad luck that he hadn't prepared to leave town. He had been overconfident. Now he would have to hole up somewhere in Paris until the search cooled. In a way he was lucky Vladi hadn't been able to shoot down the A380 — the manhunt from a splash like that would have gone on for months. The French government wouldn't like losing a helicopter and crew, but would tolerate it, while the loss of a big airliner would be intolerable. He was certain the areas at the ends of the runways would become impenetrable security zones, but the airport would soon operate again. As for his own escape, he could always go to Brussels or Frankfurt.

∫

But where in Paris to hide? He needed a place that was unlikely to be searched.   -

Jamal? No, the Lincoln would be traced back to him, if it hadn't been already. That ruled out his entire old network, the one he'd carefully built up over the years. And it was that bastard Eddie Grant who'd cost him all those good connections.

He considered the crypt under Madame Nguyen's store and rejected the idea immediately. It was too uncomfortable, and there was no way to escape. It was a dead end, and by now might be known to the police as well.

He waited, trying to appear more patient than he felt, as three soldiers in blue berets passed him, their eyes searching the crowd, their hands on the stocks of their loaded rifles.

"I'm glad it's not the police," he told himself. "I bet they all have my picture. These guys are just doing the job they've been doing every day for ten years."

He slowed as he walked toward the top of the escalator, trying to look down it to the turnstile entrance to the RER tracks. It didn't appear anyone was checking IDs, but he kept looking as he went to one of the yellow machines against the wall to buy his ticket.

The schedule board on the platform told him the next train would leave in five minutes, but it was a local that would stop at every station between the airport and the Gare du Nord. He would have preferred the express, but the next one did not leave for ten minutes and a lot could happen by then.

The train waited, doors open, so he stepped aboard and found a seat with no window, so he couldn't be seen from outside. The RER trains were designed to carry massive numbers of commuters into Paris every day, so are more like inter-city trains than the métro. But unlike the world-famous TGVs, which are as comfortable as they are fast, the RER was designed in the 1970s for mass transit, not for luxury.

Three more soldiers ambled down the platform, but showed no interest in him. For the first time he began to relax and make plans for the next stage of his escape — and for his revenge against Eddie Grant. He'd sworn vengeance in 1991 when Eddie killed his son in Kuwait, but there had never been enough time to plan, so his one attempt had failed. He'd had to settle for Eddie's wife Lauren and son Sam, and he'd taken great pleasure in cutting their throats, first the boy, then his mother, so she could watch. If Sonny had done his job then Eddie was dead now, so Khan had nothing left but those closest to the man: Aurélie, and his mother Margaux. It wasn't enough, but it would have to do.

∫

Gare du Nord is the most active of Paris's six railway stations. A crowd waited more or less patiently on the platform as half the passengers pressed their way through. Khan stayed with the largest group as long as he could, then veered away toward the front entrance of the old station.

It was a contradiction, he thought. The poor dark-skinned residents of the suburban housing projects came into this dirty, noisy terminal every day to mingle, however briefly, with the swells waiting for the Eurostar to carry them under the English Channel to London.

He walked briskly toward Boulevard Magenta, the main street of the neighborhood, and after two blocks turned into a narrow cul-de-sac, more of an alley. Four doors down on the left, between a locksmith and a travel agency whose signs advertising flights to Morocco were half Arabic, half French, he pushed open the door of a tiny clothing store. Its bedraggled and dusty window display said it specialized in clothes for North African workingmen, who were plentiful in this neighborhood. It was in fact a service bureau for Muslim immigrants in need of false papers.

A wizened old man wearing an embroidered prayer cap and a long brown tunic sat calmly on a stool behind a battered wooden counter that showed decades of hard use. His dark eyes watched closely as Khan walked carefully around the racks of cheap shirts and trousers.

He greeted Khan with a respectful, "Bonjour, Monsieur."

Khan inclined his head slightly in response. "It is good to see you again. These days one can never be certain who is still in business." A pause. "I need your help again. I must return to the homeland of my father and I must not be found before I leave."

"I see," the old man said, rising from the bench. He limped to the door and locked it, then returned and led the way through a curtain into a long, narrow room with clothes hanging all along one side. "Did you know the police came to see Jamal?"

"I did not know, but I am not surprised. Was he arrested?"

"No. He said he had no useful information for them so they left him in peace, although he is afraid they will be back."

"For that reason, and others, I must go home, but not quite yet. I have one more job to do, and cannot use my own name."

"Would a German passport be good? You could pass for a Turk."

As they talked, Khan ran his eye over the clothes. He selected a pair of dark trousers and a blue worker's shirt, then chose a well-used brown leather belt from a batch hanging from a wall hook. Without a word his host offered him a bottle of black hair dye and a pair of scissors, then watched dispassionately as he changed clothes.

"Austrian would be better. Do you have that?"

The old man opened a file drawer under the workbench and withdrew a large envelope tied with red cord. He rummaged inside and withdrew a burgundy passport, an old-fashioned one with the picture pasted into it.

"This is the last one. Do you still have the Bulgarian document? We can use its picture. It will look more authentic than a new one, and take less time."

Khan handed over the Bulgarian passport. "May I return at the same time tomorrow?"

"Of course. I am proud of my prompt service."

∫

Khan unlocked the front door and stepped quickly back into the narrow alley. During the six-block walk to the Barbès-Rochechouart métro station, he dropped the clothes he'd been wearing piece by piece into street-side *poubelles*. He took the métro two stops to Pigalle, where a Babel of languages greeted him as he emerged from the stairway, then turned to the south, walking past a row of bars offering an ethnic rainbow of naked women.

The century-old stone buildings stood just as they had during his childhood, but they had grown steadily shabbier over the years. In the last decade, the trend had reversed and now a few new buildings stood where the land had been vacant, and many of the old cut-stone Haussmannian buildings had been upgraded with new windows and awnings. It made him a little sad that he had to leave.

He had fled once before, in 1960, but had returned to make his fortune. Now he would return to the desert to nurture it.

∫

He knew exactly where he was going — an old and unrenovated no-star hotel on the tiny Rue Musique, an alley running between Rue Baille and Place Clichy. There he found the narrow Hôtel Ave Maria — an incongruous name for an establishment that catered almost exclusively to North African men. They knew his Arab side wasn't from their tribe but they were willing to accept any paying guest, and they could keep a secret.

Khan requested a tiny room at the back of the third floor, which he had used before. He liked it because its single window looked over the roof of a small two-story apartment building next door. In an emergency he could slip through his window and across the roof, then either go down the building's stair to the street or take his chances scaling a drainpipe to the courtyard below. Either route would be dangerous, but either would be better than being trapped like a cornered rat. It gave him a tiny feeling of security.

The room was just the way he remembered it: small, under-furnished, and last redecorated a half-century before, if then. A narrow bed stood against a wall papered in a fading Victorian floral print that once had been mainly blue. A shaky table and a single straight wooden chair, its seat covered with a tiger-stripe fabric that clashed violently with the wallpaper, completed the furnishings. Two small rugs did nothing to cover the stains and scratches of the old wooden floor, and a single bulb hung low in the center of the room. There was no place to hang clothes, which made no difference to Khan because he had none.

After a few minutes, he left his key at the desk and walked around the corner to a Franprix, where he bought sausage, bread, cheese, bottled water, and a toothbrush. He wanted enough food to last for several days, time he would need to plan his next move.

When he returned, he carefully locked the door, undressed to his underwear, and walked to the stained white sink in the corner. In the light from the single dirty window, he cut his hair to an uneven spiky mass, then poured the dye over it.

"A new man," he said with satisfaction.

CHAPTER TWENTY-EIGHT

Restaurant Charles-Victor

W here do you think he's gone?" Eddie threw the question out for Aurélie, Philippe, Paul, Jeremy, and Jen. Heads shook all around the table he'd reserved in a back room of Charles Victor, a neighborhood restaurant near the catacombs.

Philippe was the first to respond. "He'll turn up. With the news today the pressure will build. He's spent the last four days crammed in somewhere uncomfortable and is probably about ready to start moving again. Did everybody see this?" He turned his iPad around to show the black headline from *Le Figaro*: "Two More Missiles Found at Airport."

"I called Walker and told him about it. He asked me to tell everybody that he's doing well and we can visit him tomorrow. My suspicion is that he's going stir crazy after three days in the hospital. He thinks Khan was the second shooter, but got scared off when the Tigers arrived."

"That's the most likely explanation, especially after Sonny Perry departed this earth," Jeremy said. Jen grimaced at the mention of Sonny's name.

Philippe continued. "I think — I hope — he's burned his entire network. Jamal obviously hates him and is talking to us, and he hasn't been back there, so he's probably holed up in a safe house of some sort. We know it's not the one Madame Nguyen kept for him, but there probably are others."

Aurélie interjected, "The only person we haven't accounted for is the driver who brought the missiles to Paris."

"We found the van," Philippe replied. "It was burned down to the bare metal in the northern suburbs, a much more thorough job than our neighborhood hooligans usually do. Somebody intended to destroy the evidence. My guess is that the driver just disappeared into the neighborhood."

Paul added, "It seems to me our best chance is still to catch Khan on the way out of town. Between the police and the Army, all the airports and rail stations are being watched, and the bus lines are under surveillance. Munich police are watching the ruins of his house just in case he doesn't know about the fire."

Jen threw out an unexpected question. "Do you think he might go to Ahmed?"

"Wow. That would be something," Aurélie said. "Would Ahmed take him in?"

"He's an important customer, and to a businessman the customer is holy. Ahmed probably recognizes on an intellectual level that Khan is dead as a customer, but he would do a lot to keep his business alive. Without Khan the business might fail, especially if Ahmed is sucked into the investigations."

"The police have searched his warehouse twice and his home once," Philippe said. "His wife made quite a stink when she found them going through her lingerie drawer. No luck in either place.

"But this interesting bit of news did come out. She was the leak who told Khan that Eddie had interviewed Jen in Munich. She says Khan just called one night looking for Ahmed and she happened to mention that he was meeting a friend from Paris. I don't know if it was that innocent, but it might have been."

Jen added, "I did get some news from Icky earlier today. He's found out how the gold is being moved. Part of it goes to Dubai with a Saudi diplomat who has his own A320. It's diplomatic baggage so it's not searched at either end, although I suspect everybody knows what it is because of the weight.

"That's a pretty small part of it, though. Most of it goes by ordinary ocean freight, usually from Hamburg. It all goes into a bullion locker in Dubai. Even though it's a lot of gold by anybody's standards, it's a drop in the bucket in the Emirates.

"But here's what's most interesting: the shipping arrangements are made quite openly by Henri Gascon's bank. There's nothing illegal or even unusual about that, except the quantity. A *lot* of gold has been shipped in the last six months, and it's been increasing."

"In other words," Eddie said, "the shipment Paul and I saw in Bulgaria was just a small part of the whole scheme?"

"It sure looks that way. At about that time gold was moved from Bulgaria, Greece, the South of France, Vienna, and Amsterdam. It's an immense conspiracy. If all that gold were dropped on the market at one time, it would destabilize gold prices and every stock market in the world for weeks."

Philippe added, "Khan doesn't want that to happen. His deal is that he gets a big commission if the gold is sold for more than 1,500 dollars an ounce. If he sold now he'd have a nice profit but he's a true believer and probably thinks the price will go higher yet, even if his plan did fail.

"Do you think he might stiff his European investors, pay the Arab ones, and just settle into Kuwait or Iran or somewhere like that? He'd just be one more fish in the sea, but a rich one. We know he's a chameleon, and he'll certainly never be able to come back to France if he does escape."

"I'm sure that's just what he'll do, at least for a while," Eddie said. "The price of gold has gone up fifty dollars an ounce since the airport attack and looks ready to go higher — and that's because of an attack that *failed*. He could still wind up getting what he wants if we don't stop him.

"But what's he doing right now? How can we find him? Philippe, I know your people are watching, but he's such a crafty bastard he could just slip through our fingers and we might not find out until the CIA gets wind of him after it's too late. The Saudis certainly aren't going to give him up, especially if one of their princes is helping him smuggle out the gold."

Aurélie asked, "Where do you think we should start?"

"I'd put my money on Henri Gascon the Fourth. He has the motive and the means. Philippe, could you watch him, maybe wiretap him?"

"Not a chance. I mean, I could try again but I asked about it once and got shot down. Maybe the additional information about his bank and the gold shipments would help, but the interdiction last time came straight from the president's office. They aren't really radical enough for Henri, but they are in power and they're up for re-election next year, although that cause looks pretty hopeless. I'd need a picture of Khan in bed with Henri, or maybe with the president. That's the reason we're having to meet in a restaurant instead of at the préfecture — I need your input, but some of my colleagues don't see the need for outside help."

"Okay then," Eddie said, "we'll have to do it ourselves and try to bring the political types in if we develop more information. Who do we have?"

Jeremy said, "Us, I guess. We could use some younger blood, though."

"And I'll have to keep my distance so it won't look like an American intelligence operation, much as I'd like to be involved," Jen said.

"I've been staying in touch with the taxi driver who helped out when Khan's goons tried to run you two down — Thierry Delabie," Paul said. "I'll talk to him."

Eddie said, "Let's see if we can get everybody together at our place. Noon tomorrow. Put Thierry on the school payroll, tell him there will be a bonus."

"I think he'd do it for nothing. He was really pissed about what happened to the two of you."

"But he shouldn't have to, and this could be dangerous, at least a little. We'll pay him. Let's start right now. Aurélie and I will take the first shift — is that OK with you?" He raised an eyebrow and looked at her. It was.

"I'll call with a schedule later so the area will be covered all the time, and we can meet somewhere nearby but out of sight tomorrow."

CHAPTER TWENTY-NINE

Île Saint-Louis

Nothing had happened during the six hours they watched the Quai d'Orléans, and at midnight Aurélie and Eddie lay in a flushed and sweaty post-coital glow, the lights of Notre Dame across the rooftops providing a dim illumination through the open window. She moved slightly to press her breasts against him and moved her thigh closer.

"Careful there," he said with a smile.

"You have twenty minutes," she said.

"That's pretty quick for a guy well into his forties."

"If it's a problem it will be the first time. I have confidence in you."

"I'll try to rise to your expectations. But seriously. Are we ready for tomorrow?"

"I think so," she said. She closed her eyes as she felt him respond to her light caress. "Our shift was the weakest one, with only two of us. Tomorrow we'll have somebody at all four corners of Henri's block, and if Khan comes through the center of the block I'll be waiting in the little park across the sidewalk. We don't know what he'll be driving, so we have to find him. Then we'll just follow him. At that point we can call in the police."

"Is Philippe okay with that?" Eddie asked.

"He's unhappy he can't be on the stakeout himself, but when I talked to him this afternoon he was satisfied. He'll find some way to have a flying squad in the neighborhood just in case."

"And Jen?"

"She's going shopping. And your twenty minutes are up. You're ready. Kiss me."

∫

Eddie was almost unrecognizable the next morning when he appeared at the short bridge connecting Notre Dame Cathedral and the Île Saint-Louis. He'd fished a tattered old overcoat out of the back of a closet where it had hung since one of Icky's projects years before. With a dirty plaid flat cap he looked more like a *clochard* than a tourist, and the outfit was far too heavy for September. Two policewomen walking behind Notre Dame gave him a suspicious look.

If anything, Aurélie was less recognizable. She had pinned up her hair and put on a dark-colored scarf and a long smock she borrowed from one of the maids in the hotel. "I can't decide if this getup makes me look more like a nun or a Muslim housekeeper," she said.

"Either way," Eddie responded, "You sure as hell don't look like Aurélie."

She would patrol the western end of the quai and the park below it along the river while he watched from the other end of the street, near the busy Pont de la Tournelle, which he and Aurélie had crossed just before Khan's men tried to run them down. He stopped a minute to reflect that it had been only ten days since that party at the banker's home had begun the whole drama. Both he and Aurélie had been kidnapped and very nearly killed and an airliner had escaped disaster only because two alert policemen had taken decisive action when they saw Vladi prepare to fire his missile.

Now there was only one step left and his ten-year nightmare would be over. He knew Khan wanted to kill him and intended to do it, but he was fully determined that Claude Khan would not survive the day he was found.

He borrowed Jeremy's Glock. "Double backup," he said. "Belt and suspenders. You may not see this again."

"No problem," Jeremy replied. "Icky has a closet full of them. I'll tell him to send you the bill."

The day was an exercise in boredom. They watched as Henri walked out the door to a waiting Peugeot in the morning, on his way to work. They expected to see his wife leave later in the morning because Jeremy had learned that she went almost every day to a suburban tennis club, but on this day she didn't appear. Philippe was able to learn that she had left the day before to visit her sister in Germany for a week.

At noon, Jeremy relieved Eddie and Thierry Delabie took over for Aurélie. They walked around the block out of sight of Henri's windows to a small café on the Right Bank, where after a *baguette jambon* and a fragrant expresso, and a visit to the surprisingly clean toilets, they rotated positions to let Paul and Jeremy go to lunch.

And so it went through the day. As the afternoon wore on, Aurélie texted Eddie that she'd heard from Philippe. Henri had a ticket that night to the Comédie Française and would have to leave well before 7 p.m.

The same black car drove up to the door a few minutes after six and let Henri out. The liveried driver spent ten minutes wiping invisible dust from the gleaming body, then took up his position near the rear door. After a few minutes he looked at his watch, then resumed waiting. It looked to Eddie like he had been a soldier — he knew how to get the maximum relaxation out of a few minutes' forced waiting.

After fifteen minutes he walked to the building's door, pressed a code, and watched as it opened. He stepped back for a short man who brushed past him and walked rapidly down the sidewalk toward the one-lane street that ran through the block.

That's Khan! Eddie said to himself as the man disappeared down the alley. He quickly followed, dialing Paul, who had parked the family's Peugeot 206 at the corner of the street behind Henri's building. Paul rapidly went to the car, notifying Thierry at the same time, while Eddie called Aurélie.

They watched Khan get into a small red Renault with a parking ticket on its windshield. Paul slipped into the driver's seat of the Peugeot and Eddie sat quickly next to him. Aurélie climbed into the back seat. Eddie tossed his overcoat and cap next to Aurélie. The two other men would follow in Thierry's cab.

"He's been in there since before we started watching, so Henri must have been hiding him," Eddie said. "When we see where Khan is going, we'll call Philippe."

"Shouldn't we do that now?" Aurélie asked, pulling her phone out of a pocket of the smock.

"NO!" Eddie raised his voice. Abashed and surprised, Aurélie put the phone back.

To Paul, he said, "Stay as close as you can. He'll probably turn right onto the Pont Louis-Philippe and try to get onto the Pompidou Expressway. If he does that, at this hour there's a real risk we'd lose him. If that happens at least we have the license number to give to Philippe."

The light turned red and Khan stopped, second in line. Paul stopped a dozen feet back but Eddie told him, "Closer. Get right up behind him."

As the car stopped, he opened his door and put one foot out on the pavement. "Now tap him pretty hard. I want to surprise him." He waved away Aurélie's effort to object and stepped out, closing the door gently. He bent low to stay out of sight.

As soon as the door closed Paul moved up quickly and tapped Khan's rear bumper, hard enough to make the Renault jump. Khan sat up straight and looked in his mirror, then turned and started to open his door.

At that moment, Eddie pulled open the passenger door and sat down beside him, his gun held low, out of sight of curious pedestrians.

"Hello, Khan," he said. "This is going to be the worst day of your miserable life, and it's hardly started."

CHAPTER THIRTY

The Seine

K han's surprise lasted only a heartbeat.
        "You're supposed to be dead!" His left hand emerged almost instantly holding a small silver automatic but Eddie was prepared and parried quickly, trapping the little gun in his large hand and twisting it toward the roof. Khan managed to pull the trigger once, and Paul and Aurélie saw the thin sheet metal pucker as the bullet passed through.

"Oh!" Aurélie took a deep breath.

"Eddie knows how to handle that. Don't worry. The tough part will come when it's just the two of them, no gun," Paul said reassuringly.

"What do you think he'll do?"

"Both of them must have plans, but I'm pretty sure they aren't the same."

With the gun successfully turned away, Eddie called on his weight and strength advantage to end the fight. He continued to twist Khan's hand back until he heard the unmistakable snap of bone breaking, and the atmosphere in the car changed instantly.

Eddie quickly unloaded Khan's gun and tossed it out of the window into the middle of Rue Saint-Louis en l'Île, where it bounced to the gutter. A half-dozen well-dressed shoppers stopped to look in surprise as it came to rest, and a parking agent stopped writing a ticket and raised her radio to her lips.

Eddie said, "So now it's just us, bastard. Is this a more even fight than a woman and a young boy? Or how about a ninety-year-old man? Did killing them make you feel powerful?"

"It sure did..." Khan got three words out before Eddie balled his fist and hit him forcefully in the temple.

"I should just shoot you in the head right here and be done with it, but I have bigger plans. Something more like what you're used to doing.

"Let's see how you like being on the receiving end, you bastard. You don't have much time left and I plan to make good use of it."

"You won't kill me. You don't have the balls for it."

"Just keep thinking that. I just wish I still had that combat shotgun. I'd love to see your guts spattered over the landscape, but you deserve something slower."

Eddie switched the pistol to his left hand and stuck it into Khan's ribs.

"Don't even think about pulling anything now, bastard." He tilted the gun down. "I'll shoot you through the guts and balls. It won't be quick."

He looked back to be sure Paul and Aurélie were close behind and felt Khan move.

"Bad mistake." He pressed the muzzle of the gun viciously into Khan's side. "Oh, and did you know? Jen Wetzmuller killed Sonny Perry. She killed him with her own hands. He turned out to be just another punk, like the rest of the losers you had around you."

Khan looked at him in surprise. He was trying to drive with his injured hand, steering with his palm while he tried to protect himself with his right.

"You didn't know? She was hoping you'd be there for the same treatment. But I'm glad you weren't. I've been waiting for this moment for ten years and now it's here — your last day. From now on you'll just be remembered as the bastard son of a Nazi and the terrorist who couldn't shoot straight, a failure in everything you did. And it's going to be very painful. You have no idea.

"Turn right here, asshole," Eddie told him as they reached the street leading to the Louis-Philippe Bridge. "Then turn right onto the Pompidou."

Paul and Aurélie were only a few yards behind. The Peugeot bucked as Paul accelerated around the corner onto the Rue Jean de Bellay, then through another right onto the approach road for the Pompidou Expressway and its long route along the Right Bank of the Seine.

Aurélie slid to the right seat and held tight to the doorpost as Paul pressed hard on the accelerator.

"Why the Pompidou?" Paul asked over his shoulder, shouting against the noise of the wind.

"This is where we run early in the morning. He knows it like the back of his hand. And once they're on the expressway, there aren't many places to get off. That will give the police time to catch up."

"Yeah? Well, they're here. I see a blue light behind us. I'm not going to stop, and they show no sign of it, either."

"Don't."

Paul thought there was very little chance Khan would ever see a policeman again, but he kept it to himself.

The Renault dashed down the entrance ramp to the expressway. A line of cars waited at the bottom for a red light to change.

"Go around them, bastard. There's room," Eddie said. "On the right. Faster."

Khan squeezed the little car as far to the right as it would go, finally putting two wheels up on the curb. Eddie pressed the horn button, a long blast to warn a pedestrian who was about to step off the curb. The man looked up in alarm and scurried back from the road.

Khan turned to look at him, his face a mask of fear and pain.

"Don't do this. It won't get you anything. I'll give you half the gold fund."

"You offering me money? That's rich. You took lives and you ruined more. No, this story goes to the end, wherever that is. Who knows, you might just get out alive. Watch where you're going!"

They brushed a plumber's work van as they edged around it, then missed a car on the expressway only because the driver braked frantically to avoid them. He honked angrily as the Renault flew in front of him and pulled away.

As they flashed past a floating restaurant tied to the riverbank, then under the Pont Marie, Khan tried to cut left to take an exit ramp leading to the dense warren of narrow streets in the Marais.

"No you don't, not quite yet," Eddie said as he pulled the wheel back to the right. The little car careened dangerously for a few yards before it stabilized.

"Now's your time," Eddie told Khan calmly, and hit him again in the right temple, then immediately pulled the wheel sharply to the right. Khan shook his head, trying to clear it, but the situation was completely out of his control. He sat back in resignation as the car bumped over the curb, barely missing the concrete bollards designed to prevent exactly what was about to happen.

The car covered the twenty yards to the river in less than a second. It sailed over the edge, landed ten feet from shore, and began immediately to sink. Just as water began to pour through the window, Eddie reached out and threw Jeremy's pistol as far as he could toward the deepest part of the Seine.

∫

Aurélie had anticipated Eddie's plan when he turned down the Pompidou. "He's going to take Khan into the river — Jen told him water is what he fears most," she told Paul quickly, and started to rip off her clothes.

The scarf and the long coat already lay on the seat beside her. She quickly unbuttoned her white blouse and pulled it off, then struggled out of her slacks. By the time she was down to her bra and panties, Paul had stopped on the riverbank.

The Renault disappeared into the murky water of the Seine, leaving only a stream of bubbles marking its location.

Aurélie ran a few yards upstream. "Call Philippe," she shouted at Paul, then stepped back a few paces to get a running start and cannonballed into the river, as far away from the bank as she could.

By the time she came up, the current had carried her to the small fountain of bubbles marking the car's location.

"I'm going down," she shouted, then took a deep breath and jackknifed, using her strong breaststroke to carry her toward the bottom. Her hand felt the car's top before she could see it, but as her eyes became accustomed to the darkness she could see that it was perched at a precarious 45-degree angle at the edge of the channel. *Merde!* The Seine through Paris averages thirty feet deep. If it fell further into that trench it would be much harder to reach, if not impossible, and certainly not in time.

She swam quickly to the passenger-side door and felt inside for Eddie. Nothing — the seat was empty, but was pushed back in full recline.

Hand over hand, almost out of breath, she moved to the rear window. By pressing her face close to the glass she could barely make out the dim image of Eddie, his head out of the water in an air pocket that was shrinking as the water rose.

He was peering closely at the surface of the water. Then he pulled something up into the air pocket. It was Khan, and Eddie was holding him by the hair.

She saw him look directly into Khan's eyes. His lips moved but she could not hear his words. Then, very deliberately, he forced the head back under water.

Her lungs were about to burst as she fought her way to the surface and shouted, "Paul! Eddie's in an air pocket. I think I can get him out."

"The *pompiers* are on the way," he replied. At the same moment she heard the siren of the firemen's boat coming from the river fire station downstream. The police car following them had stopped behind Paul. Both gendarmes were talking animatedly into their phones.

By the time she returned, the car was almost completely full and rocking dangerously. She swam blindly in through the passenger door, feeling ahead for Eddie. Her head struck the back window and she found herself in the much shrunken air pocket, so small it allowed her only one short breath.

There she found Eddie, barely conscious. She put her arms under his and pulled him slowly toward the door.

"Take a deep breath, Édouard. You'll be on top soon. The doctors will get you patched up again, but if we don't get out of here there won't be anything left of either of us to patch."

As gently as she could, she squeezed him through the door. Then she freed one arm and pulled as hard as she could, straight up.

They surfaced a dozen feet from the fire department's Zodiac. Two divers were waiting to take Eddie gently from her.

"He's really weak," she told them. "Please be careful."

"Is there anyone else down there?" one of the divers asked.

"There was another man in the car but I didn't find him. Be careful if you go back. It's just about to tip over into the channel."

"Got it," he said. His fins flicked spray on her and he was gone.

The remaining diver put his buddy mask over Eddie's face and watched for a few seconds. "He's breathing fine. No problem there." Then he and Aurélie strapped Eddie's limp body to a rescue board. Two muscular firemen pulled him aboard the Zodiac, then reached down to pull Aurélie up over the gunwale. The crew chief wrapped a blanket around her then steered the boat toward a landing ramp a quarter-mile away where an ambulance waited, its blue light turning slowly.

Eddie squeezed Aurélie's hand. "Thanks again for saving my life. I can always count on you." She kissed him. Her eyes were burning — say what you will about salmon returning to the Seine, it's still not the place to go for a swim, she said to herself.

"Who was in there with him?" the crew chief asked.

"A man named Claude Khan," Aurélie responded. "He's the one who tried to shoot down the airliners at De Gaulle. I felt around the car for him but didn't find him."

"That explains it. My dispatcher says Commissaire Cabillaud has been asking, and he's not someone you keep waiting."

"Tell me about it. He's my father."

"He's on his way."

CHAPTER THIRTY-ONE

Hôtel-Dieu

"The *pompiers* pulled Khan's body out of the river this morning, drowned," Philippe told the group assembled around Eddie's hospital bed. "One of the tourists trying to attach a love lock to the Pont des Arts caught a glimpse of an arm sticking up above a pile of junk caught on one of the pillars. He called the fire department. Oddly enough, the same firemen who pulled you out of the water recovered the body. It scared the hell out of the tourists, but they'll be telling their friends about it for months. It will be their favorite Paris story."

Philippe stood at the side of Eddie's bed in the Hôtel Dieu. Aurélie sat at the opposite side of the bed holding Eddie's hand tightly.

"Dr. Santange will be in later, but he says you can come home tomorrow. You got some water in your lungs and were pretty badly chilled, so they want you to stay in bed a few days. There's no reason to stay in the hospital, though."

"We can't go running along the Seine?" Eddie smiled. He was alert and, since he'd heard first-hand that Khan's body had been found and identified, he was content.

"Well, maybe the day *after* tomorrow," Aurélie replied with a smile.

"There's one other thing," Philippe said. "Henri Gascon is dead. We found him in his apartment tied to a chair, which is why he couldn't meet the driver. His throat had been cut, and there was a bloody antique curved sword lying on the floor nearby. It looked like he put up quite a fight."

"Was it the Persian scimitar he had mounted on the living room wall?" Eddie asked. "If it was, there's a sort of rough justice to it, since Khan gave it to him."

"Probably," Philippe said. "We won't know for sure until the lab finishes its work, but we're not out looking for any other suspects right now.

"We did find out how Khan got in without being noticed. He bribed the crew of a garbage truck and went through the alley door. Henri told the *gardienne* to show him upstairs. Khan blackmailed Henri into taking him — it was an expensive misjudgment.

"But there's more. One of Henri's partners came to see me this morning. It seems that Henri lent a lot of the bank's money to Khan's hedge fund. Funds like that all work with borrowed money, but in this case it looks like Henri may have over-extended the bank, especially since the collateral may be hard to find. It's squirrelled away in Dubai."

"Won't that be a gnarly foreign-policy puzzle to solve?" Eddie asked.

"Oh," Aurélie said. "I almost forgot. Jen and Icky said to give you their best wishes. She left on an early flight this morning to brief him."

"Jen and Icky?" Eddie sounded perplexed.

"I think there's something going on there, but I don't know for sure. Anyway, she said they would both come to see us in a month or two."

"I suggested, very privately, that she leave," Philippe said. "I had a call or two from the German police about Sonny and the fire. Much better to let things cool down. Icky can handle it on an official level, and if they want to talk to her they can do it in Washington. I think you'll have to go there to visit them if it's any time soon.

"And by the way, a detective will be in this afternoon to ask you a few questions. He's pretty clear about what happened and why, but like all of us he wants to hear it from the main player."

"No problem. I tried to stop the car against one of the bollards but Khan was fighting me and I missed it. When we hit the water the seat flipped back and the next thing I knew was when Aurélie came to get me. I didn't see what happened to Khan."

"That's the way it looked to me, too," Philippe said. "It should be plenty of detail. Aurélie, can you add anything?"

"Not a thing. I just saw it go into the water and jumped in, then I found Édouard in the air pocket, very disoriented and damn near drowned himself. Maybe the *pompier* who went in after that knows something about Khan. As far as I'm concerned it's good riddance, like taking out the trash."

CHAPTER THIRTY-TWO

Washington, The Watergate

Eddie and Aurélie stood at the balcony door of Icky's apartment admiring the view across Washington. He had bought it only three months before, when Jen left Paris and moved in with him.

"Icky, I think you found a view Margaux might even admire," Eddie said. His mother lived across the street from Les Invalides and Napoleon's Tomb, one of the most spectacular gilt-heavy buildings in Paris.

Icky stood behind them with an arm around each of their shoulders, three old friends together in calm circumstances for the first time in years.

"I dunno, sport. It's hard to beat her panorama. How can you top a view that goes from the Eiffel Tower all the way around to Notre Dame, with the entire city in the middle? Her place is one of the reasons we looked for this view. The Watergate apartments are an old name with a lot of baggage, but we like it here."

Jen was on her way back from the kitchen carrying a bottle of Cabernet when Aurélie asked her, "I had no idea Icky was your secret lover, but it does seem like a really good match. Where does it go from here?"

"Well, we're officially engaged and plan to get married this winter. But that's not the big decision. I mean, I'm forty years old, so if we're going to have a family we need to get on it right away."

"We must be reading the same tea leaves. I had my IUD taken out the same day the city buried what was left of Khan."

"Any luck?"

"Looks like it. We'll know soon."

Icky raised his glass for attention. "Enough kiddie talk. Everybody sit. Bring us up to date on your house hunting and then we can exchange juicy tidbits about the unmourned Mr. Khan, may he burn in hell."

Aurélie and Eddie had been in New York for the last week looking for a place to live while she taught French history and literature at Columbia for the spring term.

"We've just about decided on a brownstone in Harlem, on West 143rd Street," she said. "It's a charming old place with a carved stone doorway, and it's just a couple of blocks from the subway, which is only two or three stops from Columbia. It's near a nice neighborhood of small shops, a lot of them ethnic."

Jen asked, "Are you going to rent?"

"We thought we'd buy. Eddie looked at the New York real estate market and likes the prices, and if we buy we can re-do it the way we want. Right now the second floor is one huge master bedroom. We'll put in some walls and build a nursery."

"Nursery! How things have changed. A new job in a new country along with a new baby. All that's left is for us to move to the suburbs."

"It's good to be planning something ordinary," Eddie said. "I feel like my old self for the first time in years. It's time I went back to serious work on building the schools. Maybe we'll expand over here — I need to reconnect with my American side."

"Enough about us. We were pretty surprised to find out about you two," Aurélie interjected. "Flabbergasted is more like it. I suspected *something* was going on but I had no idea it was this far along."

"We started dating when I came to Virginia for training, after Roy died," Jen said. "I'm sorry I couldn't tell you earlier. And I'm sorry I had to act like such an ass in Munich."

"That was my doing," Icky said. "We couldn't afford any leaks. Khan had worked for years to find back-door information sources about everybody he dealt with. For example, did Philippe tell you Halime was passing information back to Khan?"

Eddie said, "Yes, and Ahmed called me about it, too. Did it affect anything you were doing with him?"

"It was touchy for Jen. It was Halime's leak that let Sonny Perry know you'd visited Ahmed, so he knew we were on to him. It could have been serious when Jen was alone with him in the house."

"Serious?" Jen retorted. "It could have got me killed."

"But you did handle him pretty neatly, didn't you?" he said gently, touching her arm and pulling her closer to him on the sofa. "Intelligence is a world of close calls. But it did get Ahmed's friend Gregor killed. The information he was bringing out would probably have tied Khan to the Chechen missile deal much earlier in the game."

Jen added, "That was after I stupidly told Khan that Ahmed was meeting a plane. He grilled Halime and found out about Gregor, whose name he already had from Albert Cate, so he had Vitaliy set up the Chechens to make the hit. That slip was my mistake, and it was a costly one."

"We still have an hour before dinner," Icky said in an effort to divert the conversation to something more comfortable. "I made reservations at the French restaurant downstairs, so we don't have far to go. Let's use the time to update each other."

"We hear things aren't going well for the congressman," Eddie replied. "We had Gloria Tennant over for dinner a couple of weeks ago and she told us she's filed for divorce and will spend at least part of the year in Paris."

"You probably know more about her than I do here," Icky said. "It's been a big political mess on the Hill. He should be prosecuted for money laundering but it looks like he may dodge that. However, the *Washington Post* confirmed the other day what we knew already — he'd borrowed money from our friend Boris in Miami using the hedge fund as collateral, and now that that's evaporated he's in deep financial trouble. He was also touting the hedge fund without a securities license, so the SEC may go after him, not to mention some of the suckers who bought it."

Jen asked, "Will they let him stay in Congress?"

"Not a chance. Last I heard he was looking for a job at a couple of nonprofits. His best shot seems to be one I'd never heard of — a gun group that's even to the right of the NRA. That's the sort of thing our disgraced ex-congressmen seem to find these days."

"I hope Ahmed doesn't do too badly in all this," Eddie said. "Even if his loyalties are a little iffy, he was our classmate."

Icky said, "I'm not certain they were all that divided. He's just been in business so long sometimes he can't see beyond the money. Halime may have been the problem. Khan seduced and used her, although she was pretty willing. She passed on anything interesting Ahmed told her."

"Can he continue to work for you?" Eddie asked.

"I don't know yet, but needless to say we're keeping a close eye on him. He's filed for divorce, and the German authorities told Halime she'd be charged as Khan's accessory unless she moves back to Turkey. I think that's what she will do, because stupid she's not. Ahmed also knows we're trying to help him keep his business alive. For example, he just got some new financing from Henri Gascon's old bank."

"How in hell did you work that?"

"Easy. The bank was bankrupt because of all the money Henri lent Khan to buy gold. Only Khan knew where it all went, although we'll untangle it eventually. The gold has disappeared somewhere in Dubai — so the bank's collateral is so impaired it had to find a buyer or close. As it happened, we knew somebody."

"So now it's a CIA bank?"

"They probably wouldn't phrase it *exactly* that way."

"And the Mafia brothers?" Eddie knew part of the answer but wanted to hear all of it.

"That's more complicated, like those Russian dolls nested inside each other, the *matryoshka*. Boris didn't fare very well. Some of the more conspiracy-minded members of Congress were convinced the loan to Congressman Tennant was effectively a loan from the Russian government, because the picture of Putin on Boris's wall proved to them he was a Russian government agent.

"He wasn't. He's just a crook with crooked friends, but all the talk spooked the Russian secret services so much they spirited him out of the country on a chartered plane a month ago. I haven't been able to find out where he is, but I'm certain it's somewhere cold and unpleasant."

Aurélie added, "It sounds like he did worse than his brother in Nice."

"That's where it gets interesting. Vitaliy was really the one working closely with Khan, and together they provided a whole lot of weapons to the group of Chechen nationalists you saw pick up the missiles in Bulgaria.

"And, by the way, the FSB and the Russian Navy met the ship a couple hundred miles offshore, took off the missiles, then scuttled it. We think they put a half dozen of the crew in one of the cabins and welded the door before they sank it, but that's just rumor."

"And Vitaliy?" Aurélie asked again.

"Vitaliy has left Nice for points unknown. I don't blame him — Philippe found out he made the call that tipped Sonny off to move Aurélie after the Chechen lawyer alerted him. He was looking at hard time, and the French prisons are not a bit like our federal country clubs. A dozen of his friends who were also funneling gold to Khan have disappeared, too. Interpol is looking for them, but good luck with that.

"There's more, and it's interesting. Vitaliy had a big mortgage on the restaurant, and of course the local bank is pushing it into foreclosure — but it appears that Ben Pelonie was smarter than we knew. It's not final yet, and there will be courts involved, but it looks like Vitaliy's debt to Barbara will come ahead of the bank's loan, and Barbara will get her money back before the bank gets anything."

"That's a relief," Aurélie said. "I haven't talked to Philippe in a while, but last time I did, he thought Barbara would have to sell the big house."

"She may do that anyway, I hear," Icky said. "Since Philippe wasn't interested in stretching their one-night stand into even two nights, she and Walker have been seeing each other — in fact, it was Walker who figured out how cleverly her husband had structured the loan. And after Ben died her accountant started cooking the books, so Walker put a stop to that as well. I hear it was messy.

"They'll be a storybook couple among all the Russians and Arabs on the Côte d'Azur — the ex-spook and the gangster's moll. It will be high times again."

Aurélie said, "She's my mother and Walker is a nice guy, so I can't help but wish her well, but I'm glad Philippe didn't go back to her.

"But that's a detail. I'll always be grateful to the three of you for putting yourselves on the line to get rid of Khan. That's what really counts."

"Don't forget your own close call," Eddie said. "Without that and Jen's very astute suspicions about Khan we might have 500 dead airline passengers, gold over 3,000 dollars an ounce, and Khan as king of the world, at least in his own mind.

"But now let's put it behind us and go down to dinner. Tomorrow is a new day, and thanks to you — thanks to all of us — it will be better for junior." He patted her stomach gently and she beamed.

What happened to *Portrait of a Young Man?*

Raphael's famous self-portrait has been missing since the end of World War II, when Hans Frank, the governor-general of occupied Poland, supposedly included it in a shipment of art treasures he dispatched from Krakow to his home near Munich. After the American Army arrested him in Bavaria, soldiers searched his home and found many of the missing artworks, but not the Raphael.

Frank went to the gallows in Nuremberg the next year without revealing what happened to it.

From that point, the history is murky. Frank's son, in a bitter book condemning his father, theorized that the painting arrived and his mother exchanged it for food in the bitter post-war period.

In 2012 the Polish Foreign Ministry said the painting had in fact survived the war and was hidden in a bank vault in a part of the world with a functioning legal system. Where that is, or even if it's true, remains a mystery.

The painting appears from time to time in popular fiction. In the George Clooney movie "The Monuments Men," for example, one of the final scenes shows it being destroyed by the Germans, which almost certainly is a screenwriter's invention.

However, despite the best efforts of its owner, the Czartoryski Museum, it remains lost, along with thousands of lesser works.

Did you enjoy *Last Stop: Paris?*

Thank you for reading the sequel to *Treasure of Saint-Lazare.* If you enjoyed it, please leave a review on Amazon, at this link:

http://j.mp/LastStopParis

Made in the USA
San Bernardino, CA
13 November 2017